UNDER THE MISTLETOE

Shayne felt her mouth touch his. Oh yeah, life was good, damn good.

She was tentative. Jerky. As if maybe she hadn't kissed in a while. It was the most arousing sensation, but right then and there, he knew. The one quick peck? Not going to be enough.

Dropping the mistletoe, he cupped her face, his fingers gliding into her silky hair to hold her head as he better lined them up.

Her hands lifted, hovering in the air for a beat before settling on his chest. A soft little murmur of wanting escaped her, and just like that, he went insta-hard. Her fingers dug into the material of his shirt, holding on just a little, telling him she felt the same, telling him he wasn't alone in this odd sensation of not wanting to let go, not ever wanting to let go.

And he didn't even know her name . . .

The novels of Jill Shalvis

Aussie Rules

Get a Clue

Out of This World

Smart and Sexy

Strong and Sexy

Superb and Sexy

Instant Attraction

Instant Gratification

Instant Temptation

Anthologies featuring Jill

Bad Boys Southern Style

He's the One

Merry and Bright

JILL SHALVIS

STRONG AND SEXY

The Sky High Series

KENSINGTON BOOKS
http://www.kensingtonbooks.com

KENSINGTON BOOKS are published by

Kensington Publishing Corp.
119 West 40th Street
New York, NY 10018

All Kensington titles, imprints, and distributed lines are available at special quantity discounts for bulk purchases for sales promotion, premiums, fund-raising, educational, or institutional use.

Special book excerpts or customized printings can also be created to fit specific needs. For details, write or phone the office of the Kensington Special Sales Manager: Attn.: Special Sales Department. Kensington Publishing Corp., 119 West 40th Street, New York, NY 10018. Phone: 1-800-221-2647.

Kensington and the K logo Reg. U.S. Pat. & TM Off.

ISBN-13: 978-0-7582-2183-4
ISBN-10: 0-7582-2183-5

First Kensington Books Mass-Market Paperback Printing: April 2013
First Brava Books Trade Paperback Printing: January 2008

eISBN-13: 978-0-7582-8908-7
eISBN-10: 0-7582-8908-1

First Electronic Edition: April 2013

10 9 8 7 6 5 4 3 2 1

Printed in the United States of America

Prologue

She rushed into Shayne Mahoney's party as if there was a firecracker on her ass, wobbling on heels she clearly wasn't comfortable in, wearing a little black dress that revealed pale, porcelain curves most people found unfashionable these days.

Not Shayne. Nope, he loved curves.

The woman's dark hair was piled haphazardly on top of her head, held there by two yellow pencils. Interesting choice for a formal cocktail party. So was the way she moved into the large reception lobby, her gait a little awkward, her smile broadcasting her nerves.

Very interesting.

She wasn't his type. Not because she wasn't tall, stacked, and model-ready, but because she pretty much screamed *fish out of water*.

All of the women he'd dated lately—hell, ever—had been confident. Bold. Overtly sexy.

And, as Brody and Noah would tell him, none of

the women he'd dated had managed to hold his interest.

There was a message there, he knew, but he didn't care. He shifted to move away, but then something had him turning back, just as the woman tripped over her own feet. As he started toward her, she managed to catch herself, then furtively glanced around the crowd to see if anyone had noticed, a self-conscious gesture that made him smile.

Definitely not confident, bold, or overtly sexy.

And yet something about her seemed incredibly appealing, and not just because in a sea of pedigreed roses she stood out as the lone wildflower, but because she seemed familiar.

He hadn't slept with her, he knew that much. He hadn't flown her in one of his planes, or for Sky High Air, and he hadn't worked with her.

So who was she?

A server passed her, and she took a flute of champagne, flashing the guy a quick smile that could break a heart at fifty paces because it was real. It made her more than just pretty, but someone he couldn't take his eyes off.

And yet the server didn't smile back, which pissed Shayne off. Granted, she wasn't fake tanned or gym toned like the other women here, and no, she wasn't especially graceful and clearly felt out of her element, but she was a guest, and as such, deserved the same respect the others received.

Shayne would talk to the server, that was for damn sure, though it would do little good. The people here tonight were shallow, all of them. Hell, Shayne himself had been hit on no less than three times before the party had even gotten started, including once by Michelle, a woman he'd stopped seeing when she'd gotten a little too possessive after two dates.

But this woman wasn't hitting on anyone, she was trying to be invisible. Interest definitely piqued for the first time in days, he kept his eye on her. She was attempting to tuck some of her wayward hair back into its constraints, not being successful in any way as the strands immediately slipped free again, brushing over her throat, her shoulders.

Yeah, she was a complete wreck.

An adorable, sexy, complete wreck.

Who was she, and how did she fit in with the elegant, sophisticated crowd that was here tonight? Since he was the one throwing this party for one of Sky High's wealthiest clients, he'd held the guest list in his hands, a list that was a virtual Who's Who of Los Angeles because Sandra Peterson loved nothing more than a good party in her honor.

And if anyone thought it odd that Sandra had Sky High host her engagement party and not her family, Shayne understood. Sky High Air's flexibility, dedication, and ability to meet any client's demand had put them on the map. He'd seen to it himself. Sky High provided service at the highest level, a fact a client like Sandra appreciated since her own family couldn't have put together a party of this size and caliber. Or wouldn't. Her stepkids were too spoiled, and her daughter? It was rumored that she was a little off her rocker.

Not a surprise, given how rich Sandra was. Her trust fund made even Shayne's seem like a tween's weekly allowance. Such an embarrassment of riches often had some pretty serious effects on people.

He should know. His own family was a pack of paranoid snobs, and the women he'd dated had had many a gold-digger in the bunch. Luckily he rarely dated anyone more than once or twice. Mostly that had been his choice, but lately, not so much. He'd gone out with three women after Michelle, all of whom had turned him down for a second date.

It was entirely possible he was losing his touch, not a pleasant thought for a guy who'd relied on his touch all his life.

Adorable Sexy Complete Wreck Woman moved farther into the elegant lobby, her dark eyes darting left and right, still looking as if she'd rather disappear than be seen.

Given that people had been trying to get into this high-society event for days and days, willing to do just about anything to be seen here tonight, her attitude fascinated him.

Craning her neck, she checked behind her, apparently not taking into account the speed with which she was moving, because just as she looked forward again she nearly plowed into a potted tree. She managed to catch herself before she hit, but one of her heels snapped right off, and she uttered a four-letter word that made Shayne grin.

Nope, she didn't belong here. But he was damn glad she'd come, whoever she was.

Chapter 1

She'd promised herself she'd do this. No running, no avoiding, just face it head-on and get it done. But as Dani Peterson bent for her broken-off heel, she felt her resolve slip.

Running like hell would have been so much easier.

Damn it.

All she'd asked of herself was to get through this with a shred of dignity, but that would be a little tough now, wouldn't it, while minus a heel.

Ah, well. Her family already believed her a little off, why not just go ahead and prove it by looking the part.

But then came the voice.

The low, husky male voice asking, "Are you okay?"

She sighed as she eyed her offending heel. "That depends."

"On?"

On whether or not she could find room in her budget to replace the shoes. "Nothing. I'm fine. Thanks."

Blowing a strand of hair from her mouth, she glanced over just as he crouched at her side.

And felt the most ridiculous schoolgirl urge to blush and stammer. Because wow.

Seriously wow.

He smiled at her. And although everything about him—his confidence, his clothes, his ease—all projected old money and class—not to mention a sophistication she couldn't have faked on her best day—he wasn't *GQ* perfect.

No, nothing as easy to shrug off as *GQ* perfect.

Instead, his hair had been finger combed at best, the sun-streaked wheat strands shoved back off his face, where it fell in unruly waves to his collar. His mouth was wide, quirked in a half smile that revealed a single heart-stopping dimple on the left side, the same side as the scar that slashed his eyebrow in half over a set of golden eyes with laugh lines at the corners.

He apparently smiled, and often.

His nose had been broken at least once, the bump only adding more character to a face that already had it in spades. He was bigger than her last boyfriend, but truthfully it had been so long she could hardly remember if she'd had to go up on tiptoe to kiss him. She'd definitely have to get up on tiptoe for this guy, and why she was even thinking such a thing was ridiculous.

"I'm fine," she repeated, hoping that by saying so multiple times she could make it true. "Really. Just fine." Uh-huh, and now she sounded like an idiot as well as looked like one. "So fine . . ."

God. She rambled when she was nervous, and she was very nervous now. "Super fine." *Shut up, shut up.*

With a smile, he put his hand on her arm. It was a

big hand, warm and strong, much like the rest of him. He had to bend because he was well over six feet, and while she was noticing that, she couldn't fail to continue to notice the rest. He definitely had a build to go with the height, an athletic one, not a gym-made one, the kind that under normal circumstances would have made her swallow her own tongue.

But since she'd embarrassed herself enough already, she told herself no tongue swallowing, and to make sure of it, avoided looking directly into his face. It should help the problem of finding his . . . maleness so utterly unsettling and intimidating.

Movements easy and fluid, he pulled her to her feet, still touching her in a way that woke things within her, things that had been dormant for a long, long time. Yes, he was attractive, but also astonishingly, remarkably . . . *male.*

And as if all that wasn't potent enough, he looked right into her face, and whoa baby, those golden eyes were full, deep, and direct in a way that said he could read her all the way to the bone.

If that was the case, she was in big trouble.

Around them, the party was noisy, festive with holiday cheer and decorations, complete with sprigs of mistletoe. It was crowded with happy revelers—everything that she usually avoided. Mostly, she'd rather have a root canal without the benefit of good meds than dress up and make nice with rich, spoiled people, but she'd used that excuse last time.

So here she was, being physically supported by one of them, no less. Since she barely came to his shoulder, she had to balance on her one heel for some desperately needed height.

He smiled, and while maybe he wasn't exactly *GQ* material, he'd certainly dressed for the cover, wear-

ing gorgeously cut black pants and a soft-looking
whiskey-colored shirt that matched his eyes, clothes
that had clearly been made for his long, leanly muscled body.

They were not in the same tax bracket. Not even
close.

"Let me find you a place to sit," he said. "It's too
nice an evening to be rushing around."

She sensed he didn't do a lot of rushing. There
was something relaxed and laid-back about him.

And gorgeous. Let's not forget gorgeous. "I'm good,
thanks."

"Would you like a drink?"

After which he'd likely vanish as quickly as he
could. It was nothing personal, she knew. She just
wasn't the sort of woman to keep a man like this interested for long, though she spared a second to
wish that for once she could act like her mother's
daughter. That for once she could simply go after
whatever she wanted.

Because what she wanted was a chance beneath
the mistletoe, if only for a moment . . . "So why
aren't you out there having fun? Drinking or dancing, or . . ." As was its habit, her tongue ran away
from her brain. "Or making the most of that mistletoe?"

His eyes lit with good humor, and that dimple
flashed. "Maybe I don't have someone to make the
most of it with." He glanced out at the party, and behind his back she smacked herself in the head. *Making the most of that mistletoe?* Had she really said that?

When he looked at her again, she forced a smile.
"So, about that drink."

"Yes, thanks. Anything," she said, allowing his escape.

But not hers. She was doing this. No matter what. She was going to forget about Perfect Stranger Guy and make nice here if it killed her, no matter how much she really hated these silly get-togethers her mother was always having thrown in her own honor. Tonight, it was to celebrate her latest catch, her fourth—or was it her fifth?—fiancé, and Sandra had insisted her daughter be present.

Well, here Dani was, even though she actually could be having her own celebration because she'd finally gotten promoted today, from mammal keeper to head mammal keeper. Yay her. But her celebratory carton of ice cream would have to wait, and with Perfect Stranger Guy heading to the bar for her drink, she limped through the lobby to make her appearance.

The building was new, all steel and glass, with a wall of windows looking out onto the tarmac, lined with million-dollar jets. Beyond that, an incredible view of the LA nighttime skyline. The place belonged to Sky High Air, a luxury jet service to the stinking rich, and these days her mother was indeed as stinking rich as they came, a far cry from the trailer park they'd started out in.

As Dani hobbled along, trying to look like she fit in, she took in more than her fair share of curious glances. Yeah yeah, so she didn't have a spare pair of Choos in her trunk and her hair was out of control, so what. She was here to support her mother, not to have a bad high-school flashback.

But just like high school, the few guys who glanced her way looked right through her like . . . like she was a nobody.

Nice to know that she was still registered so high on the desirable scale.

Except not.

Okay, maybe the shoes and hair mattered, at least to these people, who'd probably never had a bad hair day in their collective pampered life. Feeling more than a little off her axis, and a whole lot clumsy and unattractive, she forged ahead. She could do this. She could smile and make merry, and as a reward, later, she'd plow through that carton of Ben & Jerry's.

Determined. That's what her epitaph would read. Ahead of her, her mother appeared out of a circle of people, moving with all the elegance and grace that she hadn't passed on to Dani. As one of the most wealthy, powerful women in the area, Sandra Peterson had a reputation to uphold, and she knew it. After all, she'd married up the ladder, several times, trading husbands for upward rungs as she'd gone.

Well, Dani had gotten that determination from somewhere.

As usual, Sandra's dark hair had been carefully coiffed, and unlike Dani's, remained firmly in place, framing a gorgeous, well-preserved face. The smile seemed real enough, which surprised Dani, considering Sandra had been telling people her daughter was just a little crazy—her mother's way of accepting their differences in lifestyle.

Her mother was flanked by her stepsiblings from a previous marriage to some Italian count. Tony and Eliza were in their twenties, both dressed to the hilt, with noses tilted to nosebleed heights. Since they'd inherited God only knew how much from their father and rarely spoke to mere mortals including, maybe especially including, Dani, she looked at her mother first. "Hello, Mother."

"Darling." And to her surprise, Dani received an air kiss in the region of each of her cheeks.

Tony and Eliza smiled, though Dani could only call it such because they bared their teeth. Maybe their purse strings were too tight, choking them. Or maybe they really disliked her as much as she imagined they did. Most likely it was lingering concern over their trust funds, which were so huge they couldn't have spent all their money in their lifetimes. Or in their children's lifetimes.

Or their children's children's lifetimes . . .

Once, a year back or so, Dani had suggested the two unemployed socialites go into philanthropy. They'd stared at her blankly, mouths open so wide Dani had practically seen the hamsters running on their wheels inside their brains.

Give away money? they'd asked in horror, having never once in their lives been strapped for cash. Why would they give money away . . . ?

When their father had gotten cancer and had revealed he planned on leaving Dani a share of his estate, people had been shocked. But then he'd died without finalizing his new will. The probate court had given everyone eighteen months to make a claim against the estate, something Dani had never even considered doing. She made her own way in the world, always had. But until the eighteen months were up, people were waiting for her to make a move, whispering about her, thinking she was odd to say the least for not wanting the money.

When she greeted her stepsiblings, their lips barely curved, not a single laugh line or wrinkle in evidence, making them a walking *Don't* ad for Botox.

Meanwhile, Sandra was giving Dani and her appearance the eagle eye. "Go ahead, Mother. Have your say."

"I wasn't sure you'd come, seeing as you hate me these days."

"I don't hate you."

"Soon as I got rich, you disowned me."

If that wasn't a twisting of the facts to suit the woman. But then again, her mother was the master of twisting things to suit herself. "I simply asked you to stop controlling me with your newfound money. And then you reacted by disowning *me*."

"Controlling you with my money?" Sandra shook her head and sipped her champagne. "Honestly."

"That *was* honesty."

"Okay, yes, fine. I'm guilty. I admit it. For you, my daughter, I wanted the right clothes, the right college, the right job—"

"There's nothing wrong with my clothes—"

Her mother sniffed. "That dress is at least four years old. Not to mention off the rack."

Five years old, but who was counting. She was just grateful to still fit in it. "And Cal Poly was a great college."

"Please. With your grades, you should have gone to Harvard."

"They didn't have a zoology program."

"Yes. And I know how important it is for you to play with your elephants."

Ah, there it was. Dani pinched the bridge of her nose and drew a deep breath. She was a mammal keeper. *Head* mammal keeper now, which still meant a pathetic salary but she didn't care. She was doing what she loved, what she'd always dreamed of, and she wouldn't apologize. "Look, have a great evening. I think I'll just go." And for once she was going to make an exit on her own terms. Turning, she ran smack into a solid brick wall.

Or the chest of a man.

He was holding two drinks, or had been holding, along with a sort of lazy wicked smile that spoke of a confidence such as she'd never experienced, and as she plowed into him, the champagne flew out of the expensive-looking flutes and right on her, splashing down the front of her off-the-rack, five-year-old little black dress.

Her mother gasped.

Dani's Perfect Stranger Guy swore and began to apologize, setting down the flutes, gesturing to a waiting server for assistance, but she backed away.

She didn't need assistance. She needed a lobotomy for thinking she could come here and even partially fit in. Waving good-bye to her mother, nodding to the man she could happily look at forever but hoped to never see again, she moved away, more carefully this time, searching for her most direct escape route.

The iced champagne down her front made breathing difficult. Or maybe that was just humiliation choking her. Pulling her soaked dress away from her torso, she grabbed her own flute from a passing server and tossed it down the hatch as she hobbled on. There. Maybe that would help bolster her spirits.

And maybe Santa would really visit this year.

Just ahead, in front of the coat check where she'd left her coat, two women glanced at her, then back at each other, exchanging a look.

It didn't matter what the Paris Hilton clones thought, she told herself. She was far more than anyone here saw. She knew it, and repeating it to herself, she passed them by without stopping to get her coat, forcing her head high, smile in place. It wouldn't have fooled the mammals she trained, and it wouldn't have fooled a single one of her friends, but it would fool people here in the Land of Fake Smiles.

At the front doors, her fake smile faded as she stumbled to a halt.

It was raining. Not just raining, but pouring, huge buckets of water falling out of the sky, hitting the pavement with such velocity the drops bounced back up again, nearly to her knees.

Damn it, and she'd forgotten to get her coat.

Turning back, she took in the party. People were dancing, talking, laughing, in general having a good time. There were several couples nearby, beneath various sprigs of mistletoe, kissing. Another couple about to kiss . . .

She sighed. Just once, she wanted to be beneath the damn mistletoe, just long enough to boost her failing confidence. Perfect Stranger Guy came to mind, but no doubt he had women lining up holding mistletoe over his head, their pulses racing, panties already wet.

With another sigh, she moved back to the coat check.

"He's the hottest man here."

This from one of the Paris Hiltons as the woman eyed no other than Dani's Perfect Stranger Guy.

"You're going to have to fight me for him," Paris Hilton Number Two said.

"From what I hear, he's ready, able, and willing. Why don't we just share him?"

Okay, ew. Dani moved down a hallway, thinking she'd just find a ladies' room to give herself a pep talk, and then, hopefully, the coat check would be clear. She opened the first door she came to, which turned out to be an office. A rather lush office, with candles strewn across a huge glimmering black desk, and behind it, a gorgeous man in the desk chair wearing a Santa hat. Perfect, really. Except he was clearly already taken, presumably by the beautiful woman in the Mrs. Santa hat, straddling him.

Whoops.

"Noah," the beautiful woman said with a gasp. "You didn't lock the door."

"Sorry, I thought you did."

"Excuse me," Dani whispered, trying not to notice that the man's hands were up the woman's skirt, and Ms. Claus's hands were . . . oh boy.

"My fault." Dani shut the door and winced, even as a little part of her yearned. What she'd give to be in the lap of a man who couldn't keep his hands off her. Shaking her head at herself, she kept going.

The next door wasn't a bathroom, but a storage closet. A big one, the shelves filled with office supplies, organized and neat.

And then suddenly there was a hand at the small of her back as a big, tall male form squeezed in behind her.

"Hey—"

"Hey yourself." Flicking on the light, he shut the door, then leaned back against it, flashing that lazy, wicked boy smile.

Perfect Stranger Guy.

Chapter 2

Dani gaped at him, the man who'd seen her graceless entrance to the party, who'd witnessed her social skills, all none of them. "What are you doing?"

"You looked like you could use a moment alone."

"Yes, but I'm not alone," she said pointedly.

He smiled.

Her happy spots stood up and tap-danced, but her brain beat them back down.

Then he stepped closer, and her happy spots won the battle. All around her, the closet seemed to shrink. The shelves closed in, the light dimmed, and she couldn't see anything but this man looking at her, smiling easily, relaxed, laid-back.

Sexy.

Trying to be cool, she smoothed back her hair and attempted to balance on her one heel—and nearly went down. At least she caught herself before he could, at the expense of her pride.

And her hair.

It fell in her face and over her shoulders as one of the pencils she'd forgotten about hit the floor.

A pencil. The one she'd shoved in at work to hold her hair off her head when she'd been vaccinating a panda. God, she was such a hopeless geek.

Before she could beat herself up about it, he bent for the fallen pencil and handed it to her. "Yours?"

"Um. Yeah." *Be cool. Please, be cool.* "It's a new thing. You know, a casual/formal thing—"

At his arched brow, she sighed. "Fine. I was late and forgot to do my hair."

He flashed that dimple, and just like that, her other senses kicked in. Mostly the lust sense. But she cut herself some slack because he was fairly dazzling. So dazzling that her skin was feeling too tight for her bones. Or maybe that was just her dress, shrink-wrapped to her body thanks to the champagne.

Following her thoughts, his smile faded. "I'm so sorry about the drinks. How can I make it up to you?"

Oh, let me count the ways. "No," she told herself.

"Excuse me?"

"Nothing. Talking to myself. Bad habit." She realized she was inviting him to think she was as nuts as her family thought her. "I mean . . ."

"That's okay. I talk to myself sometimes too. Look, can I get you something? Anything?"

Confidence on tap, please. "I'm good. Wet, but good."

He laughed.

She blushed. "I mean—"

"I know what you mean." He studied her for a moment. "You're like a breath of fresh air, you know that?"

She started to squirm, then stopped and looked

at him right back. Was he . . . flirting with her? "How many times has that line worked for you?"

Leaning back against the shelves, he flashed that dimple, looking fairly off the charts while doing it, but not very abashed. "Quite a few, actually."

She laughed. *Laughed. Ask him to stand beneath the mistletoe,* her body begged. She opened her mouth to do just that, just as he pushed away from the shelves and brought that leanly muscled body closer.

Oh boy.

His chest pressed into hers, and his arms, when he lifted them, surrounded her. Oh, God. Someone here *did* look at her, *did* see her . . . *desire her.*

He was going to kiss her.

"Oh," she whispered, thrilled, even as her breath backed up in her throat. Yes, he was going to kiss her and she hadn't had to ask. That was the very best kind, and she stared at his mouth. "Thank you," she whispered. *Thank you? God, be quiet. Don't ramble now!* "I'm just so glad—I mean . . ."

His mouth curved quizzically. It was a good mouth, an enticing mouth. Despite her reservations, despite the insane evening, she couldn't wait to feel it on hers, to have him take her out of herself and make her feel wanted. Waiting for it, she closed her eyes, and—

"Here you go."

She opened her eyes and met his golden ones.

He'd pulled something off the shelf behind her and was handing it to her.

A towel.

"You've got to be soaked through," he said.

Well, her brain certainly. She took the towel and pressed it to her torso, because yes, she *was* soaked through. And that was the reason her nipples had gone all happy. The only reason.

God, she really was an idiot.

Pulling yet another towel off the shelf, he glided the soft material along her throat. "I'm really so sorry," he murmured, his gaze on the task at hand.

Which was not kissing her.

"It's okay." Maturely, she closed her eyes again and wished for a huge, giant hole to swallow her up. "It wasn't your fault."

She heard him toss the towel aside, but she didn't open her eyes. Couldn't bring herself to. Until she felt his hand, his big, warm hand, cup her jaw. His fingertips were at her hairline now, just the simple, easy touch making her knees a little wobbly.

Damn champagne.

"Why do you look so familiar?" His mouth was close to her ear, close enough to cause a whole series of hopeful shivers to rack her body. He was rock-solid against her, all corded muscle and testosterone.

Lots of testosterone.

"I don't know," she whispered, still hoping for a big hole to take her.

"Are you sure you're all right?"

"Completely." *Except, you know, not.*

"Because I can't help but think I'm missing something here."

Yes, yes, he was missing something. He'd missed her whole pathetic attempt at a kiss seduction, for instance. And the fact that she was totally, one hundred percent out of her league here with him. But his eyes were deep, so very deep, and leveled right on hers, evenly, patiently, giving her the sense that he was always even, always patient. Never rattled or ruffled.

She wanted to be never rattled or ruffled.

"Am I?" His thumb glided over her skin, sending all her erogenous zones into tap-dance mode. "Missing something?"

"Yes. N-no. I mean . . ."

He smiled. And not just a curving of his lips, but with his whole face. His eyes lit, those laugh lines fanned out, and damn, that sexy dimple. "Yeah," he murmured. "Definitely missing something."

"I'm a little crazy tonight," she admitted.

"A little crazy once in a while isn't a bad thing."

Oh boy. She'd bet the bank he knew how to coax a woman into doing a whole host of crazy stuff. Just the thought made her feel a little warm, and a nervous laugh escaped.

"You're beautiful, you know that?"

She had to let out another laugh, but he didn't as he traced a finger over her lower lip. "You are," he murmured.

Beautiful? Or crazy?

"You going to tell me what brought you to this closet?"

"I was garnering my courage."

"For?"

Well wasn't that just the question of the night, as there were so many, many things she'd needed courage for, not the least of which was standing here in front of him and telling him what she *really* wanted. A kiss . . .

"Talk to me."

She licked her lips. "There's a man and a woman in that first office down the hall. Together. And they're . . . not talking."

"Ah." A fond smile crossed his mouth. "You must have found Noah and Bailey. They've just come home from their honeymoon. So yeah, I seriously doubt they're . . . talking."

"Yeah. See . . ." She gnawed on her lower lip. "I was hoping for that."

"Talking."

"No. The *not* talking."

Silence.

And then more silence.

Oh, God.

Slowly she tipped her head up and looked at him, but he wasn't laughing at her.

A good start, she figured.

In fact, his eyes were no longer smiling at all, but full of a heart-stopping heat. "Can you repeat that request?" he asked.

Well, yes, she could, but it would make his possible rejection that much harder to take. "I was wondering your stance on being seduced by a woman who isn't really so good at this sort of thing, but wants to be better . . ."

He blinked. "Just to be clear." His voice was soft, gravelly, and did things to every erogenous zone in her body. "Is this you coming on to me?"

"Oh, God." She covered her face. "If you don't know, then I'm even worse at this than I thought. Yes. Yes, that's what I'm pathetically attempting to do. Come on to you, a complete stranger in a closet, but now I'm hearing it as you must be hearing it, and I sound like the lunatic that everyone thinks I am, and—"

His hands settled on her bare arms, gliding up, down, and then back up again, over her shoulders to her face, where he gently pulled her hands away so he could see her.

"I saw the mistletoe," she rushed to explain. "It's everywhere. And people were kissing. And I couldn't get kissing off my mind . . . God. Forget it, okay? Just forget me." She took a step back, but because this was her, she tripped over something on the floor behind her. She'd have fallen on her ass if he hadn't held her upright. "Thanks," she managed. "But I need to go now. I really need to go—"

He put a finger to her lips.

Right. Stop talking. Good idea.

His eyes, still hot, and also a little amused—because that's what she wanted to see in a man's eyes after she'd tried to seduce him, amusement—locked onto hers. She couldn't look away. There was just something about the way he was taking her in, as if he could see so much more than she'd intended him to. "Seriously. I've—"

He turned away.

Okaaaay . . . "Got to go."

But he was rustling through one of the shelves. Then he bent to look lower and she tried not to look at his butt. She failed, of course. "Um, yeah. So I'll see you around." Or not. Hopefully not—

"Got it." Straightening, he revealed what he held—a sprig of mistletoe.

"Oh," she breathed. Her heart skipped a beat, then raced, beating so loud and hard she couldn't hear anything but the blood pumping through her veins.

His mouth quirked slightly, but his eyes held hers, and in them wasn't amusement so much as . . .

Pure staggering heat.

"Did you change your mind?" he asked.

Was he kidding? She wanted to jump him. *Now.* "No."

With a smile that turned her bones to mush, he raised his arm so that the mistletoe was above their heads.

Oh, God.

"Your move," he whispered.

She looked at his mouth, her own tingling in anticipation. "Maybe you could . . ."

"Oh, no. I'm not taking advantage of a woman in a closet, drenched in champagne." He smiled. "But if she wanted to take advantage of me, now see, that's a different story entirely."

He was teasing her, his eyes lit with mischievousness and a wicked, wicked intent.

"I'm a klutz," she whispered. "I might hurt you by accident."

"I'll take my chances."

She laughed. She couldn't help it. She laughed, and he closed his eyes and puckered up, making her laugh some more, making it okay for her to lean in . . .

And kiss him.

Chapter 3

Shayne felt her mouth touch his. Oh yeah, life was good, damn good.

She was tentative. Jerky. As if maybe she hadn't kissed in a while. It was the most arousing sensation, but right then and there, he knew. The one quick peck? Not going to be enough.

Dropping the mistletoe, he cupped her face, his fingers gliding into her silky hair to hold her head as he better lined them up.

Her hands lifted, hovering in the air for a beat before settling on his chest. A soft little murmur of wanting escaped her, and just like that, he went insta-hard. Her fingers dug into the material of his shirt, holding on just a little, telling him she felt the same, telling him he wasn't alone in this odd sensation of not wanting to let go, not ever wanting to let go.

And he didn't even know her name . . .

She opened her mouth a little, but that was all the invitation his tongue needed, and then her tongue

and his were doing a slow dance, an age-old imita-
tion of what he really wanted to be doing, and she
was right there with him, and when they finally both
pulled back, her eyes fluttered open. "Wow," she
whispered.

Yeah. Definitely wow.

"That was . . ." At a loss, she let out a low laugh. "I
don't even have the words."

Him either. That kiss had just registered off the
scale for first kisses. Not really understanding why,
he stroked a strand of hair from her face, then left
his fingers on her because she was tightening her
grip on his shirt, tugging ever so slightly, her gaze
back on his mouth . . .

"That was . . ." she repeated.

"Wow," he reminded her.

"So wow." She licked her lips, and then they
lurched at each other and went at it again, deeper
than before. Wetter.

Hotter.

Her hair fell the rest of the way, assisted by his fingers, and the second pencil hit the floor. She arched
against him, bumping into the zipper of his pants.
Apparently she liked what she felt behind that zipper because she let out a little gasping "oh," and
then a sound of pleasure from deep in her throat as
her arms tightened around his neck, her hair flying
all around them.

God. He was in a closet, with an entire lobby full
of people on the other side, important people that
he'd brought here with his family connections so
that he could further Sky High Air's business, and
what was he doing?

Making out in a closet like a high-school kid.

Only there was nothing high school about the

mystery kisser in his arms. Christ, no. She was all woman, straining up on the tiptoes of her one-heeled foot to get closer. Closer worked for him. He hoisted her just a little higher so that he could rock his hips into hers, so that her breasts pressed into his chest.

Her shoe hit the floor.

It didn't stop her, didn't stop either of them. She let go of his shirt to entwine her arms around his neck. He let go of her head to slide his hands down her arms, up her slim spine, bared by that dress so he was touching smooth, silky skin. Hauling her closer, he turned, pressing her back against the door, where they strained against each other some more, the champagne from her dress soaking into his shirt.

He didn't care.

But she slowly pulled back, breathing hard. Her eyes fluttered open and landed on his, glazed and dazed. Her gloss was gone, her mascara smudged. One of the thin straps on her little black dress had slipped off her shoulder, hanging down to her elbow.

God, she was sweet. And hot. And such a sexy, wonderful mess.

"That was some powerful mistletoe," she whispered.

He laughed. "I don't think that had anything to do with the mistletoe."

Her gaze locked on his lips. "No?"

"No."

"Maybe we should make sure."

That worked for him. The mistletoe lay where he'd dropped it, near their feet. He nudged it beneath the shelving unit, out of sight, prompting her to let out a low laugh that sounded like half anxiety, half anticipation as she stared up at him.

He stared back, tracing her temple with his finger, stroking a strand of hair back . . . and then suddenly they were leaping at each other again, mouths fused, hands fighting for purchase on each other—

Until a knock on the door behind them nearly gave him a heart attack. *Jesus.*

"Hello in there?" came a woman's voice.

Maddie. *Shit.* Shayne pressed his forehead to the woman in his arms and closed his eyes.

"Hello?" Maddie called again. "Is anyone in there?"

Shayne set a finger to his mystery woman's lips because maybe, if they were very, very quiet, maybe Maddie would go far, far away.

"Shayne, is that you?"

Ah, hell. Who was he kidding? It was Maddie, bull-dog terrier. Once she'd locked her jaw on something, she never let go. "How did you know?"

Through the door, she laughed. "When are you going to learn that I? Know everything."

"Know this. Go away."

"Touchy, touchy. What are you doing in there?"

"Maddie?"

"Yeah?"

"Code Pink."

"Did you say Code Yellow?"

"You know I didn't. Code Pink, Mad."

There was a beat of silence, then nothing but the beautiful sound of her heels clicking as she walked away.

The woman in his arms slid out from between him and the door. "Your girlfriend?"

"No."

She nodded. "Code Pink?"

Maddie was Sky High's concierge, as well as assistant to Sky High's three partners—Brody, Noah, and himself. Maddie was the best of the best, even if she was a pain in his ass. Code Pink was their private code for Back The Hell Off. As opposed to Code Yellow, which was SAVE ME. "It's a work thing. Watch out—"

But she'd already backed right into the shelving unit. A stack of towels rained down on top of her, and with a little squeak, she ducked. "I'm sorry," she gasped, trying to catch everything as it fell and put it back.

He watched for a moment because there was something so watchable about her. Her necklace had turned itself around and was hanging down her back. A tiny, delicate gold chain dangled between her shoulder blades, the pendant a capital *D*. As more things rained down on her, she swore, having absolutely no luck catching anything. Stepping close to her, he reached above, helping to stanch the flow.

She shoved the strap of her dress back up but it immediately slipped again, still giving off that whole slightly messy but adorably silly thing she had going, which he'd never imagined would be attractive.

But it was. And not just because her sweet ass was snugged up to his crotch.

Okay, partly because of that.

He touched her necklace, let his finger slip beneath the pendant, and dropped it over her shoulder so that it slid back between her breasts where it belonged.

At the touch, she went very still, and then, in that tight, small space, turned to face him, slowly lifting her face.

The only sound in the room was their breathing.

"I really thought it was just the mistletoe," she finally whispered. "You know, the whole holiday spirit, or something like that, and we just got caught up in it."

"I think we already proved that theory wrong."

"Maybe it's the closet."

Clearly, she needed it to be something. But it wasn't the mistletoe, or the closet, and he slowly shook his head.

"What, then?"

"I'm thinking Chemistry 101."

Her mouth was still wet from his. He had no clue what was so sexy about that, but he couldn't tear his gaze off her.

"So." She lifted a shoulder. "You're Shayne."

"Yes. And you're . . . ?"

"Dani. Dani . . ." She hesitated. "Peterson."

"Peterson."

"That's right."

Peterson. A bad feeling began to worm its way to his gut, and his hands, which had been moving lightly up and down her arms, went still on her. "As in Sandra's daughter?"

"Yes."

Oh, Christ. Sky High Air had been built on love and sweat, lots of sweat. In the first lean year—last year, in fact—he and Brody and Noah all had been mortgaged to their eyeballs, scrapping their way out of the red and into the black by sheer determination alone.

And Shayne's trust fund.

But even that hadn't been enough. They'd needed connections, and Shayne's family had them. Sandra Peterson had been one of these connections, and she'd brought her rich friends to Sky High, garnering them many new clients. And one thing those clients did was gossip.

A lot.

Sandra included. How many times had Shayne heard her talk about her daughter? Brilliant, she'd always said. But crazy. "I didn't know you'd be here tonight."

"Neither did I." Dani dropped her hands from his chest. "And I can tell from the look on your face that you're ever so thrilled to find out who I am."

Well, let's review. He had the daughter of their most valued client in a closet, shoved up against a shelving unit, his hands—*Christ.*

He yanked them off her and opened his mouth to apologize, but she laughed harshly and shook her head.

Now he understood why she looked familiar—she *was* familiar. She was a dead ringer for her mother, minus twenty-odd years and four husbands. He'd just kissed his most valuable client's daughter. His most valuable client's *crazy* daughter.

"I see you've heard of me."

Yes. Yes, in fact he had. "I fly your mother."

"So you're a pilot."

And that's when he realized. While he knew exactly who she was, she had no idea who he was, that he was one of the three owners of Sky High. That was new. New, and . . . oddly refreshing.

"I'm not a good flier," she said, completely unimpressed by him. Another first.

"I've gotten many people over that hump," he said, and something in her changed. Her eyes shuttered from him, and she crossed her arms.

"No. Thanks."

Interesting. Usually once a woman found out who he was, her eyes lit up.

This woman hadn't even completely realized it, and her eyes were lit.

"I've got to go." She moved past him for the door.

"But—"

The door shut behind her with a decisive finality.

Nice going, he told himself. *Using mistletoe to kiss your client's crazy daughter. Really. Good job.* When his cell phone rang, he glanced down at the readout and sighed.

"You about done in there, stud?" Maddie asked in his ear.

"I'm not doing anything."

"Hey, I'm not here to judge."

He pinched the bridge of his nose. "What do you need?"

"To talk to you. But I can wait until you finish." She sounded amused.

"I'm not doing anything!"

"There's nothing to be ashamed of." She was out and out laughing now. "Men have needs. I get that."

"Okay, you did *not* talk to Noah like this when *he* was in the closet several months back with Bailey."

"That's because Bailey had a couple of goons with guns after her. You have goons with guns after you, Shayne?"

"Why do I pay you again?"

"Because, wait for it, I just signed the Clark family's Learjets to a six month lease. *And,*" she continued, "I told your stalker that you've left the building."

"Dani?"

"Who? No, Michelle."

"She's still here?"

"Was. She said she had plans for you tonight. I

corrected her, and she's not too happy with you. But she's gone now."

"Scratch what I said earlier," he told her gratefully. "Whatever we're paying you, it's not enough."

"I'll memo that. Now you might want to make an appearance out here before our guest of honor wonders what the hell you were doing with her daughter in a closet."

Not only in the closet, but up against the door, tongue buried deep in her mouth. "How the hell do you know *everything*?"

He could practically hear her grin through the phone. "It's a gift."

Dani headed toward the large double front doors of Sky High, adrenaline still rushing through her veins, along with a shocking amount of yearning.

Had that just really happened?

Had she really just made out in a closet with a stranger named Shayne? A pilot—a frigging pilot!—whose demeanor said laid-back trust funder? Seriously? Because he was so far out of her league that they weren't even on the same planet.

He'd heard the stories about her. She'd seen it in his eyes when she'd told him her name. He knew everyone thought that her elevator didn't go to the top floor.

But she'd made a career out of not letting what people thought get to her. Nope. Not getting to her. She was simply moving full speed ahead in one heel toward the front doors for her health. Because that's what she did. She ran when the going got uncomfortable.

She'd made a career out of that too.

It was still pouring buckets outside, but she no longer cared. Escape was more important than comfort. Pulling open the doors, getting slapped in the face by the icy wind and rain, she stepped into the night, where there were no recriminating stares from stepsiblings, no couples kissing beneath the mistletoe.

No sexy pilots.

God. She'd wanted a diversion, she'd wanted to feel something, wanted to need, to yearn and burn, and man, oh man had she needed, wanted, yearned and burned for him . . .

The kiss had been amazing. So had their second one.

It'd been more than amazing, it'd created a soul-deep longing for things she knew she couldn't really get in a closet with a stranger, but there for a second, for one single tiny mindless second, she'd been *so* willing to try—

Nearly plowing into a figure standing there in a dark cloak, the hood up, she staggered to a surprised halt. "Sorry," she said, pushing her wet hair from her face. "I'm—"

There wasn't one person standing there, but two. And one of them was slowly slipping to the sidewalk, just as something flashed from beneath the first person's cloak.

A gun.

Chapter 4

Shayne closed his cell phone on Maddie and eyed the mistletoe still lying on the floor. It made him smile, for no real good reason other than Dani had been right. Insane or not, those kisses had been every bit as wow as she'd said.

For the second time in as many minutes, his cell vibrated, making him sigh. This time it was Brody. *"What?"*

"Maddie says you're abusing yourself in there. Dude, the porn is in the mechanic's bathroom, not the closet."

"Funny." Brody was more than a partner, he was his best friend, and had been since that fateful day in middle school when the three of them had landed in detention. Noah had been fighting, Brody had been caught with a girl four years his senior, and Shayne? Cheating in chemistry. "What do you want?" he asked, crouching down to clean up the things that had fallen from the shelves.

"Maddie said you gave her a raise. Tell me that's not true."

News always traveled fast at Sky High Air, mostly due to the fact that they were all apparently still in high school. "She signed the Clarks' three Lears for six months."

"Thought that was your job. Maybe we should switch your job descriptions. You'd look good in that pink miniskirt Maddie wears."

"Shut up." They were all equals at Sky High, him, Brody, and Noah. And all pilots, though Brody handled the majority of their flights. Noah specialized in personalized adventures, finding and fine-tuning them for their clients. And though Shayne loved to fly and did plenty of it, as the people person of the group, he handled the business end of things; bringing in new clients, acquiring new planes, leasing said planes, etc. Together, they made the whole package, and whether that meant flying a turboprop or a jet on a moment's notice, taking a charter flight to Santa Barbara, or a business group to Alaska, it got handled, efficiently, discreetly, and luxuriously.

Not a bad gig, especially for Shayne, the black sheep of an affluent family who'd always seen him as the youngest, the daydreamer.

The weak link.

His family would be surprised to know that every single one of Sky High's clients had been brought in by him. *Because* of him.

But now Maddie had brought in a client, a big one, and Shayne was nothing but grateful. For the first time, he wasn't the sole provider, and damn, that was a relief. "She deserves a raise, Brody."

"We already pay her a fortune."

"So now we'll pay her a fortune and a half."

"Can't bleed a turnip."

Brody had been born poor, had grown up poor, and starting Sky High Air had nearly gutted him. He couldn't stand the thought of debt, couldn't wrap his brain around the fact that they were on their way to making it, and making it big.

They were going to do it, shocking as that seemed for three fucked-up kids once headed directly for juvy without passing go.

But it was more than money on the line and they both knew it. Brody, the ultimate guy's guy—and commitment-phobe to boot—had allowed Maddie to get beneath his skin.

Not that the big guy would ever admit it. Hell, no. Show a weakness? Brody? He'd rather gnaw off his own arm. "She's saved our ass time and time again," Shayne reminded him.

As he knew this to be true, Brody fell silent. Maddie *had* been a godsend. At twenty-six, she was a few years younger than them, and probably a helluva lot more mature, even with her current choice of magenta hair. She'd been going through a biker stage lately, and with that came a lot of black leather, which he had to admit had been fun to look at. She was more than their concierge and assistant, she was an all-around miracle worker. The woman could get her fingers on anything and have it delivered before the client even knew it was needed. "We can vote on this," he said. "But I know Noah will agree with me."

"Shit. Noah's so pussy-whipped he can't even see straight. They're still in his office, you know. Him and Bailey. Someone's going to have to send food in there to sustain them."

"Jealous?"

That made Brody laugh. "Of having a wife? Are you kidding me?"

"How about for having sex whenever you want it?"

"You don't need a wife for that, so why should I? And who are you in there with anyway? Not Maddie, not Michelle. Kathleen?"

"Left the country."

"Dude."

"What does that mean?"

"That's what a girl says when she dumps you."

"I did not get dumped." He'd so been dumped.

"So you're in there with someone new, then," Brody decided. "Big surprise."

"Hey." Shayne might have the reputation for going through women like some went through fine wine, but he'd always used discretion and was careful to be only with women looking for the same thing he was—a good time.

Dani had certainly seemed to fit that bill. She'd come on to him, always a fun bonus, and had seemed lucid enough at the time, but now that he knew who she was and that the world in general considered her to be crazy, he felt uncomfortable, as if he'd taken advantage of her somehow. "I thought you said I was in here alone."

"Well if you are, self-gratify on your own time. You've got at least fifty socialites out here, drinking and being merry, all way too close to million-dollar planes." Brody was extremely protective of the planes. "People are all over them, carrying flutes of champagne and tiny plates of fancy shit masquerading as food. So please, get your ass out here and flash that poster-boy smile as you tell everyone to watch the damn planes. Ah, shit—"

"What?"

"Maddie, three o'clock," he hissed. "Heading right for me." The big, badass Brody sounded terrified. "She's got that look in her eye too. The gonna chew me up and spit me out look."

Shayne had to laugh. "She's a whole foot and a hundred pounds lighter than you. Suck it up, you chicken shit."

"You have no idea—*Fuck*. Gotta go."

Shayne slipped his phone back in his pocket and had no sooner reached for the closet door to go out and rescue the planes when it opened and someone slipped inside.

Dani.

"Oh, thank God you're still in here." She gulped. "Houston, we have a problem." She was drenched, shaking, and sobbing for breath as she turned and slammed the door before whipping back around, eyes so wide there was nothing but white all around her dark irises. If he thought she'd looked like a mess before, it was nothing to now, with water streaming down her face, her hair plastered to her head, her dress sucked up against her like a second skin. "Ohmigod, Shayne—"

"Dani." Jesus, what had happened? With no other choice, he put his hands on her, drawing her close even though she was wet as hell, and making him the same. "Are you all right?"

"Yes, but"—she gulped again, pointed to the door— "out there—" Burrowing against him, she shuddered.

She felt so small and cold, and her whole body was racked by her next shiver. He tried to warm her up with his body heat. "What happened?"

"I saw—I need to call the police but I don't think

I can dial. Can you dial?" Pulling free, she patted herself down.

He saw the exact second that it registered, she had no pockets in that little black dress, and most likely no cell phone.

"My phone's in my car," she whispered. "And my car's in the shop. I need a phone. He needs help. We have to help."

Her eyes were fully dilated, twin balls of horror, and he pulled out his cell. "Who needs help? Tell me, and I'll call."

"There's a dead body. I saw the gun." She covered her face. "I saw it happen, ohmigod, Shayne, I saw it happen."

His gut went cold. "Where?"

"Out front."

Jesus. "Wait here." Sounds from the large party filtered over him as he ran down the hallway; laughter, music, talking, sounding all so surreal as Dani's words ran through his head.

A dead body.

A gun . . .

Passing a server who tried to offer him a tray of hors d'oeuvres, he headed out the double front doors. It was raining like a mother, coming down in slashing sheets that blocked out much of the light from the two lamplights on either side of the walkway. As the doors closed behind him, shutting out the sounds of the party, all he could hear was the rain slapping the concrete.

There was absolutely no one else around. No engines running, no people, nothing. Turning in a slow circle, he took a second look, and a third. He even moved down the steps, directly into the rain, getting soaked within seconds as he walked into the parking lot, up and down the aisles of parked cars, looking, searching . . .

Finding nothing.

Slowly heading back, he blinked past the water in his face, taking in the parking lot one last time before the front doors opened.

Dani.

"Did you call the police?" she demanded, hugging herself. "We have to get them out here right away."

She needed a coat. And a warm room.

And possibly, a straitjacket. "Dani."

She stared at him with dark, tormented eyes, then turned to look at a spot only five feet from him, her gaze glued to the sidewalk.

The empty sidewalk. "But . . ." She didn't say what he'd already discovered.

No dead body. No gun. No bloodstains.

Nothing.

As if to emphasize this, the rain increased, hitting the ground like bullets, pounding into him with painful velocity.

Shoving her hands into her hair, Dani pushed the strands off her face, then stepped to some invisible mark and slowly turned to him. "It was here." She hunkered down to get a closer look at nothing. "Right here."

"What was that, exactly?"

Straightening, she turned and hobbled into the parking lot, limping on her one high-heeled sandal.

"There's nothing there, Dani."

"But only a few minutes have passed. Not long enough to dispose of a body and all the evidence, right?" Standing in the downpour, she turned in a slow circle as he'd done, taking in the parking lot, the area all around them, her bare limbs gleaming with rain water, pale and shimmering as she hugged herself.

"Dani—"

"There were two of them," she said hoarsely, eyes still wild. "They were . . . fighting, I think. Or maybe not. One of them shot the other. I saw the gleam of the gun. I saw that person fall."

Again he eyed the spot she was talking about. Nothing but wet pavement. No bloodstains, no sign of trouble . . . "Did you hear the gun go off?"

"No. The rain is too loud. I think." Lifting her head, she leveled him with those eyes. "I know how it sounds, but I swear it, Shayne. I saw somebody die."

He wanted to believe her. Her terror was genuine. But then there was his reality. Half of the people inside had heard about her. Her own mother had told them.

The girl was crazy.

Was this how she was crazy? Did she get perfect strangers to kiss her and then make up wild stories? If he went off sheer odds alone, he'd have to admit, the cards were stacked against her.

She was staring at him, clearly reading the thoughts all over his face. "Damn you." She covered her mouth, her hand shaking. "Damn you." Then as if she couldn't quite get enough air, she bent over and breathed like a person on the very edge.

"Dani." He put his hand on her back, and she straightened. Glared at him.

"I am *not* making this up, Shayne."

Maybe not, but she was in full panic mode, complete with near hyperventilation, dilated pupils, possibly going into shock. Keeping his hand on her, he pulled out his cell, hitting Brody's number.

"Hey," Brody complained. "I'm in the middle of a plate of food here."

The only thing Brody loved more than his planes was his food. "Is everything okay in there?"

"I don't get these little appetizers. They're just teasers. We need some real food in here, you know? Want to get a pizza?"

"Jesus, forget the food. There's no problem in there, nothing at all?"

The good humor dropped from Brody's voice. "No. Why? What's wrong?"

"I'm not sure." He watched Dani, who walked away from him, again crouching down, peering at the sidewalk, rain pouring down her face.

"Shayne?"

"Stay tuned," he said, shutting the phone, walking toward Dani.

"I'm not crazy," she said, without looking at him. "I'm not. I saw someone die, right here."

She absolutely believed it. Which begged the question—did he believe it too?

Chapter 5

Dani shivered as she kneeled on the sidewalk, the rain pouring down over her. She was so wet now it no longer mattered. All she wanted was to get to the bottom of what she'd seen.

But that wasn't going to happen, she could tell by the look in Shayne's eyes. Oh, God. He thought she was nuts, and for one beat in time, she felt nuts. But she'd seen what she'd seen.

She *knew* it.

Still, with no evidence, what could she do? Nothing. Nothing at all.

Knowing that, it was time to get out of here, time to get back on solid ground. She needed to go home, back to her comfort zone.

Shayne had been talking on his cell phone while carefully watching her, but he closed it now and slid it into his pocket. He was as drenched as she, his hair plastered to his head, his whiskey-colored shirt and dark pants clinging to his long, hard body, and yet he somehow managed to look as elegant and sophisticated as he had perfectly dry.

Pushing the hair from his brow, he came toward her, his eyes giving nothing away of his thoughts. "Dani."

A few moments ago, she'd been able to read him like a book. But that had been when he'd been holding a sprig of mistletoe above her head, his eyes bright with wicked fun and enough heat to melt her bones.

He'd delivered on the promise of that heat and then some.

But she didn't expect him to deliver now, not with that unfathomable look in his eyes, and could she blame him? She had a reputation for being a loon, and she'd just told him she'd witnessed a murder.

Without evidence even remotely supporting such a claim.

"I'm sorry," she said, turning away before he could see how shaken she felt. "I'm just going to go."

"Wait—"

"It was a lovely party. I'm sure my mother is very happy with you and will continue to hire you to fly her on her every whim." She had no idea where she was going; she'd gotten ready for the party at work, and thanks to her car being broken down again, she'd taken a cab here.

But she had to go.

Unfortunately for her, Sky High's fixed operating base wasn't on the main side of the Burbank airport, but across the terminal, on the private sector side. She could see the road from the lot, but it was quiet. No lights. No cars.

And per the usual, she'd left her cell phone in her car in the shop, which was really going to piss off

Reena because Dani had promised to call her with a play by play of the rich and famous. Even worse, Dani's coat was in the coat closet in the building behind her, but even though she couldn't afford a new one right now, she wasn't going back for it.

Not now.

Not ever.

Except . . . damn it. Her keys were in her coat pocket.

"Dani."

You know what? She didn't need her keys. She had one hidden beneath the mat at her apartment. So she kept moving, quickly. Or at least as quickly as one could move with only one heel. She was halfway through the parking lot, her feet splashing through the water pooling there, when a hand closed around her elbow, gently pulling her around.

"Where are you going?"

She looked up into Shayne's face. His golden eyes were definitely no longer twinkling with good humor and that bone-melting lust, but were full of dark concern that threatened her composure, as tenuous as it was. And that mouth, the one that had been so adept at amping her heart rate, was no longer sensually curved, but grim. "I'm going home."

"Where's your car?"

Pulling free, she shook her head. "I'll catch a cab. I'll be fine." Probably.

Hopefully.

He actually let her take a few steps away before he spoke. "You saw something tonight."

She nearly tripped, but didn't. She did, however, slow to a stop, staring straight ahead into the dark night. "Yes."

She heard his footsteps as he came up behind her,

his fine shoes hitting the water pooling in the lot. He'd ruined them, no doubt. *She'd* ruined them.

"Something that terrified you," he went on. "So don't tell me you're going to be stupid enough to go walking off into the night alone."

She blinked past the rainwater in her face, still looking straight ahead at nothing, nothing but the scary night.

"Let me give you a ride at least."

Turning, she met his gaze. He'd shoved his hair off his forehead again, but water was still running in little rivulets down his face. His lashes were inky black and stuck in little spikes. Rain dripped off his nose, along his jaw.

Good God, he was something to look at. "Why would you do that?"

"Because I want to."

"Shayne, you don't have to do this. You don't have to baby-sit the crazy chick."

"It's just a ride, Dani."

"Yes, but—"

"Maybe we could talk about it in my car. In my *dry* car." Without waiting for an answer, he slipped his fingers around her elbow again and steered her around, back toward the building.

"I'm not going back in there."

"No." His car was parked in the front row, a gleaming, fancy, gorgeous Porsche as sleek and sophisticated as the man who owned it. He fished through his pockets and found his keys, opening the passenger door for her.

She glanced inside at the plush leather interior. "I'm too wet. I'll ruin it."

He let out a soft huffing laugh that broke through her panic and scraped low in her belly. "Just get in."

"Shayne—"

"It's pouring rain, Dani."

"Yes, but . . ."

When she trailed off, he leaned in, his mouth close to her ear. "Just a ride . . ."

Just a ride . . . Only for her, it felt like more, a lot more. It felt like a great leap of faith. But he'd moved in, his body close enough to hers to share body heat. He wanted her to get in, but it felt, just a little, like going from one danger to another. And yet with one last long look into his eyes, she slid in.

"You're just going to leave the party?" she asked when he'd come around and slid behind the wheel.

"Yes. Where to?"

She gave him directions to her building in Burbank Hills, and he drove them into the gloomy, tempestuous night.

"If when you get back, something's happened—"

He slid her a glance. "You mean like someone finding a dead body?"

"I know what I saw, Shayne."

"If when I get back, something's happened, I'll call you."

"I left my coat."

"I'll make sure you get it." He made the turn onto her block and parked at the curb. She lived on a street right out of the turn of the century, but not the current one. The houses here were three-story Victorians dating to the early 1900s, all having been renovated into duplexes. Most had been redone many, many times, and though they were old and quaint—a polite word for small as a postage stamp— they possessed great character and had a good view of the city below.

She'd lived here since college, and loved it. It was

more home than anything had ever been before, that being because her mother had been fond of living off her husbands, and they'd moved around.

A lot.

But Dani wasn't going down that particular memory trail tonight. Nope, all she wanted now was a mug of hot tea, a bathtub full of bubbles, and then bed.

Alone.

As soon as Shayne stopped the car, she reached for the door handle. "Thanks." Then, before he could say a word, she scrambled out into the storm and shut the door.

Behind her he turned off the Porsche.

She hurried, going as fast as she could with one heel, but she heard the driver's door open and then shut. She sped up, not wanting him to walk her to her door, not wanting to look into that face and see the mixture of wariness and pity.

Because after all, she was crazy.

But she wasn't, damn it. She didn't have an explanation for what she'd seen, but somehow, she'd figure it out—

"Dani."

How he'd caught up so quickly, she'd never know. Probably those ridiculously long legs of his. Or her lack of a heel. "I'm fine. There's no need for you to walk me up."

"Well, if it's all the same to you, I'm going to anyway."

A stubborn gentleman. That would have made him all the more attractive if she wasn't uncomfortably close to a breakdown and wanted to be alone to have it, thank you very much. But she remained silent until they took the steps to the second floor.

There was a hallway here, and two apartments. A head popped out of the first one, and she was just spooked enough to nearly jump right out of her skin.

Alan was a high-school geometry teacher who'd moved in a few weeks back, and Dani had done something completely out of character. She'd made him welcome brownies. He'd bought her a pizza and they'd watched a basketball game on her TV. He'd like her to go out with him in a more formal way, but something held her back. He was cute and funny and sweet, and she wasn't sure what her problem was.

He smiled when he saw her, that warm, kind smile—

Which dimmed as he then took in Shayne, and then her disheveled state. "Dani? You okay?"

She went with her standard. "I'm fine, thanks." Well, other than the fact that she'd kissed a stranger in a closet, seen a murder, and was frozen solid as a Popsicle . . . she was fine. Fine, fine, fine.

Her apartment was right next to Alan's. At her door, she paused. Alan was still watching her. Shayne had moved in close behind her, also watching her. "Good night," she said. To both of them.

Only neither budged.

"I can take it from here," she assured them.

More of neither man budging. The only sound was the rain and the water dripping off herself and Shayne. "Oh, for God's sake." She bent to reach beneath her mat for the key she kept hidden there.

A sound of disbelief came from Shayne. "You're kidding me. You can't hide a key there." He glanced back at Alan. "And he's watching."

"Hey," Alan said, frowning. "I'd never just—"

"I'm just saying." Shayne stepped in close, blocking Alan's view of her. "Look, I'm really beginning to worry about you."

She shot him a look, then put the key in the door. "Good night," she said again, more firmly.

Or so she tried. But her damn voice shook. *Okay, definitely time to be alone . . .* She turned the key and stepped inside.

With Shayne right on her heels.

"Oh, no. No way." Putting a hand to his chest, she halted his progress, but that left them standing in the doorway, incredibly close, his head bent down toward hers, their mouths nearly touching.

Alan nearly fell out of his own doorway trying to get a better view. "Dani? Are you sure you're okay?"

"Still fine," she called out, eyes on Shayne as she gave him a push.

Like a brick wall—or a stubborn ass, pick one—he didn't budge. "I want to walk you inside."

"Not necessary."

"I think it is."

"I can get myself inside, I manage to do it every day. I'm not crazy, damn it."

"Okay," he said agreeably. "You're not crazy. Explain tonight."

"Before or after the closet? Because that part? That *was* crazy."

His mouth twitched. "*After* you kissed me."

"*You* kissed *me*."

"No."

"Yes. You held up the mistletoe and leaned in and—"

Oh, God. *She'd* kissed *him.*

He let out a sound that might have been a half

laugh, half growl as he stepped forward, into her, slipping an arm around her waist.

"Hey—"

Whipping her around, he shut the door and pressed her back against it, trapping her between the hard wood and the even harder length of his body, which freed up his hands to cup her face as he kissed her.

Really kissed her, and holy smokes, she was out of her league here with him. So out of her league.

He nibbled at her mouth until she opened for him, a feat that took less than a heartbeat because damn, he knew what he was doing. She found herself wrapped around him like shrink-wrap, kissing him back with everything she had, which caused a low, sexy rumble from deep in his throat. His hands got very busy, gliding down her arms, her hips, her bottom, which he squeezed, before moving up again, to her back bared by the dress.

The feel of his fingers on her skin brought a shiver that had nothing to do with the fact that they were both chilled and dripping water on the floor, nothing at all—

His industrious fingers played in the black velvet strings crisscrossing her back, entangling with the knot, and she went still. If he loosened it, the thing would release the entire top half of her dress.

He kept playing.

She stopped breathing.

Lifting his head, looking into her eyes, he smiled, as his fingers dallied with the string, and then . . . oh, God and then, very lightly pulled.

Still not breathing. "Shayne—"

His eyes were sexy and slumberous as his hands

slid down her body one last time before falling away. "*Now* you can say I've kissed you."

She was breathing again, like a marathon runner now. The only thing that made it even halfway acceptable was the fact that he wasn't breathing any too steady either.

"Dani?"

"No, I don't think so."

He cocked his head to the side. "You have no idea what I was going to ask."

"You were going to ask me out. I don't think so."

He let out a low laugh of a genuine amusement. "I was going to ask you not to leave your key under the mat."

Her face bloomed. "Oh."

"But just out of curiosity," he murmured, still looking amused. "Why wouldn't you go out with me?"

"Doesn't matter, since you weren't asking."

"Why, Dani?"

She sighed. "You don't want to know."

"No, I do. I really do."

"Okay." She shook her head. "You're a ten."

"A ten?"

"Yeah. And tens? They date tens. And sixes date sixes. If a ten dated a six, then the six is pretty much just asking for a heartache."

He blinked. "Was that in English?"

"Never mind." She tried to open her door to kick him out but he blocked it with a palm on the wood above her head.

"You think you're a six?" he asked.

She controlled her wince. "I know I presented as a three, but on a better day, I can be a six."

He looked at her for a long moment, then reached into his pocket and pulled out a card, pressing it into her hand. She looked down. A business card.

His.

"My cell-phone number is there if you need me." Leaning in, he put his mouth to her ear. "And on your worst day? You're a ten plus."

Her knees wobbled. He was strong and smart and sexy—and colossally wrong for her. She recognized it, he had to recognize it, and she just hoped she was also smart enough to remember it. "I won't be calling, Shayne."

Something flashed across his face. Resignation? Regret?

Lingering heat?

Definitely lingering heat.

Fine. Great. So they were both still a little turned on. They were adults. They could deal with it. Yanking open the door, she gave him more than a push this time, it was far closer to a shove, and she knew the only reason she was able to budge him at all was because he let her.

Gaze still locked on hers, he stepped back, opening his mouth to say . . .

She had no idea because she shut the door. Shut the door on a hot man who thought she was hot too.

Ten plus? She fanned her suddenly hot face with her hand. Maybe she really was crazy. Dragging a deep breath, she moved into the living room, kicking off her worthless shoes.

God, what an evening. She'd left a few dishes in the sink, and she had some reports from work spread across the kitchen table, but the place was warm and cozy. Home sweet home. Grabbing a spoon and her carton of ice cream, she headed toward her bedroom. She needed to ditch the little black dress ASAP, get a hot bath, and then fall into bed. Just as soon as she consumed a thousand calories or so.

Chapter 6

When Shayne got back to Sky High, the last of their guests were just leaving and Maddie was pouring the happy, and quite drunk, bride-to-be into a cab. Sandra caught sight of Shayne, dragged him close and gave him a smacking kiss on the cheek. "Thanks." She was a little goofy and a whole lot drunk. "Best party ever." She would have given him another kiss, right on the mouth this time, if Maddie hadn't rescued him and shut the cab door on Sandra.

When the cab had driven off, Maddie turned to Shayne with her hands on her hips. "What is it with you and women? It's like you're irresistible or something."

"Maybe I am."

She laughed.

"Hey," he said, following her back inside to help clean up. Walking around the lobby with a trash bag, he took a good, long look around, shocked at what he saw. Looked like the disasters at one of the frat parties he and Noah and Brody had had in college. "For a bunch of rich people, they sure were slobs."

"Hello, Mr. Kettle." This from Brody, who was sprawled on one of the couches, tie loosened, working his BlackBerry.

"Just because I grew up around these people doesn't mean I'm one of them."

Brody snorted.

Shayne looked at Maddie, also walking around with a trash bag, then back to Brody. "Who's the one *not* getting their hands dirty?"

Brody didn't bother to answer.

Shayne threw him an empty bag. "Feel free."

"Yeah, I don't do trash."

Maddie righted a tipped-over potted plant, the trash bag at her hip definitely clashing with her teeny, tiny, heart-stoppingly clingy silver cocktail dress. "Tell him you want a raise, Shayne. Let's watch his blood pressure rise."

Brody narrowed his eyes at her. "What does that mean?"

"That you're looking quite comfy on that leather couch. If Shayne is Mr. Kettle, I think you're Mr. Pot." She moved to a wall to straighten two crooked pictures. "And a cheap one at that."

"All I said was that we pay you a helluva lot of money. I didn't say you weren't worth it."

"That's because you *can't* say that. Not when you know I am worth it, every single penny. Why are you still here anyway? I thought you had a date. You get stood up?"

"No." But Brody scowled. "Maybe."

"What a shock, what with all those pretty words and heart-stopping smiles."

Brody looked at her, the air crackling between

them. The silence grew, until Shayne opened his mouth to suggest they just knock it out like a pair of horny teenagers to see if that helped, but Maddie asked him a question.

"How did your rescue mission go?"

"What rescue mission?" Noah asked, coming out of his office, holding Bailey's hand. His shirt was wrinkled and half untucked, and Bailey's hair had a definite I've-just-been-thoroughly-screwed-on-a-desk look.

Brody took one look at him and shook his head in disgust. "Aren't you two tired of jumping each other's bones yet?"

Bailey blushed and tried to fix her hair.

Noah flat-out grinned. "Hell, no. What rescue mission?"

"Nothing," Shayne said.

Noah looked back and forth between them. "Okay, what did we miss?"

"Only the entire party." Brody tucked his Black-Berry away. "Maybe I ought to get a wife too, so I can miss all the social shit."

"You couldn't get a wife if you tried," Maddie told him. "Too curmudgeonly."

"Seriously. I sign your paychecks."

"And I earn every penny."

"You could dress the part."

She looked down at her sexy dress. "What's wrong with this?"

"Absolutely nothing," Shayne told her.

Brody glared at him. "I'm just saying you could dress like an assistant once in a while, that's all."

"Tonight was social, you moron."

Noah laughed and pulled Bailey to the door. "You kids play nice."

"Curmudgeonly?" Brody said to Maddie after they'd left. "Moron?"

But Maddie followed after Noah and Bailey, grabbing her purse and coat as she went.

"Hey," Brody called after her. "Where are you going?"

"Out. Because I? Didn't get stood up."

"I didn't get stood up either." Brody frowned. "And I'd make a great husband! If I wanted to wear a ball and chain!"

From over her shoulder, Maddie waved a hand, sashaying across the lobby in that silver clingy dress that seemed to be defying gravity to stay up—

"She's our concierge," Brody hissed to Shayne. "Stop looking at her ass."

"I wasn't doing anything you weren't doing."

"I was *not* staring at her ass."

"Please. You've made a career out of staring at her ass."

Maddie turned back. "Maybe the both of you could stop staring at my ass. Hot as it is . . ."

Brody grimaced and shoved Shayne. Shayne decided to let that go, because while he'd been just having fun, Brody was not. The guy was sporting a crush on Maddie, one of gigantic proportions.

And one of these days, the guy might even face it. Maybe he and Maddie would figure out a way to go at each other, and it just might be the real thing.

Then Noah would have Bailey, and Brody would have Maddie, and Shayne?

Odd man out.

A little twinge hit him at that, which was stupid. He had everything, anything he could possibly want right at his fingertips, and yet . . .

And yet he felt a restlessness he couldn't deny.

Odd, since he'd never given much thought to the far-off future, or even tomorrow, and yet he felt like he was missing out on something.

But hell if he knew exactly what.

Maddie turned back. "Oh, hey, playboy?"

Brody lifted his head.

"Not you. Shayne."

Brody looked affronted.

"Gotta live it to earn it," Maddie told him.

"I could live it." He sank further into the couch when both Shayne and Maddie laughed. "Well, I could."

"Okay," Maddie said and rolled her eyes. "Shayne, I forgot to tell you, when Michelle was looking for you, she asked me to have you stop by her place tonight."

Which was pretty much the last thing he wanted to do.

She read his face. "I figured you wouldn't want to, what with your whole date-a-woman-once thing."

"I've dated women more than once."

"Really? Name one."

"Michelle. I dated her twice."

"Because you didn't sleep with her until the second date. Face it, Shayne, you're allergic to relationships."

"Hey, after Michelle, I went out with Marie, Suzie, and Kathleen, remember?"

"And your point?"

"I asked each of them out on a second date, and . . ." He grimaced. "And each turned me down."

"Wow. Three whole rejections." Maddie shook her head. "After the hundreds you've rejected."

His cell phone rang. Pulling it out, he stared down at the name on the ID.

"Dani Peterson," Brody read over Shayne's shoulder.

Maddie. "She's hooked."

"Damn," Brody said. "How do you do that so fast?"

"Guess she didn't get the memo about the no-second-date thing," Maddie offered.

"Maybe she has another closet she needs you to check out," Brody added.

Maddie laughed, and Brody smiled at her, and for a moment she seemed to soften.

Shayne shook his head, and turning his back on his so-called friends, answered. "Hello?"

"Shayne?"

She was in panic mode again, he could tell. "You okay?"

Dani opened her mouth to respond to Shayne, but nothing came out. She was scared. Terrified, actually. She'd taken her bath and gone to bed, but had awoken suddenly, heart pounding.

And though she hadn't heard a sound, hadn't seen a thing in her darkened bedroom, she'd felt it.

A presence.

She hadn't been alone in her apartment.

She'd grabbed the baseball bat she kept in the corner and had gone still, listening. A soft rustling had come from her bathroom. Heart kicking hard, beating at a rate that had to be near heart-attack inducing, she'd left her bedroom, pausing in the hallway but no longer hearing a thing, not even a whisper of sound.

It was as if someone had been holding his breath, waiting.

Well, that person wasn't the only one. Dani had

grabbed her cordless phone and the business card
by it and had run out her front door, going straight
to Alan's, torn between pounding and a light tap because she couldn't decide which was more important—that Alan hurry, or that she not let the stranger
in her apartment know where she was.

But Alan's place was dark, and silent, and he didn't
answer. She was hunkering in the shadows between
his door and hers so she didn't run out of range on
her phone, planning on dialing the police.

Who would have actually been helpful. She hadn't
meant to call Shayne, but she'd looked at his card
and read his name in embossed print.

Shayne Mahoney
President of Operations

Calling his cell while his title played in her head,
along with the implications.

He'd told her that he was a pilot. So why had she
turned to him? Bad fingers. Bad decision, calling the
man who'd let her think he was nothing but a pilot
for hire, when in fact he ran Sky High Air.

The only reason for that—he'd been slumming.
With her.

And still, she'd called him. Clearly her brain had
gone AWOL on her.

"Dani?"

Hunkered there in the dark shadows in the up-
stairs walkway of her building, she considered hanging up on the man she'd kissed in a closet.

And against her front door . . .

"Talk to me, Dani."

Just his voice did something, brought her a sense
of calm when she didn't think she could ever find

her calm again. "I didn't mean to call you. Just a re-
flex, I think. So if you could forget this whole
thing—"

"Just tell me what's wrong."

She squished herself farther into the shadows, but
no one came out of her place. Had she imagined the
whole thing?

"Dani."

She glanced at Alan's apartment again. Now
would have been a really nice time for him to poke
his head out.

No such luck.

She wasn't far from work, about a mile. Sometimes she walked there, but doing so now in a T-shirt
and men's boxers didn't appeal.

"Dani, damn it. Talk to me."

"I fell asleep," she whispered. "And when I woke
up, I think there was someone in my apartment."

"Where are you now?"

"Between my place and Alan's."

"Alan . . ." He tried to place the name. "Stalker
Alan?"

"He's not a stalker," she whispered and rubbed
the baseball bat for courage. "Listen, I'll call the police from here, okay? I'm sorry. I really shouldn't
have called you. Please, forget I called."

"Dani—"

"Thanks." She winced. *Thanks?* "Bye, Shayne."
She hit the off button and resisted smacking her
own forehead with the phone.

Shayne gritted his teeth at the unmistakable click.
"Hello? Dani? Don't you hang up on me—" She'd

hung up on him. "Damn it!" He pulled his cell phone from his ear to look at the readout. "She hung up on me."

Still sprawled on the couch, Brody shrugged. "Saved you some time."

"This is serious. At least I think it's serious." Shayne brought up the last number received on his phone, then called it.

"Interesting," Brody noted to Maddie. "He's calling her back. I think that constitutes date number two." He looked at Shayne. "Aren't you worried you'll get your, what is it now, fourth rejection in a row?"

"Brody?"

"Yeah?"

"Shut up." *Pick up,* he silently urged Dani, while letting Brody's teasing roll off his back. So he hadn't been the most reliable of men where women were concerned. He'd never been a good bet. He didn't stick. Ask his family. Ask any of the women he'd dated.

But this felt different. This wasn't about sticking. Or at least that's what he told himself as he waited. This was simply about helping someone who needed it.

Dani's phone rang and she nearly lost a year of her life. Still against the wall between her apartment and Alan's, she looked at the caller ID screen, felt her stomach quiver, and answered. "Shayne."

"You call the cops yet?" he demanded.

"I—" Oh, God, was that a scraping sound behind her? Flattening herself to the wall, she squinted into the darkness and saw nothing. *Breathe. Just breathe.*

She'd just half convinced herself she'd made this whole thing up, but she hadn't manufactured that noise. "I'm fine," she whispered.

"So fine your voice is shaking with terror. So fine you accidentally called me instead of the police."

"I would have called them now," she pointed out. "But you keep chatting."

"You're giving me gray hair as we speak. Gray hair, Dani."

"Don't worry. Gray will blend in nicely with your color."

"Not funny."

Through the phone, she heard a car start up. A Porsche. "Shayne, seriously. Stay put. I'm calling the police right now. I'm getting out of here."

"Where to?"

"The zoo. I work there. It'll be fine." There was that word again, fine. She'd used it so much tonight it didn't even sound like a word anymore.

"Don't tell me you are going to walk."

"Okay." She winced. "I won't tell you."

"Jesus Christ. Another ten gray hairs just popped out on my head."

"Look, I was going to knock on Alan's door, but his place is dark."

"That's because it's the middle of the night. Can you get to the street? Near one of the lights?"

"Yes." Glancing behind her as she took the stairs, she saw no one, not a person, not another car, nothing. Sort of becoming a thing with her tonight. She got to the ground floor and moved toward the street. With a little distance, she began to breathe easier. "Seriously. This is silly."

"If it turns out to be silly, then we can laugh and move on."

"Gray hair and all?"

"Gray hair and all. But for right now, go with scary, and stay out of dark places. I'm nearly there."

She didn't know what to say or how to feel about the fact that his rushing over without question had brought a lump to her throat, so she quietly nodded. "Thanks," she whispered, but the phone had died. She'd gone outside the parameters. Completely alone, she hugged the wall behind her and hoped he hurried.

Maddie sat at a bar looking at her date, wondering what the hell she'd been thinking. She'd met him at the party tonight, had agreed to this drink because he'd been funny and gorgeous and smart, but as she watched his lips moving while he talked, she wished . . . *hell*.

She wished it was Brody who'd wanted the nightcap with her.

Stupid.

She'd taken the job at Sky High out of desperation. She'd needed money, and more than that, she'd needed security, both of which had been in short supply most of her life. So she'd bullshitted her way into the job, thinking how hard could it be to make flight reservations and keep the clients happy?

Turned out to be a lot more complicated than that, and a lot harder. The guys—Noah the sexy intellectual, Shayne the carefree playboy, and Brody the wild pilot rebel—had seen through her B.S. immediately, of course, each of them being just as street-smart as she, but still they'd hired her.

They'd taken a real chance on her.

But it turned out that she had a real knack for the organization required, for making things happen. For making people happy.

Who'd have thought?

She'd saved the guys' collective ass in their first year, and they'd saved her too, without even knowing it. They'd given her that sense of security she'd craved, and a place where she'd been accepted, no matter what. She'd love them for that alone, but it went deeper. They trusted her, and in return, she'd been able to learn to trust again as well.

And in a shockingly short amount of time, Sky High Air had become home, and the guys her brothers.

But nothing about Brody felt as comfortable as a sibling or a kid. Nope, the man made her sweat, pure and simple.

She hated to sweat.

The problem was her own, of course. Yes, she was damn good at what she did, and yes, she'd made herself completely indispensable. But in doing so she'd also made herself a part of the family.

As a result, there was no way in hell that Brody would touch her now, not the way she dreamed of him touching her. It made her ache, but if she had to choose between having him or having the job, the job would win.

Every time.

Cold consolation when she excused herself from her date and walked toward the front of the bar just as Brody was coming in, with a tall, gorgeous brunette.

So tall. *So* gorgeous.

Damn.

He'd taken her advice. He'd started to "live it." Terrific time for him to listen to her.

He didn't see her, he was too busy laughing with Barbie Doll—as he never did with her.

All about the job, she reminded herself. Not the man. Which was really just more cold consolation . . .

Chapter 7

Distance, Shayne reminded himself on the drive to Dani's. The trick was to remain a little distant. Shouldn't be a problem, he was a master of distant, and any who knew him would be able to swear to that in a court of law.

But no more than six minutes after Dani had hung up on him, he pulled up to her apartment building.

For the second time.

He had no idea what to expect, or what he thought he could do, and twice on the way over he'd nearly turned around, and would have, except for one thing.

She'd been genuinely terrified.

As he parked, she came out from beneath the awning on the front porch and into the rain, moving like a shimmering wet dream. Her hair was down, still wet, clinging past her shoulders. Out of her black dress now, she wore only an extremely wet T-shirt and boxer shorts, no longer looking awkward and out of her league, but like a hot, drenched, curvy woman who deserved the trophy at a wet T-shirt contest. *Holy shit.*

Yeah, that was some great distance he was maintaining.

She opened the passenger door of the Porsche before he'd pulled the parking brake, and certainly before he could get out of the car to open her door for her.

"Sorry," she gasped, shoving back the streaming wet strands of her hair. It fell in tangled, wet waves past her shoulders, as wild as her eyes.

He tore his own off her body. "For?"

She lifted her hands helplessly. "For making your car all wet for the second time tonight. For calling you in the first place. For kissing you. I don't know, pick one."

Reaching into the back seat, he handed her the coat she'd left at the party. "Yours?"

"Yes." She shrugged into it and hugged herself tight.

"There's no need to apologize for any of this."

Her gaze dropped to his mouth. "Okay." She licked her lips, an entirely innocent and uncalculated gesture, but it still shot a bolt of heat right through him. "If you're sure," she said softly. She hadn't buttoned her coat, and with her hands fiddling in her hair, it fell open enough to remind him—hot, wet female.

No bra.

And, he could only figure, no panties. Though why he even went there, he had no idea.

"Shayne?"

He had to clear his throat and forced himself to look away. "Yeah?"

"Thanks for the ride."

Distance. Keep it. Repeating the words like a mantra to himself, he turned off the engine.

"What are you doing?"

"Going up to check out your place."

"That's not necessary."

Arching a brow, he turned to face her. "Did you call the police, then?"

"No."

"Why not?"

"Truth?"

"Please."

"I think . . ." Embarrassment crossed her face. "I think I probably just imagined everything."

He studied her for a long moment. Her eyes were haunted, her mouth grim. "You don't believe that."

She lifted a shoulder, and he sighed. "So what's your plan? Go to work in your pj's?"

Again she lifted a shoulder.

"I can't just leave you here, Dani."

"Yes, you can."

"Is there someone you could call to come stay with you?"

"No."

"You're the queen of no's tonight, you know that?"

She let out a self-deprecating laugh. "I just . . . I don't like to lean on people."

"Trust me. I get that. Hell, I live that. But you shouldn't be alone. Not tonight."

Turning to him, she flashed those wide, gorgeous dark eyes, filled with . . . ah, hell, *hurt.* "Because I'm crazy?"

Crazy beautiful. "I didn't say that."

"If you could please just take me to the zoo, I'll handle it from there."

"Dani—"

"Please."

She had a strand of hair stuck to her jaw, another along her throat, curling down to her collarbone. She had a drop of water on her nose, and as he watched, it fell to a breast.

Her T-shirt, white and thin, was really quite sheer. He was certain he should tell her, or at least reach in and close her coat.

Be the gentleman.

But he didn't say a word, which undoubtedly made him a jerk. She'd been right not to want to go out with him.

"Shayne?"

"Yeah." He shook his head at himself. "Yeah, I'll take you to your work."

"Thank you."

He put the Porsche back in gear and pulled away. "So what do you do at the zoo?"

"I'm a mammal keeper."

He arched a brow, surprised. "As in feed the bears?"

"Feed, clean, monitor . . . and not just the bears. Today I was with the elephants. Tomorrow I'll be with the primates."

"You're not quite dressed for that."

"I have things to change into there."

Good. Great. He didn't care because look at him, he was keeping his distance. "But we really should check out your apartment."

"No. I imagined it. I know that now. I'm sorry."

She was lying, but what could he do? Distance. Repeating that, he pulled out of the lot.

The highway was deserted, and as he drove into the dark, stormy night he told himself he was doing the right thing, and that he would not, repeat *not* try to change her mind regarding getting involved, because getting involved would lead to things, things like more kissing, and that would be a bad, very, very bad way of maintaining his distance.

Dani let out a relieved breath and leaned back into the soft, toasty interior of Shayne's car. The heated leather crinkled around her, pulling her in, and she let out a shuddery sigh that undoubtedly gave away her relief and lingering fear. Going still, she glanced at him.

Looking unruffled and perfectly at ease as he drove, as if he could be modeling for a car ad, Shayne cut his eyes to hers.

He remained quietly calm, which she greatly admired. She wanted to be quietly calm. And he smelled good. How she could notice such a thing was beyond her, but he smelled yummy and looked even yummier with that hair tousled just enough that she wanted to run her fingers through it.

"You're staring at me," he murmured.

A short, mirthless laugh escaped her. "Sorry."

What he did next surprised her. He reached out and took her hand in his.

She stared down at their entwined fingers, his long and tanned, work-roughened. And warm. So wonderfully warm. She pictured them gliding over the parts of her that were chilled, imagined how that would feel, and shivered again.

"You really should have let me go up there," he said, cranking up the heat.

"No, it's all right."

"Or called the police."

"If I'd called the police the two times you'd wanted me to tonight, I'd probably be at the station being held for a psych eval."

His silence was his agreement, and she sighed again. The rain had picked up even more, if that was possible, and when a large truck came at them, splashing copious amounts of water across the windshield, Shayne let go of her hand to put both of his on the steering wheel, fighting the slick road and wind.

Feeling frozen from the inside out, she slipped her hands into her coat pockets—

And went still as stone.

Oh, God. "S—Shayne?"

Still fighting the road, he didn't glance over. "Yeah?"

Heart kicking into full gear, she slowly pulled out what she'd found . . .

A gun.

Cool to the touch, surprisingly lightweight, it gleamed in her hand. As if it being lightweight was her biggest worry. Unable to believe she hadn't felt it in her pocket, she just stared at it. "Um, Shayne?"

He glanced over and executed a double take. *"Jesus."* He jerked the car to the side of the road with a squeal of tires. "What the fuck is that?"

She held it in the air between them as if it were a ticking bomb. "A g-gun?"

"Why are you holding a gun, Dani?"

"I don't know!"

"Okay." Watching her as if she was a spitting cobra, he nudged it aside. "Which is infinitely better than saying 'I'm going to use it on you, Shayne.' "

"You thought I—*Ohmigod.*"

With the same slow care he'd have given the snake, he reached out and took it from her, then let out a long breath. "That's better."

"I wasn't going to—Is it real?"

"Oh yeah." He was staring at the gun in his fingers. "Definitely real."

"Oh, God." She couldn't even wrap her mind around it. *"How did a gun get in my pocket?"*

"Yeah, now see, I was kinda hoping you were going to tell me that story." He held the gun with just his thumb and first finger, clearly trying not to get any more fingerprints than absolutely necessary on it now that he understood it wasn't hers.

And thank God he understood. She had to give it to him for his composed, relaxed nature. He hadn't freaked.

Which was good because she was freaking enough for the both of them. "It isn't mine," she whispered. "I swear it."

Leaning past her, he opened his glove box and pulled out a small towel, which he used to hold the gun. Then he did something to it, and a part of it clicked open.

He was checking to see if it was loaded, she realized, and leaning in, she caught a flash of a bullet.

Oh, God. She covered her mouth with a shaking hand.

It was loaded.

Their eyes met, Shayne's grim and determined as he wrapped up the gun.

"It was loaded," she said very softly.

"Yes."

"I could have shot off my own foot with it in my pocket like that."

"Yeah."

She swallowed hard. "I could have—"

"But you didn't."

Right. She'd focus on that. But she had to swallow again. "Do you think it's the same gun that I saw someone use tonight? At Sky High?"

He closed his eyes briefly and rubbed his forehead. "What does it say about the way the night has gone that I actually forgot about that part of the evening?"

"That it's been a long one?"

He opened his eyes and shook his head. "If it's the same gun, and it's not yours—"

"It's not!"

"Then someone wanted it to look like yours."

She just stared at him.

Swearing softly, he shifted in his seat to more fully face her. He put his hands on her arms, and she could tell by the look on his face that she wasn't going to like what he said next.

"Dani, my brother is a cop, a detective, high up in the ranks—"

"Shayne—"

"No, listen to me. There's something going on. What you saw tonight at Sky High, whatever happened in your apartment, and now this. It's time for help."

Staring into his face, she saw the concern there. Not for himself, but for her. And somehow that reached her. "I really did try to convince myself I imagined it all."

"Well, you didn't imagine the gun."

"No."

"Dani, we have to call the cops. It might as well be Patrick, who can—"

"Yes." Her hands went to his chest, because he was solid. He was a solid piece of ground beneath her as she balanced on a spinning, out-of-control world. "I . . ." She closed her eyes. "I need help. Your help."

Silently agreeing, he pulled out his cell phone and hit a number. "Patrick. Yeah, it's Shayne. I have a problem." He listened, then rolled his eyes. "No, I didn't call you to take care of a speeding ticket— Look, it's complicated. You available? Good." His eyes cut to Dani. "I'm on the 134, between Victory and Zoo Drive, and there's a gun—That's right, a gun. It was found in the coat pocket of . . ."

A crazy woman, Dani silently finished for him.

But that's not what he said. "A friend."

Dani let out the breath she'd been holding and resisted the urge to hug him. He wasn't a *friend* friend. He wasn't someone . . . someone she could call for help. And yet that's exactly what she'd done, and he'd come through.

"She's never seen it before," Shayne was saying. "And just a little while ago, she thought someone might be inside her place—Yes, we'll wait here for you." He gave his brother the address, then slipped the phone back into his pocket and looked at her.

She tried to smile, but couldn't, so she gave up. "Now we wait?"

He nodded, still holding her gaze in that way he had that convinced her that not only could he read her mind, but he could see right through her.

Inside her.

To the real Dani Peterson, the one who felt more comfortable in pj's than a fancy dress, the one who scooped elephant poop for a job and wouldn't know a Prada item if it bit her on the ass.

The most surprising part of that was he seemed to

be okay with that woman, as okay as he'd been with the one who'd kissed him in a closet. That felt lovely, so lovely, which was bad because she couldn't do this with him. Not without getting hurt. "I'm not a good waiter."

"It won't be long."

She looked into his eyes, feeling her heart sigh just a little. He'd been so patient tonight. She'd bet he was a good waiter. The best of waiters . . . which brought her mind back to his kisses.

"Dani." His voice sounded soft, a little husky, as if he knew where her thoughts had gone.

And she felt a catch in her chest. He'd been such an amazing kisser.

His fingers were playing with her coat, and then one of her shoulders was bared as he nudged it, and in spite of herself, she leaned in. "Help me wait, Shayne." Sliding her hands up his chest, into his hair, she entangled them in the wavy strands.

His eyes darkened, and her body reacted to that and the unbelievable amounts of adrenaline in her system. "We could talk," he said.

"Talk."

"Uh-huh." He let their noses gently bump. "Talk."

They were breathing each other's air, just looking into each other's eyes, and the moment seemed so startlingly intimate, she couldn't move. "I don't feel much like talking." Oh, God. Had she just said that? Really?

"No?" He tilted his head so that their noses were no longer bumping.

Now their mouths were lined up perfectly.

"No . . ."

"Dani—"

God, she really loved the way he said her name, all raspy and extremely male.

"What else did you have in mind?"

Honestly? There wasn't a single thought in her head that wasn't a dirty, wicked little fantasy. Certainly nothing she could mention. "I can think of several things."

He smiled, that killer smile that scraped at all her happy spots.

"Shayne?"

"Yeah?"

"How is it that when I'm with you, I don't feel like I'm losing my mind."

"I don't know." He ran a finger over her ear and made her shiver. "For me, it's the opposite."

"So I . . . rattle you?" And was that good? Or bad?

But the look in his eyes told her. It was good, very, very good, and it set off all sorts of alarms inside her. "We can't really do this again," she murmured.

"No. Because there isn't any mistletoe."

Be strong. Say it. *Believe it.* "Because we're not going to date."

"Right. No dating." He nudged the coat off her other shoulder as well. "Because . . . ?"

"Because you're not my type," she said, reminding herself. So not her type.

His soft laugh brushed the hair at her temple. "Liar."

Oh, God, she thought. *Toss me a life vest, because I'm going down . . .* He was warm, so deliciously, wonderfully warm, and exactly her type. So much so that her body leaned to his like a heat-seeking missile. And this time, when their mouths touched, it was more like a homecoming than she'd ever experienced, and she opened for him, opened and let out a sound that would have been horrifying for its dark neediness except for the fact that he matched the sound with one of his own.

All by themselves, her hands slid beneath his shirt—to warm them up, she told herself as she ran her fingers over a set of abs that made her tremble, and though he sucked in a shocked breath at the iciness of her touch and let out a low "holy shit," he seemed to like her hands on him. Pulling her coat off, he bent his head and took his mouth on a hungry tour over her bared throat, her shoulder.

Her entire body quivered with anticipation.

He had all the access he needed. Her T-shirt provided little coverage. It was wet, clinging, and he easily pushed it up as his hand skimmed her belly to cup her breast, holding it for his mouth. His tongue rasped over her nipple, and the only sound was her head thunking back against the passenger seat. And then her moan, along with another of those horrifyingly needy gasps for air, as if she'd just run a 5K.

"Still not dating me?" he asked against her skin.

Oh, he sounded smug, didn't he. At least he was breathing heavy too. Yeah, that worked for her, knowing she wasn't completely alone in this. "No. Still not dating you—*Ohmigod.*" His thumb had rasped over her other nipple. *"Shayne—"*

At the knock on the window, they both jumped so high they nearly bumped their heads on the roof.

A cop stood there, looking an awful lot like . . .

Shayne.

In a moment that summed up all the moments of poor timing in her life, his brother had arrived.

Chapter 8

Dani watched as Patrick Mahoney walked through her apartment, jotting notes on a pad of paper. She couldn't tell if he'd believed a word she'd told him. She couldn't tell if he thought she was crazy.

The only thing she *could* tell was that he really did look like Shayne's twin, which is to say tall and rangy and effortlessly sexy with that untamed wavy hair and see-all golden eyes. Except his weren't nearly as warm as Shayne's.

She tightened the belt on her coat and tried not to picture exactly what Patrick had seen when he'd knocked on the window of Shayne's car. Tried not to think what might have happened if he *hadn't* knocked on the window of Shayne's car.

Seriously, she couldn't believe she'd—

That he'd—

That they'd nearly—

Strangers. They were complete strangers, she reminded herself. Strangers who couldn't keep their hands off each other.

Why was that, anyway? She had no idea, but whatever was happening between the two of them, it had to stop. Immediately. Mostly because she appeared to be in the middle of a breakdown. That, or someone was stalking her. Neither was exactly conducive to a well-rounded relationship.

Not that she was thinking about a relationship.

Oh, no. No, no, no. Because Shayne? He was a walking, talking heartbreaker if she'd ever seen one. And if she was stupid enough to even *think* about taking this to the next level, a level that she hadn't been to in an embarrassingly long time, then she had no one to blame for that certain heartbreak than herself. Because once she slept with someone, she tended to get her heart involved, and . . .

Oh, hell, who was she kidding? She hadn't slept with him, at least not yet, and already her heart felt involved. She couldn't help it, Shayne Mahoney was a combination of some of her favorite things—sharp and quick-witted, willing to put himself on the line for whatever he believed in, not to mention an even more attractive willingness to help a perfect stranger.

Or in this case, a not-so-perfect stranger.

God. She pushed back her hair and wondered how much longer she could stay awake on her feet.

And wondered something else too, something she'd already voiced to Shayne. "What if it's the same gun that I saw at Sky High?"

The two brothers, taking up all the spare room in her living room with their big, built bodies and undeniable presence, exchanged a long look.

Had she thought she couldn't read Shayne's thoughts? Because she knew exactly what he was thinking.

That she was as crazy as everyone said.

They spoke softly to each other, so softly she couldn't hear the words, and then Shayne walked Patrick to her front door, and when she looked up again, Shayne was standing in front of her, hands in his pockets, hair still wet from the rain, expression unreadable. Through all of this, his proximity had always been able to affect her, and now was no exception. He still smelled good, delicious in fact, and though he wasn't looking at her with his usual heat, it didn't matter because he was looking at her with a gentle kindness.

Devastating, really. She wanted to put her hands on his incredibly soft shirt and feel his incredibly hard body beneath. Instead, she tried to joke. "Let me guess. He recommended you run far and fast from me, right?"

He didn't respond to that, but pulled his hands out of his pockets and set them on her arms, stroking up and down over her coat. "You look beat."

"A very true statement." She resisted setting her head on his shoulder, barely. "So what did he say?"

"Who'd want to scare you, Dani?"

"Well . . ."

"You piss anyone off lately?"

"You have a lot of questions."

"Are you going to answer any of them?"

She let out a shaky breath. "Are you asking me if I have any enemies?"

"Or friends that aren't really friends."

"So . . . you believe me," she said, shocked to find her throat tight over that. "You believe that something is going on here."

"Something, yes."

"Okay." She concentrated on breathing. Breathing was good. "Okay, now I'm really scared."

"You should be. Enemies, Dani? Pissed-off family members? Scorned boyfriends? Jealous coworkers?"

Taking a step back so she could lean against the couch, she nodded.

"Which?"

She tried to smile and failed. "Well, would you believe all of the above?" When he arched a brow, she let out a short laugh. "I know, it sounds ridiculous. I mean, look at me." She spread her hands. "I'm a mess. But it's shockingly true."

"Tell me."

"I was promoted today—yesterday, now," she corrected, looking at the clock, finding it well after midnight. "To head mammal keeper. It's mostly just a title, with a joke of a pay increase, really. I'll still be poor as dirt, but I get to make management decisions and I get the good schedule."

"Anyone upset about that?"

"The only other person eligible was Reena, and she's a close friend. We got hired at the same time, so the promotion could have gone either way, but she's happy for me."

Crossing his arms, he sent her a get-real look.

"She is," she insisted.

"She can be happy for you and still really pissed off about it."

"Pissed off enough to kill someone? Enough to break into my place? To plant a gun on me? Seriously, this is ridiculous. What happened tonight has nothing to do with my work."

"Okay, so what about family?"

"You know my mother. She's a stuck-up, narcissistic snob, but she's not a gun owner. And she's not a murderer."

"Siblings? Stepsiblings?"

"I—" She closed her mouth. Tony's and Eliza's faces flashed across her mind.

"What?" Shayne murmured, watching her carefully, an unsettling thing because the look in his eyes implied he cared. A lot. "What are you thinking?"

That she was going to have a hell of a time resisting him, that's what. "I think my stepsiblings would like me to vanish, but they like their cushy trust funds too much to actually off me." She tried to smile, but didn't feel especially amused.

"Dani—"

"The point is, none of this makes any sense. My job, while lovely to me, is actually really very boring to most. I observe mammals, write reports on their behavior. I feed them and clean up after them. Not exactly glamorous work, you know? I haven't made any enemies, and though my family is richer than God, there's no reason for any of them to hurt me. The end."

"Ex-boyfriends? Current boyfriends?"

She looked away.

"Dani."

She was too busy with work to have a real life. Okay, that wasn't exactly the truth either. She was too busy being independent to let anyone in. "It's been a while."

"How long a while?"

She winced. Could this get any more humiliating? "Months."

"Months."

She closed her eyes. "Okay, a year."

"A year?"

"And a half."

Silence. She felt her face grow hot, and finally opened her eyes.

He didn't look horrified or disgusted. Just patient, and understanding. "Nothing more current?" he said without judgment. "Nothing at all?"

She hugged herself. "If I had something more current going on, I wouldn't have kissed you in the closet."

"Which begs the question . . ." He shifted closer, put his hand on her jaw, and lifted her face to his. "After all that time of going without, why did you kiss me in the closet?"

She opened her mouth, and then shut it again. It was a good question, a fair question. But how to explain that she'd kissed him in the closet to kick-start herself, and that mission had been accomplished. What she hadn't realized was that she'd want another kiss.

And another.

And despite his interest, she knew enough to know she couldn't possibly keep it. Kissing him again, or even explaining the kiss would be like opening a big, fat can of worms.

"Just an impulse?" he inquired.

His hand was still on her jaw, and she liked his touch, too much. So much. How in the world did people do this, open up and let someone in, and then casually walk away after one encounter? She needed to work on that. "I dared myself."

"Ah." He nodded. "Okay, then. That clears everything up. Thanks."

"Shayne—"

"Never mind. I get it. We're . . ."

"On different playing fields."

"What does that mean?"

"It means you're a ten, and—"

"Not that again."

"What did your brother say exactly?" she asked.

He arched a brow. "Subject change?"

"Subject change."

He sighed. "He said that just because there's no sign of a break-in doesn't mean someone wasn't here."

"So he believes me too?"

The answer was in his eyes. "Oh. I see." She turned her back to him because she didn't want him to see her disappointment. "He doesn't." She leaned on the couch. "So what about the gun? Did I plant that myself then?"

"He's going to see who it's registered to."

"And in the meantime?"

"Sleep." He was right behind her. Not quite touching, but she could feel his body heat. "You look like you could use it."

She had to close her eyes and work on controlling her voice so that it didn't shake like the rest of her was. "Thanks. Thanks for being here for me tonight, and thanks for calling your brother. I appreciate it. I'll be fine, though. You can go."

"You're going to sleep here?"

"No, actually. I think I'll go to work and sleep there. I've done that before," she said, hoping to ward off his protest. "A lot. I'm very comfortable there."

His hands slid to her hips and turned her around to face him. "How about somewhere you won't be alone?"

"I have the animals."

"I was thinking of the human persuasion. Preferably female."

"I could call Reena," she said. "But it's nearly one in the morning. Maybe I could just go knock on Alan's door."

"Is he really your friend?"

"He bought me pizza on Monday."

"Why?"

"To be nice."

He let out a sound that wasn't quite a laugh. "Dani, guys do not bring pizza to be nice unless they're gay. Is he gay?"

"No."

"Then he brought pizza to get into your pants."

She choked out a laugh. "I don't think he thinks like that."

"Please," he said with disgust. "With that sexy laugh of yours alone, he'd think like that."

She blinked. He thought her laugh was sexy?

"Yeah," he said to her unspoken question. "You're sexy as hell, okay? You're also smart, you're beautiful, and you have this way of looking at a guy that makes him want . . ."

"What?" she whispered, fascinated, overwhelmed. *Aroused.*

"In your pants," he said frankly.

She concentrated on breathing for a moment. "Is that a compliment?"

"It's a fact. What about a hotel?"

She thought of her checking account, which didn't really have room for a hotel bill. Maybe a motel. Maybe a really cheap, out-of-the-way motel—

"My place," he said. "I'll take the couch," he added when she looked at him in surprise. He stood there, big and tall and not quite as easygoing as he'd like her to believe, but the offer was genuine.

And her immediate response, which was hopeful nipples and a tightening between her thighs, was just as genuine.

And wrong. So very wrong, because she was not going to go there, not going to give him a chance to do a tap dance on her heart—and her good parts—and then move on. No, thank you. Easier to pass now, to just keep passing.

"Dani?"

"I . . ." *Desperately want to say yes.* "I'm grateful for the offer, but that wouldn't be fair to you." Before she could betray herself, she left him standing there and moved into her bedroom, where she changed into jeans and a sweater.

When she came out, he was waiting. "Fair to me?"

"I'm not sleeping on your couch, okay?" *Even if I want to.* "Or in your bed." *Which I really want to.* "Or anywhere with you."

"Why?"

"Because I don't want to." God, she was such a liar. "Okay, I want to. But it'd be a really bad idea."

Leaning back against the wall, he crossed his arms, looking bemused. "So you'll kiss me in the closet when you don't know me, but now that you do know me, you won't sleep in my house?"

"How much longer am I going to have to live down the whole closet thing?"

"At least until daylight."

She sighed. "Look, thanks. Okay? Thanks more than you know. But no to the sleepover. I'm going to my office."

Standing there in those sophisticated, elegant clothes that had been soaked two different times over the course of the evening and were still holding up—much like the man—he held out a hand. "Fine. But I'm giving you a ride. Come on," he said, wriggling his fingers when she hesitated. "Let me help you that much, at least."

She slipped her hand into his, and together they went back out into the night.

The rain had let up. It was merely misting now, falling out of the sky like a silvery spiderweb. The ride was short, and silent, and as they pulled into the zoo parking lot, the place dark and more eerie than she could ever remember it being, making her shiver as the niggling of doubt hit her.

"It's not too late to change your mind."

Her mind hadn't changed. She still wanted him. Waaaay too much to sleep anywhere near him. "I'm going to be fine." She rattled her keys and forced a smile. *See? Look at me, all fine.*

Reaching up, he flipped on the interior light of his car and leaned in. "Smile again."

"What?" She shook her head. "Why?"

"Because I want to see if it's real."

"You don't know me well enough to know what my real smile looks like."

"Now, see, I think I do. Give it to me."

"*How* do you know?"

"Because I've seen it."

"When?"

"When I kissed you." Unhooking her seat belt, he turned her to face him. Cupping her jaw, he slid his thumb over her lips. "When I kissed you, you smiled at me. Your eyes sparkled, and your face . . ." Still holding her, his lips curved. "It's so beautiful it takes my breath."

"You need your eyes checked."

"And even with all that, you know what makes you the most attractive?"

"My sweet disposition?"

His dimple flashed. "Your sense of humor."

"Ah." She nodded. "The whole 'she has a great personality' kind of beautiful."

He held her gaze. "Actually, that's the best kind." He tugged lightly on a strand of her hair, which she knew was so out-of-control frizzy from all the rain that she looked like a Q-tip head. "I bet you were a heartbreaker in high school." The tips of his fingers continued to play with her hair, stroking it, smoothing it back from her face, and she had the shocking urge to stretch and purr like a kitten. Maybe even roll over and expose her belly for him to rub there too.

No. Bad Body. "I wasn't much of a heartbreaker. We moved around a lot. I was more of a . . . sulker."

"Why did you walk away, Dani? From your family? And, I'm assuming, a trust fund?"

"Why do you assume I walked away from a trust fund?"

"I've seen your apartment."

She had to laugh. "Right. Well, my mother wasn't always rich. And in those days, we didn't exactly see eye to eye. I walked away before she married her money. And yeah, I could worm my way into the good finances now, I just don't want to. I don't want to live the socialite life, or date the right people, or be seen in the right clothes at the right places . . ." She lifted a shoulder, a little embarrassed to realize that she was opening up, with nothing more than a kind look and a touch to the face. "I want my own life."

He smiled. And if she had to guess, she'd say it was one of *his* real smiles. "Like your job."

"Like my job."

He shook his head. "I'm trying to imagine you cleaning up elephant poop."

"I do other things too. The food and water, the grooming. I keep their environment intact."

He smiled, another real one.

"I supervise and record the animals' activities so that we can understand the nuances in their behavior."

"You evacuate poop." He was teasing, but there was something else too. Awe.

He was impressed, which made her laugh. "I evacuate poop, and you fly planes. Who should be impressed here?"

"Definitely me."

Modesty. That didn't fit into the image she had of him. Or at least of the image she wanted to have of him. Turning, she looked at the sixteen-foot fence lining the zoo, the one that vanished into the hills surrounding the property.

Beyond that gate was her life.

Time to get to that life. She pulled her keys out of her pocket and noticed her car in the lot. "Hey, my car's back."

"I thought it was at the mechanic's."

"He must have brought it back for me, which means he fixed it for less than the two-hundred-dollar max I gave him." She felt one of her real smiles crease her face. "Yay me. Thanks for the ride, Shayne. Thanks for everything." She opened the car door.

"Dani—"

"It's late. Go get some sleep." And before he could say anything more, maybe kiss her again and make her melt and agree to sleep at his house, or maybe just give false promises neither of them could keep, she shut the door.

She missed the warmth immediately as she stepped out into the cold, misting night. And not just the car's warmth, she could admit as she unlocked the gate and let herself in.

But Shayne's warmth.

Shutting the gate behind her, she let herself look back. She couldn't help it. Expecting to see the car's taillights as Shayne drove back down the hill, she found the man instead.

Out of his car, standing on the other side of the gate, only a few feet away.

Watching her.

At her start of surprise, he lifted his hand.

"What are you doing?" she asked. "Get out of the rain."

"Soon as you do."

She stepped back to the gate, gripping two wrought-iron stakes, putting her face up close as she contemplated him. "Shayne."

"Dani."

She laughed. A miracle in itself, that she could laugh on a night such as this.

He stepped up to the gate too. Put his hands over hers, his face close enough to kiss.

Ah, hell. She met him halfway, and then in unison, they both hesitated. It was only for a second, with their lips a fraction apart, but anticipation shot through her. She wanted to kiss him, God, she wanted that.

So much.

She couldn't help it. So she leaned in and put her mouth on his through the wrought iron, her breath catching in surprise at the warm softness of his lips, at the scent of him, so familiar now. The surprise of that had her pulling back but his hands tightened over hers on the bars, holding her to him. Ah, damn. Damn, what a mistake, but her mouth clung to his, absorbing the promise in the stroke of his tongue against hers, so that she forgot to keep her head about her, so that she wished there wasn't a barricade between them.

Remember this, she told herself. Remember the rasp of his rough chin against hers. His tongue in her mouth. The heat of his body a direct contrast to the chill of the bars. The dark, gloomy night all around them as their bodies strained to get closer, even closer. Remember, because this was it.

The last time.

The very last time.

Pulling back, his eyes sleepy and sexy—so damn sexy—his pleasure clearly etched on his face, he sent her a soft but baffled smile. "What was that for?"

She had no idea. None.

Zilch.

But oh, God, she wanted another. If he so much as mentioned his bed again, she was on it—

"Good night, Dani," he said softly, and backed up.

She stared at him, taking a moment to swallow. "How is it you're such a player, and yet such a gentleman?"

"A player?"

"I'm not the only one with a reputation, you know."

"Ah." He looked down at his feet, then back up into her eyes, his good humor gone. "Are you crazy?"

"What? No!"

"Then maybe I'm not what people say either."

Touché . . .

Slowly, with one last long look, he turned and vanished into the night.

Watching his tall, lean body move with such easy natural grace, she stood there a moment, rooted by the sudden urge to call him back, to pull him close again. But eventually she turned too, walking the path toward the building that housed the staffing offices.

All around her was a dark quiet, which was exactly what she usually loved about working at night. There was something about being here in the wee hours, knowing that only a few acres away were hundreds of animals in their habitats. Normally it was soothing, peaceful.

Natural.

But tonight, as she let herself in the back door of her building and headed for the stairs, she felt an inkling of unease that made her pick up her steps, eager to get into her office. Hurrying now, she turned down the hallway and found her office light already on.

Odd.

Maybe she'd left it that way, but she didn't think so, and for a moment she hovered in the doorway, uncertain. She hadn't heard a thing and yet . . .

And yet she felt as she had in her apartment.

As if she was being watched.

Chapter 9

Shayne was halfway down the hill, windshield wipers proving ineffective against the mist and fog, when the doubt hit.

Or maybe it'd always been there, from the moment Dani had gotten out of his car. It was just a little niggling, really, but it wouldn't go away.

She wasn't safe.

He glanced at himself in the rearview mirror. Shook his head. "Don't do it, man. Don't go back."

But what if . . .

Damn.

He was going back.

With a sigh, he executed a U-turn. He should have hooked up with friends.

Hit a bar.

Or a party.

There were plenty this late, and plenty that would welcome him. Michelle had been texting him all night, he'd just ignored her. She'd be thrilled to see him and would be willing to show him just how thrilled with that lush body of hers.

And yet . . . that didn't appeal, not in the least. Instead, he was heading back to a woman he hadn't imagined he would be attracted to.

He'd been incredibly wrong.

Pulling back into the parking lot, he caught a flash of light. The gate. It was opening. Opening, and a figure running out into the night.

Right in front of his car.

Dani.

And as she glanced back over her shoulder behind her, he caught her pale face and the sheer terror on it as she ran from something he couldn't see. Jerking the steering wheel, he slammed on the brakes, missing her by an inch, which did not in any way soothe the heart that had just about leapt right out of his chest. Jumping out of his car, he ran around the front toward her.

"Sorry," she gasped as she bent over his hood, gasping for breath.

He pulled her around to face him. Her face was white as she gripped the front of his shirt in her fists. "Are you hurt?" he managed.

"We have to get out of here."

Something cracked the night, shocking his eardrums as it whizzed past them, pinging into one of the tall steel light poles.

A bullet. *A fucking bullet?*

"Hurry," she gasped. "We really gotta hurry."

Pretty much the understatement of the century. Grabbing her hand, he yanked her with him, opening the driver's door, shoving her in ahead of him.

On her hands and knees, she scrambled over his

seat and into the passenger's, whirling back to glue her gaze to the direction she'd just come from.

Where the bullet had come from.

"Go," she said tersely. "Before—"

Another shot rang out into the night, missing his car, though he had no idea by how much. "Get down." He emphasized this with a hand to the back of her head, shoving it to her knees as he peeled them out of the parking lot with an exhibition of speed that would have gotten him one hell of an expensive ticket.

"Shayne—"

"Stay the hell down," he commanded, simultaneously driving and watching the rearview mirror. "Are you okay?"

"The light in my office was on. I didn't leave it on, Shayne, so—"

"Goddamnit, are you hurt?"

"No." She gulped for breath. "No."

He let out a long breath of his own. "Okay." He nodded. "Okay. So what the hell was that?"

"Someone shooting at us."

"Yeah, I got that much." At the bottom of the hill, he pulled into the gas station on the right and got out his cell phone.

"What are you doing?"

"I'm thinking if Patrick was interested in taking a look at the gun you found, then he's going to be extremely interested in this."

There were questions to answer, and then the same questions to re-answer. First with Shayne present, and then without him. Dani walked through her entire evening for the police, over and over again, until she started slurring her words from sheer exhaustion. "No, I didn't see anyone, just the light in my office," she said for the hundredth time. "Then I got that tingly sensation of being watched, and I ran. And then someone was shooting at me."

Proving her words, there was a bullet embedded in the light pole in the zoo parking lot. Not to mention Shayne's earlier statement concurring that someone had indeed been shooting at her.

Finally, she was given the okay to leave, and she walked out the gates of the zoo into the damp, chilly dawn and found . . .

Shayne propping up his car, arms and feet casually crossed as if he was at a party, content as can be.

That is until she got a little closer, and in the predawn light saw the tight, grim set of his mouth, and the way his entire body was rigid with tension.

If she wasn't so exhausted, this unusual show of decided *un*-laid-backness from him would have fascinated her. "Hey."

Pushing off from the car, he stepped close enough that their toes bumped. Cupping her face in his hands, he looked into her face with such scrutiny she squirmed.

"What?"

"You okay?"

The genuine concern in his voice had her discomfort fading away, replaced by a suddenly tight throat and burning eyes. "Good news. I think the police are taking my craziness seriously now."

"You didn't imagine those bullets."

True. In spite of the terror of the night, she had that. Something *was* going on. There was no longer any doubt of that.

Shayne looked into her face for another long moment, then he slid his thumb over her lower lip. In spite of her lingering fear and unease, not to mention sheer exhaustion, the touch felt like a lightning bolt to her good parts. *Man.* She had no idea what was malfunctioning, exactly, but she needed to get it fixed pronto.

And then he surprised her yet again. Still holding her face, he leaned in and kissed her. Not the sensually heated kiss like they'd shared in the closet at Sky High, or the heart-stopping one he'd given her when she'd been squished between her own front door and his body, but a sweet, warm connection that told her she wasn't alone.

When he pulled back, she found she couldn't speak. He didn't either.

"You didn't have to wait for me," she finally said.

He just opened his car door for her.

"You probably have flights tomorrow. Today," she corrected as dawn broke over their heads, cold but blessedly rain free.

"Come on. Get in."

"I can call Reena."

"I'm right here. Willing and able."

"Right." Admittedly relieved to have him there, she collapsed into the seat, leaning her head back against the headrest, closing her eyes.

He'd stayed.

For her.

She stole a peek at him as he drove, silent. Unbelievably, he still looked as amazing and put together as he had when she'd first seen him standing in the midst of the party last night, watching her with an amused quirk of his mouth.

After all they'd been through since then, she knew she looked like a complete wreck.

Hell, she'd started out a complete wreck.

But not him. Nope, he was still as innately sexy and calm and . . . perfect as he'd started out, and she could hardly stand it. "Shayne?"

"Yeah?"

"What would it take to ruffle you up?"

He cast her a quick glance. "What?"

"You're always so calm and easygoing. Laid-back. Do you ever lose it?" Until tonight, she'd been a stranger to him, a stranger who'd claimed to have seen a murder, then an intruder, and then been shot at.

And still he'd remained cool and collected.

But she really wanted to see him unhinged, see him let go. "Do you?"

He slanted her another glance, which she took as a definite no.

But that couldn't be. Everyone lost it, at least occasionally.

Some more than others . . .

In any case, she spent a few minutes trying to imagine how it would happen. Since it hadn't while they'd been shot at, it couldn't be danger that triggered him . . .

Maybe . . . maybe it happened in bed. Just the thought made her a little tingly. Yeah, in bed . . . She was just putting together a fairly X-rated scenario where he lost it entirely, involving him being extremely naked, when she realized he wasn't taking her home, but down a very lovely oak-lined upscale street in the hills, where she probably couldn't afford to breathe the air. "Where are we?"

"My place."

She stared at the large modern house. "Oh."

He got out of the car and came around for her before she'd gathered any brain cells.

His place.

As he pulled her to her feet, she stared up into his face. "I realize that you probably have to stay in control under any circumstances when you're in the air," she said. "But—"

"Still on that?"

"Well nothing ruffled you tonight, so, yeah. I guess I'm wondering . . ."

With a little smile, he took her hand and led her up a gorgeously paved walk, pulling a key out of his pocket with his free hand.

"Maybe you lose control over food . . ." she said, fishing for insight. Also fishing for something to soothe her sudden nerves.

Laughing softly, he unlocked his front door. "Yeah. A fully loaded pizza really throws me over the edge. Oh, you should probably brace yourself."

"Um, what?"

But as he opened the door, a huge brown ball of fur launched itself at Shayne, knocking him back several feet with a pair of paws to the chest. A pair of paws the size of polar bear paws.

"Bella." Shayne stroked the animal, who panted happily and drooled. "Miss me, huh?"

Bella panted some more, then dropped to the floor in a boneless heap of joy and exposed her belly.

Shayne obliged her, hunkering down with a smile, giving her a long, hard rub. "Sorry I was gone so long. But Jan came and walked you twice."

"Jan?"

"My neighbor, and dog walker. There, Bella, that feel better?"

Dani had never been jealous of a dog in her life until that moment. Stepping close, she crouched down too. "Is that a dog or a bear?"

"Yet to be determined." But Bella let out a welcoming doggie smile, and with a huge tongue, licked Dani's hand.

"She's sweet," she murmured, staring at the biggest paws she'd ever seen. "Aren't you something?"

"Something," Shayne agreed.

Unable to help herself, Dani petted the dog, who panted with great cheer. "She must be a great watchdog."

"She's an attention slut is what she is. If a burglar came to the door, she'd show him all the good stuff for a belly rub." But he smiled affectionately down at the dog as he said this, still stroking, sending Bella into fits of moaning ecstasy.

A guy who melted over a dog . . . "Sports?" she whispered, trying to get back to their conversation instead of nursing a sudden and dangerous crush on an out-of-reach playboy pilot. "Do sports make you lose control?"

"Love sports," he said. "Play them when I can."

"But they don't make you lose it."

With a smile, he shook his head.

Nodding, her thoughts raced as she tried to find a foothold on a slippery slide right into Serious Crushville. "Nothing makes you lose it. Got it."

Straightening to his feet, he tossed his keys into a little bowl on a table in the foyer. Then he pushed the door closed and turned to her.

Oh, boy.

Bella scrambled up to her feet just as Dani's stomach did a little tap dance. Other things tap-danced, too.

Like every single erogenous zone she had.

With Bella running circles around them, Shayne leaned in until his nose just touched Dani's.

She opened her mouth to press on the whole losing-it thing, but he crooked his head to the side, then rubbed his jaw to hers. And then his mouth was near her ear, and he was breathing into it. "So you want to see me forfeit control?"

"I—" God, she couldn't think when he was breathing in her ear. "I think so."

"But you're not sure."

"No."

She felt him smile against her skin, and then for the briefest second in history, his mouth slid against hers in a far too fleeting kiss. "Don't ask until you're sure." Then he stepped back.

She concentrated on gulping in air while he told Bella it was time for food. The dog barked with happiness, while she? Stood there trying to control her body's needs.

Note to self: don't stir the beast unless you're ready to tame it.

She didn't plan on doing that.

But a small part of her *so* wanted to.

Chapter 10

Shayne walked into his kitchen to feed Bella, incredibly, erotically, aware of the woman who followed him.

He was also incredibly, erotically aware of her inner struggle.

Do him.

Don't do him.

She was giving him a damned complex, but he didn't mention it as she watched him feed the dog or as he led her through his house.

He'd only purchased the place about three months ago, and hadn't exactly made it a home yet. There was nothing in the living room but a huge-screen TV and an even more huge soft comfy couch and chair. He had only bar stools in the den, which opened to the kitchen, where Bella was busy chowing through five pounds of food. He hadn't gotten around to finding a table he liked.

He had a bed, though, a large, lush bed that he wasn't having any trouble picturing Dani sprawled across, her wild hair all around her head, his sheets smooth beneath her lovely, hot bod, and then that same body beneath his . . .

"I can't."

He tore his brain away from the fantasy and looked at her.

Eyes glued to his bed, she swallowed and shook her head. "I'm not taking your bed."

It was barely dawn and they needed a few hours' sleep. He especially needed a few hours' sleep, since he had a full schedule ahead of him for the day, including a flight to Santa Barbara. "You're the guest," he said firmly. "You get the bed."

She stared up at him, her face unreadable. "Have you ever had a woman in your bed that you weren't sleeping with?"

"Uh . . ."

"Have you?"

"No," he admitted.

"That's what I thought." She sighed. "At least your mom taught you good manners."

"More like they were beaten into me by my father, but yeah." He smiled, hoping to see her smile in return. "Come on. Just a little shut-eye." He crossed to his dresser and pulled out a T-shirt and sweat bottoms, handing them to her. "Help yourself, if you want to be more comfortable."

Though personally, he'd be imagining her sleeping in the nude. She'd wanted to know what it would take for him to lose his control? *That.*

That's all it would take.

She hugged the clothes and continued to just look at him, her eyes filled with a longing and a hunger that made him close his.

Distance. They both wanted it.

Not going to be easy. " 'Night," he said a bit hoarsely, and left the room. Behind him, he heard her shut the door, and at the sound of the lock clicking into place, he let out a long, serrated breath.

There.

Safe.

Though who was safe from whom, he had no freaking clue. Tugging his shirt off, he went into the living room and looked at the couch as he kicked off his shoes.

Bella came out of the kitchen still licking her chops and smelling like dog food. She eyed the couch, which she considered hers.

"Not tonight, babe," he told her.

But Bella leapt up, turned in a circle three times on the cushions, then plopped into them with a blissful sigh.

With a sigh of his own, Shayne padded into the kitchen and peered into the fridge. Two beers, leftover pizza, leftover Thai, and leftover Italian.

Maybe he ought to see if he could pay Jan to keep him in some fresh food as well as walk Bella, because if his mother could see this, she'd just sigh.

She'd done a lot of sighing over the years for Shayne. There'd been his inability to deal with his older brothers and his father's constant ribbing and roughhousing. There'd been his trouble in school, not grade-wise, but attitude-wise. Mostly his father had beaten that out of him too, but it'd been a long haul because he'd been pretty attitude-ridden.

By the time he'd hooked up with Brody and Noah in seventh grade, he'd been pretty damn tired of being picked on. Then two things had happened simultaneously; he'd grown ten inches in four months, and he'd bonded with two boys who were also misfits, also different, and better yet, they *got* him. Over their mutual love of planes, they'd made promises— that someday they'd run their own private airline for the rich and famous, flying all over the world on someone else's dime.

A fantasy, nothing more.

But they believed in that fantasy, and they'd made it happen.

It hadn't been easy. It had nearly sent them each spinning into bankruptcy, several times, and no one had as far to spin as Shayne. Several times through college, and in the years since, they'd lived together because there hadn't been a spare dime, but that had worked too.

And in the end, the three of them had pulled it off.

And this year they'd paid off their last big creditor, celebrating their first month solidly in the black. A few months later, he'd bought this house for himself.

"Nice to know you didn't completely blow your trust fund," his father had said when he'd gotten his first look at the house. His mother had seconded that with "because we weren't going to replace it."

They meant well, he knew that. He also knew that he hadn't been easy on them. But all he'd ever asked of them was to believe in him, and they hadn't been able to do that, not once, not ever. So he'd gotten over it. He had Sky High. He had Brody and Noah, and now by extension, Bailey and Maddie. And he was good.

His life was full.

Very full.

With a sigh, he moved back into the living room and nudged Bella.

She cracked open one eye.

He nudged her again.

She closed her eye.

"Damn it." Snagging the blanket off the back of the couch, he sprawled out on the carpet, turning over a few times before he could get even quasi-comfortable.

Just as he drifted off, Bella jumped off the couch and stretched out at his side with a groan. She had his back and would keep him warm. She might be a bed hog with some really bad breath, but she'd never judge him, that was for sure. She'd always be there.

No man needed more than that . . .

The phone rang, jarring Shayne awake. The machine on the other side of the room clicked on, telling him he must have been sleeping pretty damn hard if the phone had rung four times, which is what it took for the machine to come on. Because he was so exhausted, he lay there, content to let whoever it was calling him at six in the morning to leave a message.

"Shayne?" Michelle's voice filled the room. "Wish you'd come by last night. I was looking forward to one of our late-night trysts . . ."

They'd had exactly one late-night tryst, one that she'd instigated, promising him that she wasn't looking for anything more . . .

"Call me," she said with promise thick in her admittedly sexy voice. "Maybe we can hook up tonight instead."

The machine clicked off, but there was another sound in the room, a light rustling that had Bella lifting her head and snuffling, but Shayne already knew who stood over him wearing—ah, man, *look* at her—wearing only his T-shirt, which fell to her thighs.

He'd fallen asleep with the kitchen light on behind her, which allowed him to see right through the material. God bless that light.

And as a bonus, from his vantage on the floor he caught a peek-a-boo hint of peach panties. Cotton? Silk?

"Hey," she said, hugging herself. She took a step closer and tripped over the shoes he'd carelessly kicked off. With a gasp, she fell.

Right on top of him.

Not so good for his supposed distance, but pretty damn great for his temporary bout of loneliness, having that hot curvy body all over the top of him. And she was all over him, her hair in his mouth, one soft thigh between his, her breasts smashed against his chest.

"I'm sorry." She tried to push off him but her hand sank into his gut, making him let out an "oof," and then she overcorrected by shifting her hand lower, and this time when she pushed up she had a handful of his package.

"Careful," he warned, wrapping his fingers around her wrist.

"Oh, God." She went utterly still, shock on her face. "I'm so sorry."

But she didn't take her hand off him.

"Dani?"

"Yeah?"

Her fingers were warm, and definitely . . . *Christ* . . . outlining him. "What are you doing?"

Groaning, she buried her face in his chest. "He has to ask me what I'm doing. That's bad. Very bad."

Fumbling for balance, she rolled to her back on the floor, thankfully managing not to un-man him in the process.

Lifting up, he eyed her. Her hair covered her face but his T-shirt had risen up high enough on her thighs to reveal a close-up and personal view of those peach panties.

Satin.

He closed his eyes as all the blood drained out of his head for parts south. "I'm sorry if the phone woke you."

"Was she your . . . girlfriend?"

"No."

She let out a shaky breath. "But you've slept with her."

Brody or Noah always said one of his many, *many* faults was being honest. Too honest. Brutally honest.

He couldn't help it. Being honest was all he had. "Yes."

"Are you still sleeping with her?"

"No." Gently, he pushed the hair from her face, and when her eyes cut to his, he shook his head. "No. It turns out we're . . . incompatible."

She absorbed that, and processed. "As in she wants a relationship, and you don't?"

"Yes."

"Because you don't do relationships, right?"

So he wasn't the only one who could do brutally honest. "Not as a habit, no."

"I do. But I'm bad at them, really bad. Guys don't tend to stick, and I've always blamed them, but lately I'm thinking it's me."

Ah, hell. "It's not you. You're perfect."

She shook her head. "Don't say stuff like that to me."

"Why not?"

"It makes me want you."

"I thought we weren't going there."

"Well, there's there, and there's there. You know?"

He really didn't, but she was looking at him so hopefully expectant, he nodded his head, which earned him a beaming smile.

"So you agree?" she whispered, not breathing, her mouth tantalizingly close to his, and then there was her warm, soft body, barely clad, lying against him.

He wasn't breathing either. Did he agree? He hadn't a fucking clue, but he nodded again.

"Oh," she breathed softly. "Oh, I'm so glad." And leaning in, she pressed her mouth to his jaw.

His world skidded to a halt.

"So glad," she murmured against his skin, her hand coming up to settle on his chest.

And then, somehow, through the fog of sheer lust, he began to interpret. She was trying to seduce him, and she'd gotten shockingly far. The knowledge pretty much ensured that he went hard and stayed hard . . .

But then she reached out, presumably to touch the hair falling over his forehead, and caught him in the eye. "Ow."

"I'm sorry!"

He'd been seduced before, but never like this, never in such a sweetly fumbling, klutzy manner, which was somehow far more endearing, more genuine, more real than anything he'd ever experienced. "Dani?"

"If you could just ignore me, that would be hugely helpful. Seriously."

He pulled her hand from her face. "Too late for that."

"No, it's never too late. Really, just pretend I'm not here. Dying."

"Dani."

"Dani has left the building."

He laughed. *Laughed.* He'd intended to keep his head about him, to keep that blessed distance she wanted so badly, and yet she'd wriggled, tripped, and fallen her way right into his heart. "Come here."

"Really? Just for tonight? It has to be just for tonight."

This time, he knew what he was agreeing to. "Whatever you want."

She smiled, and he felt his control slip.

But just a little.

Chapter 11

Dani slid into Shayne's arms and lifted her head for a kiss. She needed one, pronto. She needed that rush of adrenaline, that sense of floating, of delicious lust, and the knowledge that she could do anything.

Including seducing a man right out of himself.

It'd been a while, but she did remember the basics, plastering herself to his long, rugged length, making sure her breasts brushed his chest.

His bare chest. And wow, oh wow, was it some bare chest. With him in only his unfastened pants, she could take in all those muscles, and there was a lot of muscle. And then there was that six-pack, and the way his pants hung so low on his hips she could almost just dip her hand in and—

"Are you cold?" he murmured.

No, and that hadn't been the question she'd been expecting. Maybe "are you on the pill," or "would you like to move to some place more comfortable," but not "are you cold," because the truth was yes, she was a little cold, and a whole lot hot at the same time. "I have no idea," she said, just happy that they were on the same page, that they could scratch this itch and still be on the same page.

"Let me get a blanket—"

"No." She didn't want him to move. To that end, she wriggled. Wriggled one leg over his so that the T-shirt he'd given her rose up over her butt.

She knew she wasn't exactly Miss America, but men liked butts, and if she could just get his hands on hers, things would probably progress pretty quickly.

She wanted quickly. So she wriggled again, and he caught her knee in his hand, making her realize she'd nearly caught him in the groin again. "I'm sorry." A laugh escaped her, a very nervous laugh. "I swear I'm not out to hurt you."

"Okay, good." He brushed her hair from her face and looked into her eyes, smiling, but clearly just a little confused. "Maybe we could go over exactly what we are doing."

"Well . . ." She wriggled again, careful with her knee this time. Leaning down, she thought to give him a kiss, because that would surely remind him—

They bumped noses.

Not letting that deter her, she changed the angle of her head, leaned in and—

Bumped his nose again. "Ohmigod." Lightly slapping a hand on either side of his face, she held him still. Determined, she leaned in again, and found him—

Laughing.

At her.

Letting out a breath, she pressed her forehead to his. "Are you laughing at me or with me?"

"With you," he promised. "Definitely with you."

"Maybe you could do one more thing with me."

"Anything," he said in the most thrilling voice.

She executed another wriggle, complete with eyebrow arched that hopefully signaled "do me, do me now."

But he, the most frustrating, patient man on the planet, just lay there.

"You *know* what I'm asking," she finally whispered, beginning to sound desperate, even to her own ears. "You're a guy. A really sexy, virile guy who has women calling him at the crack of dawn. You *know*."

"Yes, but do *you?*"

"Do I know that I want to have just sex? Yes!"

"Are you sure?"

"Are you kidding me? You probably have women throwing themselves at you nightly. You probably never have to make the first move. And yet you want me to beg you."

"Whoa—"

"Because believe me, Shayne, I'm *this* close to begging you."

"Dani—"

"What?" she snapped, just a little too close to the edge.

Cupping her face, he pulled her in for a kiss. "I'm not laughing at you. I'm not waiting for you to throw yourself at me. I'm trying to resist you."

"Oh." That deflated some of her annoyance. *"Why?"*

"Because . . ." He slid his hands down her back, over her bottom, her thighs, and then up again, beneath the big T-shirt this time, and let out a low, thrilling groan at the feel of her satiny panties. "Because that's what you wanted before I brought you here. Because I don't want to hurt you." Some of the smile went out of his eyes. "Because I tend to end up hurting the women who care about me."

"You can't hurt me." Liar, liar. "This is a one-night thing only, remember?"

For a long beat he just looked up at her. "You're very different from the women I've gone out with."

"Different." But because his fingers slipped beneath that satin, this came out all breathless and whispery. "Different how?"

He didn't answer, and she lifted her head. The light from the kitchen slashed over him, and she could see the answer in his eyes. "Oh," she breathed. "Different as in not beautiful and rich—" Damn it. She tried to shift off him but his hands held her still.

"No," he said firmly. "You have it all wrong. I meant you're not . . ." Something flickered in his eyes. Discomfort? "You're not someone I would sleep with and then not call again."

The naked, raw truth of that statement was in his eyes, and finally, she understood, both his hesitation and the emotion in his voice. She wanted to hug him for it but instead she sat up. Since she'd had a leg on either side of him, that left her straddling his body.

He thought she was different. Good different, and though he could have no idea what that did for her, she felt deliciously empowered for the first time in her entire dating life. "Shayne?"

"Yeah?"

"I'm so, *so* sure."

Shayne struggled for brain cells, for *working* brain cells. Not easy with Dani straddling him wearing only his T-shirt and those peach panties. But he managed to find a few. "Dani." His voice was soft, his body not so much so. "It's just that this is out of character for you, and—"

"I've had one-night stands."

Lifting up a hand, he stroked her jaw. Her skin was like silk. "Have you?"

"Okay, no." She covered his hand with hers. "But I've thought about it."

"Dani—"

"I want to do this," she whispered, her hair falling over his shoulders and arms like a silk curtain. "I want to be held, touched. Kissed. I want to know I'm not alone."

"You're not alone."

"Thank you." Eyes luminous, thighs hugging his body, she reached down and grabbed the hem of the T-shirt she wore and slowly began to lift it up.

His heart stuttered to a stop, then jerked into motion again, kicking hard against his ribs. "I love the way my shirt looks on you."

"Held. Touched. Kissed," she repeated huskily. "I didn't say anything about talking. Did you hear me say anything about talking?"

His laugh backed up in his throat when the T-shirt revealed the gentle curve of her belly, her ribs . . . ah, God, she wasn't wearing a bra. Her breasts popped free, creamy pale and full, tipped with nipples already pebbled and begging for his attention.

He lifted his hands to start the touching part of the program, but looked up in confusion when she let out a "goddammit."

She'd gotten herself caught in his shirt. Arms lifted over her head, face covered by the cotton, she fought with the shirt, a motion that had her breasts gently bouncing. Bella, excited at the struggle—

which she interpreted as playtime—came flying over just as Shayne cupped Dani's breasts in his palms, but all laughter backed up in his throat at the feel of her. "Bella, go lie down."

Bella tilted her head to the side, studying Dani in curiosity.

"Bella."

With a sigh, the dog padded off.

"What are you doing?" Dani gasped. *"Help me."*

"I am." He gave her a nudge, and she fell forward, and look at that, one of her breasts bounced right near his mouth.

Perfect.

He opened up and rasped a tongue over her nipple.

"Oh!"

Smiling against her skin, he did it again, watching as it puckered even more. Such a gorgeous, mouth-watering sight.

"Shayne—" She was fighting the shirt again, trying to get free. "Damn it! I'm trying to make *you* lose control!"

He had her gorgeous breasts in his face, her legs spread wide over his so that he could feel her heat, which had his hips rocking helplessly upward. Control? He had none when it came to her. "Trust me. You are."

"A little *help?*"

"Sure." He stroked a hand down her smooth back and right into her panties, cupping her bare, sweet ass before slipping lower—

"Shayne!" she gasped. "That's not what I meant!"

"Ah, that's a shame." Pulling his hand free, he traced the peach panties in front now, outlining the small triangular patch before scraping the material aside to touch bare flesh instead.

Dani jerked, then went still as stone, only the smallest of sounds escaping her, the sexiest sound he'd ever heard.

He found her wet, thrillingly wet, and he let out a rough sound of his own, which seemed to galvanize her into action. Managing to rip off the stuck T-shirt, she glared down at him, hair wild, eyes glossy with hunger and desire, her breathing none too steady. "You."

"Me," he agreed.

"Are still wearing pants."

"Easily fixed." Surging up, he kissed her, his eyes open on hers. She watched him too. Watched as he sank his teeth into her lower lip and lightly tugged while his fingers stroked her again, hitting ground zero.

And given that those eyes went opaque on his, and words stopped tumbling from her lips, she liked it.

"Strip," she managed, sounding quite firm, then ruined it by adding a soft *"please."*

He'd already been in motion, rolling, tucking her beneath him, then surging up to his knees to undo his pants, all with shockingly unsteady hands.

Her hands landed on his chest, running over him as if in marvel, and he had to admit, he appreciated the appreciation. Then those hands lowered, helping him shove his pants down over his hips, freeing him as he kicked them off.

"Do you . . ." Staring at him, she trailed off. "Um."

"Um?"

"Do you have a condom that fits you?"

Again with the laugh. Laughing while getting a

woman naked was new for him, very new. "I'd usually have a clever reply for that, but my mind is blank."

"That's good, right?"

Good? How about unnerving? "It's new," he said, surging to his feet, briefly vanishing into his bathroom for a condom.

"Oh," she whispered in a very complimentary nature when he came back and dangled a strip of three condoms.

Laughing again, he scooped her up, carrying her to the big comfy chair in the corner, the one he watched movies in, his favorite place in the house. Setting her into the soft, giving cushions, he draped her legs over the arms and dropped to his knees before her, sliding his hands slowly up her body.

"Shayne—"

And down . . .

Whatever she'd been about to say vanished into thin air when he leaned forward, and with his hands on her inner thighs now, holding her open for him, kissed her belly button. Then her hip bone, then the crease of her thigh, where he paused, just to catch and absorb her quick breath of anticipation as he hovered between her thighs before lowering his head.

The sound she made when his tongue touched her, the sheer shock and undeniable pleasure in it made him even harder as he licked, nibbled, sucked, and licked some more, until she was panting for breath, pushing her hips at him in an escalating rhythm, until she fisted her hands into his hair, tossed back her head, and came.

And came.

While she was still shuddering, he tore off one of

the condoms and protected them both. Tugging her hips so that she shifted to the edge of the chair, he nudged at her center.

Gasping out a sexy little "oh" of surprise, she slipped a hand down her body and wrapped it around him and guided him home. Her head was back, her throat and back arched as she gasped in pleasure.

He pushed in a little more, then held back until she lifted her head and looked at him.

God, he loved her eyes. Loved the way they revealed everything she was thinking. "Yeah," he murmured, his voice a little hoarse with surprise. "That's so much better."

She stared into his eyes as he began to move, her cheeks going pink before she lowered her gaze and watched him sink the rest of the way into her. He did some looking of his own, coming a little undone himself at the sight of her, gorgeous and glistening, welcoming him. "You take my breath," he said, and stroked his thumb over her.

The soft sound she made undid him some more and he pulled her close to capture her mouth as he slid in and out of her, aware of the taste of her still on his lips, the feel of her soft body moving with his, the scent of her skin . . .

And then she was crying out, coming for him again, and he willingly, oh so willingly, followed her over.

Chapter 12

They moved from the living room to the shower, where they used another condom and made the most of the handheld showerhead. Afterward, Dani lay in Shayne's arms in his huge bed, listening to his deep breathing, fighting a bone-deep desire to put her mouth on his body and see how long it would take to wake him up.

But . . . *but*.

She couldn't stay. It was eight o'clock, she had to get to work. But mostly she had to get out before her heart engaged any more than it already had.

One time.

She'd promised herself one time, and she'd already had more than her fair share. *Way* more. Unfortunately, whatever she'd promised herself, the man really did it for her. The way he touched her, how he moved . . . In the shower, she'd nearly lost consciousness from the sheer pleasure of their movements, the slow slide of their bodies, how deep he went, how he'd held back, waiting until she panted out his name in desperation.

And she had panted his name.

And then cried out his name.

Sighing in bliss at the memories, knowing she'd remember these past few hours forever, she slipped out from beneath him.

He let out a long breath and she froze, but he didn't move again. Her eyes were gritty from lack of sleep. What she'd give to just slip back into that bed with the sexiest, most amazing man she'd ever met, but there was that promise—one night.

She couldn't fall for him.

Knowing it, repeating it, she tiptoed into his bathroom and found the clothes she'd left there last night. Then tiptoed toward the living room, which was where he'd removed her panties—just the thought brought a dreamy smile.

Maybe she hadn't fallen for him, not yet, but damn, she was dangerously close—

Splat.

That was the sound she made tripping over something big and furry. Sprawled in the hallway, she lifted her face, and then was licked from chin to forehead. By a dog. By a sweet, happy, slobbery dog who didn't care about morning breath or the fact that she was naked. "Thank you," she whispered.

Which got her another lick.

"Yes, good morning to you too, but if you could move—"

Bella moved. She rolled to her back, wriggling enthusiastically for more petting.

And panting. Lots of panting.

This was accompanied by enthusiastic tail wagging, a big heavy tail that whacked the wall with a thunk, thunk, thunk—

"*Shh.*" Dani tried petting her, but that got Bella even more excited. Dani sighed and sat up, reaching for Shayne's phone, which she used to call a cab while Bella whined.

"No more," Dani whispered. "I'm sorry, but as soon as I find my panties, I've got to go."

Bella snuffled, then let out one small, encouraging, hopeful bark.

Oh, God. "Shh," Dani begged, petting her some more out of desperation while she searched around for her panties. "Look, you let me out of here and you can sleep on the bed with him tonight, okay? What do you say?"

Bella cocked her head as if actually considering it.

"Good girl." Dani clutched her clothes to her naked body while turning in a circle—where were her damn panties? Oh, this was not good. She glanced at Bella, who'd made herself at home on the couch. "What if I have to leave my first one-night stand without my panties?" she whispered, horrified.

Bella snorted and licked herself.

"Thanks." Moving around the couch, Dani bent to peer beneath it, because hadn't he thrown them in this direction? Since she'd been a bit busy at the time, she couldn't be certain.

"Now *that's* a view to wake up to."

On her hands and knees, Dani froze. No. It wasn't really Shayne standing behind her while she was still on her hands and knees, head down, *naked,* providing him with a view she'd rather not think about. It wasn't him, because he was still fast asleep in his bed. She'd just imagined him, because if he was really there, she'd have to die of embarrassment—

"Dani? You okay down there?"

Jerking upright, she whipped around to face him. "Um, hi."

"Hi." His voice was rough with sleep, but his eyes were filled with heat.

And that wasn't his only reaction.

Oh, God, oh, God. She leapt to her feet and clutched her clothes to her chest. "I was just looking for my underwear."

"Ah." As naked as she, and clearly utterly and completely at ease with that, he took a step toward her. "Did you find them?"

"No."

"Sorry."

But he didn't sound sorry as he stroked a finger over her jaw. "You didn't get much sleep."

He had an erection, a really big one, and he stood there as if she couldn't see it bouncing in the morning air, brushing low on her belly, making her entire body beg her brain for one more condom . . .

"Hi," he whispered again, and with a wicked smile, brushed his mouth along her jaw, making its way to her ear.

And now her own body began to give her away but hello, she was naked. *In the unflattering light of day.*

And so was he!

Normally, she would love his lack of self-awareness, love the easy confidence, but now she only wished she possessed even a fraction of it as she took a step back while trying to shove her shirt over her head. "I was just trying to get out of here before I woke you." Damn, she'd put her shirt on inside out.

As she ripped it off and righted it, he reached for her, but she took a step backward, pulling the shirt back on, shaking out her jeans, and she couldn't help it, her eyes glued onto the part of him that was the happiest to see her. "I—I thought you'd be hard—" She grimaced. "I meant fast. I thought you'd be fast asleep. Th-that you'd want to sleep some more."

He grinned.

"Seriously," she said desperately. Damn it, he was gorgeous. Gorgeous and cute and . . . she took a peek . . . yep, still ready for more action. Her body reacted to that without her permission, but she ruthlessly pulled on her pants. Without the damn panties.

"Dani."

"Yeah." She whirled around, looking for her purse. "I've got to go."

He halted her frenetic movements with a hand on each of her arms. "Go? As in home? Where someone tried to break in last night?"

"No, not home. Work."

"Oh, okay. The place where you were shot at." He nodded agreeably, easily, but nothing in his hold was easy and agreeable. "Perfect, then."

"I really have to go." Didn't she? "I do."

"Your car isn't here. Let me get dressed—"

"I called a cab."

"Oh." He had some serious bed-head, and still looked amazing. Really, *really* unfair. And then there was that body, which she couldn't even look at because her own kept reacting to just the sight of it, like it belonged to her.

As if. "I have to go."

He stood there, naked, sexy, hot, with a bemused look on his face. Maybe no woman had ever left his bed before, at least not with him still in it, and she had to admit, she was crazy for doing so.

Crazy.

She definitely needed a new word. But the fact remained, she couldn't stay. She already felt her heart tug hard every time he so much as breathed, and that was not good.

So not good.

He'd told her himself, he was not a long-term bet. And she'd put money down that he wasn't a good middle-term bet either. Or a short one.

Yeah, she needed to get out now. Heading toward the front door, she squirmed at the feeling of wearing her jeans without panties. "I'll just . . ." *Be seeing you?* Because she didn't believe that. She'd seen his business card. She knew that he was far more than a pilot, and the fact that he still hadn't told her so spoke volumes.

She wouldn't be seeing him. "Let myself out."

"What about breakfast?"

She stopped with her hand on the doorknob. What was he doing? Why wasn't he just letting her go? "No, thanks."

"Dani—"

"Look, Shayne." Damn it, she went with frustrated to hide her sadness. "Just go back to bed, okay? And pretend you don't hear me leaving." She faced the door. Stared at the door. "It'll be a lot easier if you do that." Feeling him come up behind her, she closed her eyes. Shayne . . .

"Are you sure you don't want to talk about it?"

His mouth just barely grazed the sensitive skin beneath her earlobe. Which meant the rest of his fab bod was nearly touching, but not quite. She could feel his heat and had to tell herself not to press back and absorb it. "There's nothing to talk about."

As if on cue, the cab pulled into his driveway and honked.

"You might want to do a panty sweep before your next sleepover," she told him.

"Dani."

"Bye, Shayne." She pulled open the door. Yep, that was her. A mature one-night stand. With her shoes in one hand and her purse in the other, she smiled over her shoulder at him, albeit a weak one. "Have a good one."

And before she could weaken and give him one last kiss, which might result in her taking off her clothes again, she shut the door behind her.

In the cool morning, she gulped the air for courage and got into the cab, catching sight of herself in the rearview mirror. Her hair? Rioted. Her skin? Dewy and glowing. All of it pretty much screaming that she'd just had sex, and lots of it. She wasn't exactly looking her best, which of course directly contrasted with the fact that she felt her absolute best.

Two hours later, Shayne got out of bed for the second time and into his shower, acknowledging that he'd rather it'd have been a shower for two instead of solo. It was just that last night, with Dani, had been so unexpectedly amazing.

Which sounded as if he hadn't expected her to be amazing. But truthfully, he'd been so busy trying to hold back that he hadn't had any expectations at all.

That had been his mistake. And now, he felt something else unexpected. He felt . . . alone.

But then Bella nudged the bathroom door open, woofed a quiet "hello," one that had "feed me" all over it, reminding him that life went on. He had to feed the dog and get into work for a noon flight to

Santa Barbara. "She dumped us, Bell," he said, soaping up. "Can you believe it? I've been dumped."

Unconcerned, Bella turned around in circles on the mat and plopped down with a contented sigh.

He rinsed off, trying to get his mind wrapped around the fact that it'd happened. He'd lost his touch with women. Even the crazy ones didn't want him. Getting out of the shower, he grabbed a towel and his phone, and called his brother.

"Yo," Patrick answered. "I was just going to call you. The gun Dani allegedly found?"

"She did find it, in her pocket."

"Whatever, dude. It's not registered."

"Which means?"

"Illegal purchase. We're trying to trace the bullets now. Still no leads on who shot at you last night."

"They were shooting at Dani."

"Yeah, well, I'd stay away from her."

"Wow."

"Wow what?"

"You're a cop, telling me to stay away from someone who's obviously in danger?"

"I'm a big brother telling my little brother to watch his back. Look, she was just a girl at a party, Shayne. Let her be someone else's concern. Let her be my concern."

Which made complete sense, given who Shayne had always been and how he'd lived his life. He steered clear of attachments and all that entailed, always, so of course Patrick would suggest he do the same now.

Except he couldn't do it. He couldn't walk away this time, not while he knew she was in danger.

"Shayne? You're going to leave this in the hands of the police, right? In my hands?"

That wasn't the cop talking, that was the older brother, the one who'd bullied him and pushed him around most of his childhood, only to grow up and still think of him as the screwup.

"*Shayne?*"

"We're friends. I'm not walking away from her."

"Friends?" Patrick laughed. "Come on. You just met her. Besides, you don't do friends, not with women, not unless you're planning on having sex with her."

"Jesus, Patrick."

"What? Are you telling me you don't want to have sex with her?"

Shayne just rubbed his eyes.

"So you've already done the deed." Patrick laughed again. "Well, damn, that was fast. Even for you."

"Go to hell."

"Sorry. I'm too busy. I'll call you if I get anything else. Be smart, Shayne."

Shayne hung up. Be smart? Well no doubt, the *smart* thing to do was exactly as Patrick had suggested.

Walk away.

Hell, Dani had even helped him out in that area, by walking away first.

But damn, he'd been the black sheep of his family too long to listen to reason now. So he picked the phone back up. Yeah, he was going to call her, which was crazy all by itself, never mind the implications of *wanting* to call her. By doing this, he was sending far more than a "how are you after all the amazing sex" signal, he'd be sending a "I want to do you yet again" signal.

Which he didn't need.

Never needed.

But somehow he'd dialed her cell and the phone was ringing in his ear, and then her voice was asking him in that sweet, slightly halting tone to please leave her a message and she'd get back to him as soon as possible.

"Hey, Dani," he said, his mouth apparently having completely disconnected from his brain. "Missed you in the shower this morning." Christ, was that him? Telling her he missed her? He cleared his throat and found his balls. "Anyway, just wanted to make sure you made it to work okay. Have a good day."

Have a good day? What was he, a fucking Girl Scout? Jesus. To make sure he didn't repeat that shockingly needy mistake, he deleted her number from the memory in his cell.

Better.

By the time he got into Sky High Air, things were hustling and bustling. Maddie met him with a stack of phone messages, files, reports, and a blessed mug of caffeine. "Hey." She studied his face. "You look like crap."

"Gee, thanks. Any of these messages from Dani?"

"The damsel in distress? Nope, you're in luck, boss. No calls from her."

He lifted his head from the messages and looked into her eyes, and her smile faded. "Oh," she said, clearly taken aback. "You . . . *wanted* to hear from her."

Instead of answering, he turned away.

"Wow, that's new," she murmured.

He looked back. "What?"

"You, looking for the whole morning-after thing." She grinned, the smart-ass. "And it's so cute. What happened, she pull a Shayne and sneak out on you?"

"You do realize I sign your paycheck."

"I'm not afraid of you. You want me to get her on the line?"

"No."

"You want me to reschedule your flight so you can pull the whole stay-in-your-office-and-pout thing, like Brody does?"

"No. Brody's a woman." He headed toward his office.

"Shayne?"

With a sigh, he stopped. "What?"

"You're pretty cute when you're being the woman too."

Chapter 13

Dani got out of the cab and looked up at her second-floor apartment. At her front window. Was she scared to go in? Hell, yes. But she could do this. All she needed were panties. So she took the stairs.

She could have stuck around Shayne's longer, maybe found those panties, but she hadn't wanted him to look into her eyes and discover the truth.

One night hadn't been enough for her.

She had quite a few conflicting feelings about that. On the one hand, she felt like a woman who'd just had the best sex of her life, and she had.

No fumbling, no clumsy, klutzy, nervous movements for Shayne. Nope, the man had the moves. Great moves.

But on the other hand, she also felt exactly as she'd known she would.

Like they weren't finished.

Like maybe they couldn't ever get finished.

And that was the problem, wasn't it. Shrugging it

off, she opened her apartment door. "Hello?" she called, staying in the doorway.

No one answered. Of course no one answered. She lived alone.

"Dani?"

Nearly exiting her own skin, Dani jumped and found Alan standing in his doorway, watching her.

"You okay?" he asked, a worried frown on his face.

She opened her mouth to answer. Of course she was okay, she always showed up at eight in the morning wearing no panties, looking like she'd just had wild sex all night.

But he was looking at her so sweetly, so I-really-want-to-date-you sweetly, that she just shut her mouth and nodded weakly.

His gaze locked in on her neck. "You sure?"

She nodded again, but he kept staring at her neck. "What?"

"Is that a . . . hickey?"

She slapped a hand to her neck. "What? No. Of course not."

"Someone bit you."

Yes. Yes, Shayne had bitten her, lightly, with such heat and suction and perfect use of his tongue that her eyes had rolled back in her head with pleasure. She remembered sliding her fingers into his hair and holding his head to her, encouraging him to keep on kissing her like that.

Perfect. "Maybe it's a bug bite."

He sucked his lips inward but didn't voice the doubt that was all over his face. "Are you just getting home?"

"Yes." Which looked bad. She'd turned him down for a date, saying she was too busy with her job, and that she was going through a tough time right now, and that a man would complicate things.

But not a single one of those reasons made sense of the fact that yes, she was just getting home, she'd been with a man. She wondered if telling him it'd been a complicated man would help.

Probably not.

Nor would the fact that she'd witnessed an invisible murder, been shot at by an invisible shooter.

Oh, and then there'd been all that wild sex on the floor of Shayne's living room.

And in his shower . . .

And in his bed . . .

"Work's been a little crazy," she said weakly. She glanced inside her apartment. No sign of trouble. But still, she couldn't bring herself to step over the threshold. "Alan?"

"Yeah?"

She looked at him. "Would you like to come in for coffee?"

"Is that just because you want to have coffee, or because you're nervous about going in alone after the possible break-in?"

Damn it. He was adorably fumbling, yes. But not slow. Not by a long shot. "How do you know about the possible break-in?"

"I heard the police talking."

Okaaaay. So he'd been eavesdropping last night. That was probably just normal curiosity, right? Because Alan wasn't some kind of crazy stalker. But just in case, she shut her door and began walking back down the hallway toward the stairs.

Still extremely commando . . .

"Dani?"

"Going back to work," she called over her shoulder. *Please don't follow me with a gun.*

At the zoo, Dani let herself into her car and grabbed her cell phone, just as Reena drove up.

"Heard you had quite the night."

"You heard?"

Reena nodded. "You okay?"

Dani sighed and filled her in.

Reena listened in awed silence to the events of the night before, interrupting a few times to either ask a question or to make Dani repeat a detail.

"Tell me about the sex," she instructed.

Dani blinked. "I saw a murder, had someone break into my apartment, was *shot* at, and you want to talk about the sex? Are you kidding me?"

"Priorities," Reena said, utterly unapologetic. "Because you're okay."

"Yes."

"You're absolutely sure, right?"

Actually, shockingly, after last night, she was more than okay. In fact, she was having some trouble controlling the urge to just grin for no reason. That's what a few man-made orgasms did for her, apparently. "Yeah. I'm okay."

"Then yes, I want to talk about the sex."

"Reena."

"Come on. Was he good?"

She failed at holding back the stupid grin. Most definitely good. Off-the-charts good. So good her body was revved up and aching for more just thinking about it. "Yes."

"Nice way to celebrate your promotion."

Some of Dani's smile faded at that. "Reena, about that—"

"Look, I'm fine. I'll get the next one, or someone's going to have to die, but I'm fine. No biggie."

"Uh."

"Kidding," Reena said. "Jeez, I'm kidding. Look, are you coming or what?"

"I'll meet you in there."

"Suit yourself."

Dani looked at her cell phone, saw the missed call from Shayne, felt her heart squeeze, and put the phone in her pocket. She had work to get to.

Inside the zoo, Dani found no boogeymen, no dead bodies, nothing out of place. Just the elephants in their habitat, waiting patiently for her to observe them with their new addition—Bebo—the four-month-old baby fresh from the nursery.

So that's what she did, she settled in to watch and record. As the hours passed, she decided that yesterday and all that had happened had been some really strange episode of *The Twilight Zone.* An episode she didn't want to repeat. So when her cell rang again later, and then again, she ignored it, her gaze glued to the elephants, especially Bebo nuzzling her two-ton mama Ellie for milk.

So sweet, so simple. In the past, Ellie had pushed away the babies but today, when it was *her* baby, she nuzzled back in a show of unconditional love.

Dani watched, enraptured, awed. *Touched.*

All her life she'd been pushing people away instead of nuzzling, wanting, needing, to be independent. But now as she sat there, gaze glued to the beauty of mama and baby bonding, she couldn't justify her actions. She'd hidden behind her independent excuse so long it no longer even made any sense.

But if a stubborn mammal like Ellie had changed, didn't that mean she could as well?

Shayne flew his client to Santa Barbara, and while that client—a television producer—attempted to talk a reclusive actor into signing on a new sitcom, Shayne had a few hours to spare. Normally he'd have not wasted a single moment of that time, getting out on the waves ASAP, surfing as long as he could.

But instead he stood on the tarmac, the ocean pounding the shore in perfect five-footers, the wind rippling his hair, and tried calling Dani.

Again.

When he got no answer, he called Patrick, who also had absolutely no answer. "You're a cop," Shayne told him. "A detective. A big, badass detective. You're supposed to know all."

"Look, some things can't be explained. Stop worrying about this, Shayne."

"Stop worrying about this? The woman I was with last night was shot at!"

"Maybe you should give up the whole party-life thing, and this shit wouldn't happen."

Shayne grated his teeth. "I don't do the whole party-life thing anymore." Ah, hell. Who was he kidding? Patrick wasn't going to believe him. "If anything comes up, call me."

"I said I would."

Shayne resisted the urge to pick a fight—*see that, Mom, progress*—and did end up surfing, hoping it'd clear his head, but his mind remained a hundred miles away, back in Los Angeles with Dani, wondering what the hell she was doing and if she was safe.

After he flew the producer back to Burbank, Shayne stood in Sky High's lobby, getting a soda from the vending machine and once again calling Dani.

Still no answer.

He walked to the front counter, listening to Dani's voice mail message for the tenth time as he flipped through the messages Maddie had left for him. "Damn it."

"Flight go okay?" This from Noah, who waltzed in the front door with an easy grin on his face. The grin of a man who'd gotten lucky very recently.

Shayne had been wearing a grin like that earlier. Much earlier.

But the smile had faded in the light of day. He'd always wondered how in the hell Noah could settle down with one woman. In fact, just the thought of it boggled. But now he could admit there might be something to the notion. "You're still smiling."

"Am I?"

"I'd think you'd be tired of having sex with the same woman."

Noah laughed and patted Shayne's shoulder with mock sympathy. "Dude."

"Seriously."

"Seriously?" Noah laughed again. "Sleeping with the same woman is the best thing that's ever happened to me. No more wondering if she likes me, if she's going to go out with me, if she's going out with someone else. No more waking alone on a Sunday and having no one around, just to hang with."

"You had me."

"Okay, no one to cuddle with."

"You want to cuddle? I can cuddle."

"Have you seen Bailey, by any chance?"

Yes, yes, Shayne had. She was a leggy, gorgeous blonde. A former model, in fact. Extremely cuddle-able.

"Trust me, it's all good," Noah assured him.

"There's got to be a way to get all the good stuff without the ball and chain."

"You mean the ring."

"I mean the ring," Shayne confirmed.

"It's hard to explain, but the ring is like the icing on the cake." Noah grinned. "It's the best part."

This was news to Shayne, who'd spent years cultivating his carefree playboy reputation. Dani had known this about him. She'd known there wouldn't be icing on the cake. It's why she'd held back, why she didn't want to date him, and he respected that. He did. But suddenly he wanted icing on his damn cake, too.

Brody came down the hall, commandeered Shayne's soda, and drank deeply.

"Hey."

He slapped the now-empty soda can back to the counter. "What are you girls gossiping about?"

Shayne searched his pockets for more change, but came up empty. "Damn it, Brod."

Noah put a hand on Shayne's shoulder. "We're discussing why the laid-back surfer dude is as uptight as a guy who hasn't gotten off in a year."

"He got laid last night." Brody eyeballed Shayne. "So that means . . . *huh.*"

"What huh?" Noah asked curiously, eyeing Shayne like a bug on a slide.

"He must have gotten dumped. Again. Jesus, you're on a roll, huh?"

"I did not get dumped again," Shayne said, shoving free of Noah and glaring at Brody. "Go buy me a fucking soda."

"Yeah, he got dumped again," Noah said, nodding. "Was it the crazy chick?"

"She's *not* crazy."

"Yeah, it was the crazy chick," Brody decided, watching Shayne carefully. "Go figure."

Damn it. So he'd spent most of his life fighting off women and wasn't used to having to talk a woman into wanting him. Whatever. He'd live.

Maddie came out of the storage room wearing a leather miniskirt and two lace tops layered over each other, looking sizzling hot. She moved around the counter to sit in her chair, pulling out her keyboard, her fingers typing away.

Sizzling *and* effective.

"Don't you boys have work to do?" she asked without looking up from her work. "Planes to fly? Clients to kiss up to?"

When they didn't answer, she did glance up.

"Don't you ever dress like a secretary?" Brody asked.

Maddie arched a brow while Noah and Shayne inwardly winced. "No need, since I'm not a secretary," she said with glaciers in her voice.

"Shayne got dumped," Noah said, clearly trying to change the subject so Maddie didn't kill Brody with her eyes.

"Can't get dumped when you weren't available in the first place," Maddie noted, and when all three men blinked in confused unison, she sighed as if they were idiots. "Look, Shayne was never really available to her, right? He's never been available to *any* woman."

"And why is that?" Noah asked. "Seeing as you're the resident female expert?"

Maddie smiled. She liked the title. "Because he's the screwup."

"Hey," Shayne said.

"I mean that's what you've been told all your life." She stopped typing to squeeze his hand before going back to clicking the keyboard with dizzying speed. "You're the black sheep, the youngest, the fuckup in a large family of overachievers. You were always told you were never going to amount to anything." She shrugged. "So you decided to live up to that reputation, yadda yadda."

"Which is why you got yourself kicked out of all those schools before you met us," Noah said, ever so helpfully.

"And why you became a pilot instead of a brain surgeon or a big-shot attorney or detective," Brody added, also ever so helpfully.

Shayne stared at them. "Thanks for the trip down memory lane."

"Look, long story short," Maddie went on. "You're a commitment-phobe, hiding behind the free spirit, easygoing, laid-back bullshit persona."

"Bullshit persona?"

Maddie smiled sweetly. "Don't worry, boss. I have a bullshit persona too." She gestured to her own magenta-tipped blond hair. To her eyebrow piercing. Then, turning her back, she peeled down her already extremely low-rise leather skirt to reveal the small tattoo of a Chinese symbol, high on a first-class ass cheek.

Shayne stared, and Brody slapped him upside the head. "Don't look!"

"She said to look. And *ow*."

Maddie straightened her skirt. "It means dream big. Be whoever you want." She looked at Shayne. "Even when you're told you can't. Don't let your shortsighted family dictate your life."

"They aren't." But as he stared down at the cell phone in his hand, he shook his head. They were. Unbelievably, he was still letting what they thought of him matter enough to pretend it didn't bother him.

"See," Maddie said very gently. "The problem with being the black sheep just to spite them is that when the right woman does come along, you're not going to be able to snag her up. Because you'll be busy doing that whole no-commitment thing. You know, to prove that what your family thinks of you is true."

Noah was nodding. "Exactly. That's exactly what he's doing."

"You're all fucked up, man," Brody said.

"Bite me."

Noah took Shayne's cell phone and flipped it open.

"Hey!"

Brody leaned over Noah's shoulder as they accessed his dialed calls. "Yeah, look at that. He's tried calling her six times. *Dude*."

Shayne snatched his phone back and shoved it in his pocket. "It's nothing. This is nothing."

"It's definitely something," Noah said. "It's all over your face."

Shayne grabbed the schedule. He needed a flight. Now. And perfect, Brody had a flight to San Luis Obispo. It would get him out of here for four hours minimum. "I'm taking your flight."

"No, you're not."

"So maybe she'll call back while you're gone," Noah said.

"No. She's . . . working. She's busy."

Noah, Brody and Maddie exchanged a look of pity.

"Goddamnit, she is." Shayne tossed the schedule back to the desk. "That, or . . ." Hell. "Or she's in trouble."

"Trouble, as in . . ." Brody mimed the action of hanging a noose around his neck and jerking on the end, complete with tongue and eyes bulging out.

Maddie smacked him upside the head. "Don't you make fun of mental illness."

Shayne pivoted on a heel and walked away. It was that or kill Noah and Brody, and their investors might balk at that. On the way to the Learjet, he made one more attempt to reach Dani, but couldn't. "Fuck it," he said, and whipped around, heading back inside—

Only to plow into Brody.

"You want me to take my flight back," Brody guessed.

"I'm not taking the easy way out on this one."

"I can see that."

"She's in danger, Brody. And she's not calling back. That could just be because I'm a stupid prick, but it could also be more."

"So you're going to go find her because she might be in danger."

"No, I'm going because this is the new me. The new me who sticks."

Brody sighed again. "Go then. Go stick."

"I will." But it didn't escape him that for the first

time in his life, he was choosing a woman over a flight.

Dani recorded elephant behavior all day, and afterward, ran into Reena in the employee locker room.

"Saw you're getting Saturdays off now," Reena said, changing back to her street clothes. "Doesn't suck to be head keeper, does it?"

"I could probably get you a few Saturdays off too."

Reena shut her locker and shook her head. "I don't want any favors."

"But—"

"Seriously. Don't."

Dani began to change, hating the unaccustomed distance between them. "I have the new Depp DVD. Do you want to—"

"Can't. Some of us are going for sushi, but you can come with us if you'd like."

Dani hadn't slept in two days—except for that hour in Shayne's arms. "I really can't. I'm—"

"—Management now. Gotcha." Reena grabbed her backpack and headed to the door.

"Reena."

The door shut just a little harder than necessary.

"Damn it." Dani changed, then walked out to her car, alone. She told herself her skin was *not* prickling, but she braced herself for the sound of gunfire anyway.

Nothing.

Of course it was nothing. She'd gotten a message from Shayne's brother, saying they believed it could have been some kids playing target practice with the tall lampposts.

She wanted to believe that. With all her heart, she wanted to believe that.

Reena was just getting into her car. Dani called out to her. "Are you sure about the movie? I have double fudge ice cream to go with."

Reena smiled, but shook her head.

"I'm sorry about the damn promotion."

"No, it has nothing to do with that. Really." But her smile seemed just a little forced.

"Reena."

"Look, I'm meeting a date later. Okay? That's all it is."

Dani had to accept that. She drove home, stared at her front door with some hesitation before unlocking it. She shoved it open to prove her bravery, but once again just peered in from the doorway.

Safety first.

It looked fine. Everything was in its place. No sign of anyone having been inside while she'd been gone. She stepped inside but didn't shut the door all the way to allow for her hasty getaway if her quick inspection didn't turn out okay.

But all seemed normal. She distracted herself with the mail, and then the Visa bill, and then with a phone call from her dentist reminding her of a cleaning in two days.

Then she changed into her most comfy sweats—a pair of men's bottoms left over from a past boyfriend, three sizes too big but perfect for ice cream consumption—and a camisole top.

And while she was in her bedroom, she slopped on a facial mask. It was green and smelled like avocado, which would conflict with the ice cream, but it made her skin feel like a baby's butt and would go a long way toward lifting her morale.

This was not a pity party, she reminded herself.

Well, not officially, anyway.

She put the movie into the DVD player and plopped on the couch with a big wooden spoon and the ice cream. The only thing that would have improved on the evening would have been a big bag of popcorn, but she'd forgotten to restock from her last pity party.

Not a pity party.

Ah, hell. It was a pity party. But she could do this without the popcorn. The opening credits of her movie were just rolling when someone knocked on the door, making it creak open an inch or two.

Unbelievable. She'd never gone back to shut the damn door. So much for safety first. Heart in her throat, she looked around for her bat.

"Dani?"

Oh, good God. All her air escaped her and she sagged back into the couch. The man calling her name wasn't her invisible murderer.

Or her equally invisible mystery sniper.

But someone just as dangerous—Shayne.

Chapter 14

Slipping down onto the couch, Dani found herself stuck in place like a deer caught in headlights.

"Dani?"

"She's not here." Sinking farther into herself, she closed her eyes. "She . . . left the building."

"Uh-huh." Shayne shut the door. She heard the lock click into place.

"Go away."

"Not until I leave a message. Tell Dani that Shayne came by."

"Shayne? The pilot? The, what did the business card read, president of operations?"

He sighed. "Saw that, did you?"

"Hard to miss. It was embossed in gold."

"Maddie's doing."

"President of operations, Shayne. Not just a pilot. Not by a long shot."

"There's other things to talk about," he said. "Like why the hell is your door unlocked?"

Scrunched down as far as possible, the ice cream

and spoon still in her hand, she was rooted to the spot by several facts.

One, she was wearing huge pity-party sweats.

Two, she'd gone through nearly half the ice cream already and the sugar high was quickly turning to wooziness, a direct cause of number three.

Which was why at just the sound of his irritated voice, her entire body had gone on high red-alert status, including nipples hardening, belly quivering, and a whole host of other things too.

Good God, she was worse than Pavlov's dog. "You're supposed to knock."

"I did."

"And wait for a response!" Craning her neck, she took a peek. She couldn't help herself.

Yep.

There he was, in the flesh. Wearing his pilot gear, which consisted of blue trousers, a white button-down shoved up at the elbows with Sky High's logo on a hard pec, and aviator sunglasses, which at the sight of her he pulled off. That meant that those piercing light brown eyes landed directly on her without any barrier.

Great. So much better.

Except not. With a groan, she sank farther down in the couch and tried to vanish.

Shayne frowned at the couch. What the hell was she doing? Besides avoiding his calls.

Then the couch spoke. "Why are you here?"

"Good question."

"If you don't know—"

"Oh, I know why I'm here. Why the hell didn't you return my calls?"

"Well—"

"And why the hell is your door unlocked?"

"You already asked that."

"Still waiting for an answer that makes sense."

"Fine. I got a little distracted."

Tired of talking to the couch, he came around the front of the couch to face her. She wore green monster face paint on her face. Her hair had gone wild on top of her head, though he could see another yellow number-two pencil in there trying to hold it all together. Her entire lower body had been swallowed whole by a pair of sweats that looked like they might belong on a four-hundred-pound rapper. And then there was the ice cream, and not just a bowl either, but an entire gallon.

That was some serious ice cream consumption. "Bad time?" he asked.

"Yes, actually." She bristled a bit, which looked comical in green. "I'm . . ." She shoved the wooden spoon and ice cream behind her back, as if he hadn't already seen them. "Busy."

"Ah."

At that, she lifted her chin, playing the I-don't-care-that-I-look-like-shit game. Good tactic, one he might have taken himself, though he doubted he'd have looked even half as adorable as she while playing it.

"*Very* busy," she added.

A drop of the green mask fell from her nose and plopped to her camisole top.

"Very, *very* busy," she added, her voice a bit smaller now as she tried to surreptitiously rub the green into her sweats.

So damned adorable. "I can see that." He said this with an utterly straight face, but she rolled her eyes, set down the ice cream and the spoon, and got to her feet.

"I wasn't expecting company," she said pointedly, looking at the door.

"You didn't return my phone calls."

"No, I didn't." She took in his expression and shook her head. "That's never happened to you before, has it?"

He rubbed his jaw while trying to decide the right answer to that.

She laughed again, then put her hands to her face. "This is drying. Don't make me laugh, I'll crack."

In his pocket, his cell phone vibrated, but he ignored it. He didn't have a flight, and everything else could wait. "You smell like avocados."

"Why are you here again?"

"Are you kidding me? Last night you thought you saw a murder."

"I'm sure that happens."

"No, actually. It doesn't happen. Then you had someone in this very apartment."

"I might have been mistaken about that part."

"And you were shot at. You weren't mistaken about that."

She went on the defensive, in her big sweats and green face mask. "How do you know they weren't shooting at you, Shayne? You ever think of that?"

He gave her a long look, and with a sigh, she plopped back to the couch. "Okay, fine. What's your point?"

"My point is . . ." Actually, he had no idea. She turned him upside down and sideways, with seemingly little effort. He shouldn't have come, and yet *not* coming hadn't been an option.

Hunkering down at her side, he looked into her face. Her green face. "A call back might have eased my mind."

"Okay, well, I'm sorry about that."

"Something might have happened to you."

"It didn't."

"I was worried."

She blinked, as if that hadn't occurred to her. "Oh."

"Yeah, oh."

She looked down into the ice cream on the coffee table, and then at him, and this time, her eyes had warmed. "I'm sorry."

"It never occurred to you I might be concerned?"

"That's not what I thought you were calling for."

"What did you think I was calling for?"

Her telephone rang, shattering the sudden silence. Looking relieved to be saved by the bell, she got up, flashing him a very brief view of the top of a pale blue thong before she yanked up the slipping sweats and stalked toward the telephone.

He sank to the couch and tried to concentrate past that pale blue. He'd come to make sure she was okay. Now that he could see that she was, he could leave.

Should leave.

Damn it. He didn't want to.

Dani frowned at the phone, then hung it up.

"Wrong number?" Shayne asked, sitting on her couch like he belonged.

"No one was there." She felt him watching her. "A hang-up."

"Do you have caller ID?"

"No."

"You need caller ID, Dani."

With a sigh, she plopped at his side on the couch, tilted her head back and stared up at the ceiling. "I know. But for now, I'd like to keep pretending that it was just a wrong number."

He put a hand on her leg. Her entire body went back on high alert.

"Back to my earlier question," he murmured. "What did you think I came here for?"

It wasn't easy to think past the hand he had on her knee. In fact, it was impossible.

"Dani?"

She sighed. "A booty call."

"A booty call."

She lifted her gaze to his, and for the longest beat he just looked at her, clearly surprised.

Okay, now she didn't know which was worse. That she'd said it out loud, or that she'd been wrong.

"A booty call," he repeated. "Jesus."

She tried to get up, but he pressed a hand to her leg, holding her still. She closed her eyes. "My being mistaken makes me an even bigger loser than sitting here with a mask on, halfway through a gallon of ice cream all by myself."

"Now, see, you didn't have to admit that part." She felt him lean forward, look into the carton. "Wow. You weren't kidding."

"Please. Just go out the door and pretend you weren't ever here."

"Dani."

She didn't answer.

"*Dani.*"

With a sigh, she opened her eyes and looked at him.

"I just want to get this straight. First you were upset because you thought I was calling for a—as you so eloquently put it—booty call. And now you're upset because I wasn't?"

"That's right. I'm just doing my best to live up to my crazy reputation." She walked to the door and opened it in invitation for him to leave. It was hard to maintain her dignity with the mask cracking all over her face, her hair falling out of its tenuous hold and into her face, and also into her face mask, ew, but she did her best.

"You really want me to leave?" he asked in shocked disbelief. Clearly, this was another first for him. "Why?"

Not expecting the question, she could only stare at him as he rose to his feet and slowly walked toward her. When their toes were touching, he reached around her and shut the door.

Locked it.

Okay, this was where she said something. *Anything*. "Um." Oh, um. Yeah, that was brilliant. Really.

He ran a finger over her temple, pushing a strand of hair from her face, tucking it behind her ear, then taking that finger on a slow, seductive tour down her throat.

"S-Shayne—"

"Why, Dani?"

"Because." She cleared her throat. "Because I'm not interested."

"Bullshit."

"Okay, because you don't repeat."

Finger still on her, he went still, gaze lifting to hers.

Yep. That should do it. Any second now he'd walk out. It made her heart hurt to think of it, because despite her horror at being caught in the middle of a pity party, she didn't want to be alone.

More than that. No matter what she'd told him, she wanted his company. His. "Right?" she pressed. "You don't repeat, and I tend to do exactly that, so really, this thing is done."

"Dani."

Holding her breath, she locked her gaze on his. "Do you repeat, Shayne? Yes or no."

"No, but—"

"No buts necessary."

"But," he said again, softly. "I have a feeling this is different. *You're* different."

She stared at him. "Is that good or bad?"

"I haven't gotten that far yet." He glanced back at the ice cream. "So this whole ice cream and movie thing. Is it a party for one?"

"A pity party, you mean. And yeah. It's for one."

Holding her gaze with his for a beat, his mouth quirked, a dimple flashed. Then he broke the eye contact and leaned in so that his mouth brushed her ear. "How about one plus one?"

Oh, yes, her body said. *Great idea.* "I don't have enough facial mask for you."

He laughed low in his throat, a sound that was just as damn sexy as the rest of him. Setting his hands on her hips, he backed her into the living room, back to the couch, and as she walked, his big, bad body nudged into hers on purpose, letting her feel that she was not alone in this uncontrollable surge of need and desire.

"I'm not sharing my ice cream."

"Are you sure? Because . . ." Again he put his mouth to her ear, taking a second to nibble. "I've got a much better use for it than you could possibly have had . . ."

Oh, God. She'd just let in the big, bad wolf. "Well." She swallowed hard. "That's a very intriguing thought." She felt the couch at the back of her thighs, and just as he smiled again, she found herself falling back onto the cushions.

He followed her down, stretching his long body over hers, and there, towering above hers, with his wonderfully warm, hard length pressed to her, he still didn't kiss her.

And that's when she remembered. "The mask."

"I'm sure it tastes very yummy, but maybe it's best if you . . ."

"Yes. *God*." Shoving free, she leapt up and ran down the hallway to her bedroom and into her bathroom, where she stared, breathless, at herself in the mirror. Her eyes were bright, but it was hard to tell about the rest of her face beneath the cracked green mask. The one that made her look like a seasick smurf.

He'd looked at her looking like this. Nearly kissed her like this.

She scrubbed clean. Vanity had her adding some lip gloss. Great. Now her lips looked fabulous, but the rest of her? Not exactly at her best. She ran into her room and into her closet, ripping off all her clothes. Naked, she scrambled for something to replace the sweats with, but she hadn't done her laundry. "Damn it."

"Everything okay?" Shayne asked from the other side of her bedroom door.

God! She shoved the closet door closed and stood inside it, *naked*. "Don't come in here!"

"Why, because you might be wearing sweats and a mask?"

"You're a funny guy, Shayne." *Crap.* He'd come into her bedroom. In the dark closet, she fumbled through the pile of clothes on the closet floor for a new pair of panties. What was it with her and losing her panties lately? She didn't find any, but did locate the brush she'd lost weeks ago.

"Dani? You okay?"

She tossed the brush aside. "Peachy."

He nudged the door and she held it shut. "Don't you dare come in here."

"That's not what you said the last time you got into a closet."

"I mean it!"

"You sound out of breath. What are you doing in there?"

She found a hoodie zip-up sweater. Because she couldn't find a bra, she zipped it up to her chin. "I'm out of breath because—Never mind!" She groped for a pair of jeans and came up with a gauzy skirt she'd worn to a Renaissance Fair last summer. It was loose, with a drawstring waist, and she'd just managed to pull it up and tie it when the door was nudged again.

"Damn it, Shayne Mahoney." Why was she always commando around him? "You don't listen very well."

Completely unaware of her dilemma, he spoke with a grin in his voice. "That's what my mother always says. 'Shayne Mahoney, you don't listen.' "

She gripped the door, holding him out while she desperately straightened her clothes and tried to regain her breath. "So what did she do about your listening skills?"

"I was the last of six boys. As a litigation attorney, she was far too tired by the time she came home from work to deal with me."

Still in the dark, Dani lifted her head. That didn't fit into the mold in which she'd placed him, the one of a pampered, spoiled kid, the absolute apple of his mother's eye. "So your brothers raised you?"

"More like beat the shit out of me, regularly."

"No way. You're too big for that."

"I was a puny kid, trust me."

She pictured that, him a helpless little kid, no one to really protect him, and without her permission, her heart squeezed and engaged. "Your mom allowed that?"

"Like I said, she was tired. Of us. Literally."

"What about your father? Surely he—"

"A very busy brain surgeon. Not around much either, but when he was, he usually only encouraged my brothers to toughen me up."

"What? *Why?*"

"Because I was a classic underachiever."

She turned to face the door of the closet, even putting her hand to the wood as if she could touch him. "But you're a pilot. You run a private airport. You fly all kinds of planes and people, all over the world."

"I'm an expensive taxi driver."

"Shayne—"

"Don't get me wrong. I love what I do. I was born to do what I do. Being in the air, it . . . it feeds my soul. I'm just telling you what they think."

And she knew despite not wanting to, he cared what they thought. How well she knew the agony of that. It had her opening the door.

He was casual as could be, arms lightly crossed, his feet the same, propping up the wall. Yep, easygoing as they came.

Except there was more to him than that lazy confidence, so much more.

"There you are." He took in her zippered hoodie and the long gauzy skirt, the combination of which covered her from chin to toe. "With your armor intact."

She managed a smile and tried not to look directly at him, because he was damned distracting. "Thought I might need it." Her eyes wandered to her bed. *Bad* eyes. "So . . . did you always want to be a pilot?"

He smiled. The distraction wasn't fooling him. "From the moment I first saw a plane. What are you looking at?"

"I always wanted to work with animals," she said quickly. Not looking at the bed. "From the time I was little, animals were it for me." As usual, her mouth was running off without permission because she was nervous. And excited. Nervous and excited were a bad combination for her. "When I got my job at the zoo, my mother stopped by on my first day. I was giving an enema to a clogged giraffe."

"Let me guess. That's what she thinks you do all day. Evacuate shit."

In spite of herself, she laughed. How he did that, made her laugh when she hadn't planned on being amused, was beyond her. "Sort of like taxiing people, huh?"

He grinned too. They grinned at each other, unexpectedly unified in this. "You're happy in your job," she murmured.

"Very."

"Me too."

"I'm happy in my life," he said.

In his single life. Right. Got to remember that. She glanced at the bed again. He was happy single.

"But here's the stickler," he said quietly. "I'm happier now that I've met you."

Before she could begin to figure out how to process that, his gaze dropped to her mouth. "Much happier." Cupping her freshly washed face, he leaned in, and this time didn't stop until their lips were touching. This kiss was different from the wild kiss they'd shared in the last closet they'd stood in, and different from the kisses they'd shared at his house.

This kiss was slow and sweet, and so heartfelt she felt her throat burn, and when he pulled back a fraction, just enough to look into her eyes, hands still on her face, he murmured, "And as to your earlier question . . . I was worried about you, but I also wanted to see you again. I *wanted* to repeat. If you meant what you said, yesterday that you don't, then tell me now. Look me in the eyes and tell me you feel nothing for me, that you don't want to see where this goes."

Oh, God, don't do this. Don't be so gorgeous and *have the heart too. Don't be the whole package.* "You . . . you want to repeat."

He offered her a sweet, sort of baffled smile. "Go figure, right?"

This wasn't good. He stood there looking young and sexy, but also shockingly vulnerable, and the combination was almost too much to take.

She could fall for him.

Hard.

Fast.

And here she was without her handy-dandy, trusty safety net. Not good. Not good at all. Backing out of his arms, she moved back down the hall.

He wanted to repeat. How did she resist that? Answer—she couldn't, she really couldn't.

"Where are you going?"

"To the ice cream. I need ice cream for this."

"For what?"

She plopped down on the couch and resumed her earlier position, holding the spoon and the carton, thinking there might not be enough ice cream on the planet for this.

The couch sank as he hit the spot beside her, his thighs brushing hers. "You got another spoon?"

Turning her head, she looked into his eyes. And just like the ice cream in her hands, she melted a little. "I suppose I can share."

Chapter 15

"You're like an onion."

An onion? Confused, Shayne looked at Dani. "What?"

Her eyes were warm, her face a little flushed, whether from scrubbing off the mask or from being near him, Shayne had no idea, but he hoped like hell it was the latter.

"You have all these fascinating layers." She dropped her spoon into the ice cream. "When I saw you at my mother's party, I thought, uh-oh. Pure trouble coming right at me." She lifted a shoulder. "Sexy trouble, of course. But you were this easygoing, laid-back, too wealthy, too good-looking for your own health guy, you know? Someone who'd probably never lifted a finger a day in his life."

Hard to be insulted, when most of that had been true at one time or another. "And here I thought all you saw was my sharp wit and intelligence."

"Nope, just the whole playful playboy thing." Apparently unconcerned that her blunt honesty had a sharp edge and cut deep, she went for another bite of ice cream. "But the thing is, layers started peeling away almost immediately." And then another bite. Or rather, a lick. Her tongue delicately ran over the wooden spoon and made his eyes cross.

"Dani."

And then another lick. Without conscious thought, he urged her closer, then closer still, pulling her onto his lap.

"Shayne—"

He slid a hand up her back and she arched into his touch, even as she was careful, very careful, to keep her skirt modestly tucked around her knees as she settled in. The contradiction between that and the fact that her nipples went hard, pressing against the material of her sweater, combined to create a sensory overload.

Up and down went his hand, to the back of her neck and down again, farther this time—

And then he suddenly realized the reason for her modesty.

It was entirely possible that she wasn't wearing any underwear.

She gave the spoon another lick, which in turn gave his body a quick shudder of pleasure from just watching her. He wanted to shove up the skirt and see if he was right about her being commando . . .

"Do they?" she asked, feeding him a bite of ice cream.

What? He'd missed the question.

"I asked if all your women see right through you."

"Hope not." His hands slid down her arms all the way to the backs of her thighs.

No panties.

"I do," she whispered. "I see right through you. Past that outer layer to your inside, where you're sweet and funny and smart. I like that layer best. I decided that in the closet at the party."

"I thought you liked the mistletoe the best." His voice was just a little thick and a lot hoarse as he ran his hands up and down her outer thighs, to her hips, her waist, and back down.

Nope. No panties anywhere. What happened to the blue thong?

He was having trouble getting past that, past the fact that if he shoved up her skirt, there'd be nothing to stop him from feasting on something much, much better than ice cream.

And sitting on him as she was, she couldn't miss what else was happening with his body . . .

"The mistletoe," she murmured. "That was fun." She paused for a bite of ice cream, and wriggled her butt just a tiny little bit, so that the very core of her cradled the absolute core of him.

Yeah. She hadn't missed a thing. She knew.

"And the kissing," she added. "That was a very nice layer indeed." She fed him another bite, opening her mouth as he opened his, making him smile even though he was hard as a rock.

"But I can't help but wonder . . ."

"What?" he asked.

"Do you think . . ." She nibbled on her lower lip in a way that made him want to do the same. "That maybe it's all just an adrenaline rush? This . . . attraction? After all, there's been a lot of adrenaline."

"You really think what happened between us was just adrenaline?"

"Well, it's possible, right?"

Possible, yes. And he'd love for it to be nothing

more than that. In fact, having this all be just an adrenaline rush would be perfect.

So perfect, and to see if that was the case, he covered her mouth with his, and as his body leapt to attention, he had to agree. A good part of this was definitely adrenaline. Not to mention sheer, unadulterated lust.

But it wasn't only his body involved here. Unfortunately, his heart was too, and that meant more than just adrenaline and lust. A little stunned, he lifted his head.

She was staring at him with the same shell-shocked expression. "It should have worn off by now."

"Maybe we didn't try hard enough to get it out of our system."

"Okay," she whispered, game, so he kissed her again, deeper, hotter, wetter, and this time when he lifted his head, she let out a slow, shaky smile. "Still feel it. You?"

"Oh, yeah."

"Maybe . . . maybe you should show me what you had in mind for this ice cream. Maybe that would do it, get each other out of our system." Her smile was a little hopeful, and a whole lot hot.

But not nearly as hot as he felt. Slipping his hands beneath her, he stood and turned, then let go of her.

"Oh," she gasped as she bounced into the cushions of the couch. "Oh," she murmured again when he dropped to his knees.

Between hers.

The first thing she did was make sure her skirt was still covering her. Adorable. But so not necessary, because he had plans. Plans that did not involve the skirt. He held out his hand for the spoon. "May I?"

Looking a little breathless, she hesitated, then handed it to him. "Um, I—"

"Party for two now, remember?"

Her gaze never left the spoon. "Right." Licking her lips and fidgeting, she looked a little nervous, which only upped the anticipation. Dipping the spoon into the now softened ice cream, he touched it to her nose.

"Hey—"

And her chin.

"Shayne."

And the very base of her throat.

"Wh-what are you doing?"

"Making my very own ice cream sundae." Leaning in, he licked the drop from her nose. Her chin.

Her throat.

"Oh," she breathed with a sweet little shudder as her hands sank into his hair. "I like that."

"Good. That's good." His fingers closed on the zippered tab of her sweater, just beneath her throat. He loved how she'd zipped it all the way up to the top, as if she was all prim and proper, because he'd seen her decidedly unprim and unproper, and was hoping to get her there again.

All in the name of getting her out of his system, of course.

With one hand he slowly pulled the zipper, the other dipping the spoon back in for more ice cream.

"Shayne?"

"Yep, still right here . . ." Oh, yeah, he thought, watching as he unzipped, revealing a strip of creamy smooth skin from her collarbone to her sexy belly button.

No bra, just some great cleavage.

Holding her gaze, he slid a hand into the sweater,

gliding his fingers over her ribs, up to a breast, letting his thumb slowly circle her nipple.

Her breath caught, and she tugged her lower lip between her teeth. "Shayne."

Sliding his hand up even higher, he nudged the sweater off her shoulder, which gorgeously exposed one of her breasts.

She shivered.

"Cold?"

She shook her head, her hair tumbled around her shoulders. "No."

He felt lost in her illuminating eyes, in the rosy blush riding her cheeks, in that wild hair. Lost, and yet somehow found. "You're so beautiful, Dani," he murmured, his thumb rasping over her nipple, tugging a sigh of pleasure from her. Her eyes drifted shut as he brushed the sweater from her other shoulder, then, holding the spoon above her, he let the ice cream dribble down her ribs, over her quivering belly.

"Oh," she breathed, and then again when he brought the spoon up to her breast and painted a chocolate stripe right over her skin.

Beneath the chocolate ice cream, her nipple puckered up into a hard, tight little point.

"Okay, *now* I'm cold," she gasped.

"I've got it." Leaning in, he put his mouth to her stomach and began his dessert, licking off the ice cream, slowly devouring both it and her.

Her hands tightened in his hair as he nipped, sucked, and teased his way up to her nipple. Hovering just above it, he let out a warm breath, and she shivered.

"Please," she whispered.

Oh yeah, he'd please. He'd please her all damn

night if she let him, and he drew her into his mouth. "Good?" he asked against her skin.

Panting for air, a slight, helpless rocking of her hips against his, she didn't answer.

"Dani?"

"Good," she managed. "It's good. Lots more good, please."

Her polite tone made him smile, and he reached for more ice cream, wanting to see her come completely undone, come all over him. Slowly he bunched up the flimsy material of her skirt, slipping it up over her knees, her thighs.

Her gaze, still on his, widened. She softened the grip she had on his hair and put a hand over his, halting his progress. "Um." She tightened her legs, but with him between them, she couldn't close them. "Shayne?"

"Yes?"

"I've . . ." She blushed. "Sort of got an alfresco situation going on here."

"I know." Gently nudging her fingers out of his way, he slid her skirt up—

"You're not really going to—"

"Yeah." He got the skirt past her upper thighs, to her belly, then groaned at the sight of her, legs sprawled open, held there by his hips, no panties, nothing but Dani, all pink and glistening.

For him. "I'm really going to."

He was really going to. "But . . ." Dani struggled to form a sentence, and failed.

"Are you allergic to ice cream?" he asked.

"No."

"Then trust me."

She held her breath. An ice cream sundae. The man wanted to make her his own personal ice cream sundae. She'd never done such a thing before. To be honest, she'd never really had a lover take so much time to get her naked.

Or spend so much time just looking at her.

Not to mention the touching, and the tasting—

"Ohmigod," she gasped as the ice cream dripped from the spoon, low on her belly, over her hip, the top of her thigh . . .

And then between.

At the contact of the cold dessert on her sizzling hot skin, she nearly imploded right then and there, but then there were his eyes, also sizzling hot, watching her reaction as he leaned over and licked her.

After all, she was his dessert. But oh. My. God. In that moment, she couldn't remember why she wanted to resist, or even get him out of her system. Hell, she could hardly remember her own name.

"You're the best flavor of ice cream I've ever had."

Unbelievably, just his words brought her to the edge. Aided, of course, by the fact that she sat wantonly spread on the couch, nearly naked—which somehow felt more naked than totally naked—and him still fully dressed. Her hips kept moving of their own accord, in a rhythm she couldn't seem to stop, and though she wanted to close her eyes rather than watch him watch her, she couldn't seem to do anything but utter a soft, helplessly needy whimper.

Understanding completely, he went back to the job at hand, which apparently was to drive her slowly out of her mind. He handled the task with aplomb, using his fingers to hold her steady, his lips, his tongue, even his teeth, to drive her wild.

And she did go wild.

She came completely out of herself. And when she could breathe again, still gasping for air, she realized she had him by the ears, holding him to her, her thighs nearly strangling him. "Ohmigod." Still panting, she let go of him. "I'm sorry."

Sitting back on his heels, he smiled, not appearing to have suffered any for her abuse. "My pleasure is your pleasure."

Since that had been the case, literally, she managed not to cover her face, but she did reach for his clothes. "You are way overdressed," she told him, yanking his shirt over his head.

The sight of his chest distracted her for a moment, and she surged up to reach for the spoon. "And now it's my turn."

The look on his face defied description, a mix between amusement, shock that she wanted to return the favor, and that heart-stopping heat that never failed to sear her skin. Shifting their positions was easy enough, and somehow he managed to skim her out of her clothes while he was at it, and then she was naked in his lap, his pants shoved to his thighs, all her good parts rubbing against his good parts.

"God, you feel so good." Head back, he arched up. "So damned good—*holy shit!*"

She'd given him a taste of his own medicine with the cold ice cream, and smiling down at the trail she'd set for herself, from chest to his most impressive erection, she bent to her task.

He slid his hands in her hair, halting her progress a mere fraction of an inch from her target. "Dani—"

"Are you allergic to ice cream, Shayne?" she asked, mirroring his earlier words.

He let out a half groan, half laugh. "No."

"Then trust me." Pushing him back, she proceeded

to eat her dessert; that is, until Shayne cupped her face and lifted her up.

"Tell me you have a—"

"Yes." He held up a condom.

"Thank God." Her fingers were shaking from need, and when he took over, she saw that his trembled too. "That's what happens when you eat dessert first," she whispered, and he laughed.

And then she started laughing too, at least until he lifted her up so that she could sink down over him, because as he pushed inside her, all laughter went out the window.

A low, raw sound escaped him, incredibly sexy, and his hands urged her to move on him, up and down, and though she'd thought that since this was round two for both of them, it would be slow and sweet, apparently their bodies didn't get the memo, because it was like a freight train, hitting hard and fast, and in her entire life she'd never felt anything like it. It was as if he'd climbed inside her body, knew what she wanted before she wanted it, and knew how to give it to her. It was like being lost and coming home.

All at the same time.

Terrifying.

Yet simple . . .

And she wasn't quite sure what it all meant, except deep down she *was* sure. She was exactly sure.

Which terrified her most of all.

Chapter 16

Shayne opened his eyes. He was flat on his back on the carpet of Dani's living room.

Naked.

Dani was draped over him like a blanket, and in keeping with the evening's festivities, also naked, a state in which she looked heart-stoppingly amazing. He loved her curves, loved her creamy skin—still sticky from the ice cream—and especially loved those curves and creamy skin all pressed up against him.

While he ran his hand down her back, she let out a soft sigh and snuggled her face into his neck.

She was asleep, he realized. Fast asleep. Her hair was in his face, and if he wasn't mistaken, there was some ice cream in the strands as well, a fact that brought a ridiculous grin to his face.

Ice cream and sex. That had been a new one, even for him.

Her lips brushed his flesh, which brought both

goose bumps and another reaction, far south of his neck.

Lifting her head, she smiled at him, her eyes sleepy and sexy, a smudge of ice cream still on her jaw.

"Hey," she whispered.

"Hey back." Okay, so that hadn't been just adrenaline, and she wasn't out of his system. That was new too. He could deal with that.

"You probably have to go," she said.

Go?

"Since we, you know, washed each other out of our systems and all."

He stared at her. So . . . she *wanted* him to go. Wow. Okay. He'd do that. He'd go. Which was good, really. Because this was just sex. Of course it'd been just sex—

From the pocket of his pants on the floor, his cell phone vibrated.

"I'll get it for you."

"That's okay—"

But she'd slipped off him and reached into his pocket, handing him the phone.

The ID read: Michelle King.

"You going to get it?" she asked.

"It can wait."

"You mean she can wait?" When he looked at her, she winced. "I saw the name. Sorry."

"She's just—"

"No, don't explain." She reached for her sweater. "I went into this with my eyes open. It's okay." She grabbed her skirt and wriggled into it. "I just don't want to be the one waiting around for your phone calls, you know?"

"Aren't you the one who didn't pick up my calls?"

"I'm just saying, I don't expect you to call."

"You should. You should expect it."

She stared at him, leveling him with those soft, expressive chocolate eyes. "This thing needs rules, or something."

"Like . . . what? You get to wield the wooden spoon next time?"

The tension left her face and she laughed. "I already did that."

God, he loved her laugh.

"No, like . . . like maybe . . ." She glanced at him, chewing her lower lip.

"Like maybe what?"

"Like maybe we both have to know what we're doing here." She straightened her clothes. "With the whole just-sex thing."

"I can tell you that you seem to know exactly what you're doing."

She let out a low laugh. "That's not what I meant."

"What did you mean? What kind of rules?"

"Maybe . . . that even if we're having just sex, we're not having it with someone else until we're finished with all the sex." She said this, then held her breath, as if she might be asking for too much.

Lifting his hands, he sank them into her hair, holding it off her face as he made himself hold her gaze. "While I'm sleeping with you, Dani, I don't want to be sleeping with anyone else."

"So that makes us, what? Sexually exclusive?"

"The last time we got anywhere close to this conversation you told me you weren't going to date me."

"But then we slept together."

"As I recall it, there wasn't much sleeping."

She blushed. "I know. But the rule thing? You're okay with it?"

"I spent most of my life screwing the rules."

"Of course." Smile gone, she turned away. "It's okay. That was ridiculous of me. People having just sex don't use rules."

He managed to catch her before she ran down the hall. "Wait—"

"I've got to—"

"Wait," he said again, softly, pulling her back against him, wrestling a little with her because damn, she was strong and she did not want to look at him. "Just wait."

She didn't move, just looked at him with those eyes. Killed him with those eyes. "I like you," he said carefully. "I like you a lot. I realize I sound about twelve, but give me a minute." He gulped in some air. "I want to spend time with you," he corrected. "I want to see where this is going. But if you're asking me for a final destination, I just don't know it yet." Again, he smoothed back her hair and found himself inexplicably nervous, waiting on a response. "Is that okay for now?"

She stared at him for a long heartbeat, during which time he didn't so much as blink. Her heart seemed to be in her eyes, and it was damn hard to look at them because they made him feel things he hadn't expected to feel.

Finally she nodded, and he could breathe. "Okay." He felt this odd, overwhelming sense of relief. "Okay . . . So now it's my turn to name a rule."

She eyed him warily. "Oh?"

"I was thinking we should have a no-clothes rule. You know, when we're here or at my place."

Her eyes lit with shock, then humor. "A no-clothes rule."

"Yeah. Is that a problem for you?"

"No." She smiled, and he felt like he'd just won the lotto. "Especially since I can't seem to find any underwear around you."

He kissed her. And then again. And when they were both breathless, he raised his head. "Your turn for a rule."

"Okay." She nodded. "Rule number three," she said very seriously. "The next food item we use during sex has to be a *heated* item."

His heart actually stopped. Then kicked hard. And right then and there, he felt himself fall just a little bit. *"Deal."*

Dani woke up just before dawn to elephants bleating at the top of their lungs.

Her alarm.

Heart racing, she slapped the snooze button and turned over with a smile already in place for the man—

Not next to her.

He'd left. Which, she supposed, was only fair. After all, she'd done the very same thing to him the night before. And just because they'd talked about rules didn't mean they were going to continue this thing. So him leaving? No biggie. In fact, as far as good-byes went, it was a fairly gentle one. Gentle, and yet somehow, at the same time, a little sad.

Okay, a lot sad.

Get over yourself. In that vein, she got up and looked into the mirror. Her hair stuck straight up on one side (courtesy of the ice cream) and was flattened completely to her head on the other (also no doubt courtesy of the ice cream), making the no make-up status just that much worse. She had a beard burn beneath her jaw, which she could live with, and something stuck to her shoulder.

A condom wrapper.

Good God. She was a walking Don't Be This Girl ad. No wonder he'd run off. Any sane person would have run off.

But next time, no matter what, she wasn't going to let him in. Next time she'd—

Ah, hell, who was she kidding?

She'd let him in. She'd probably let him in and strip him out of his clothes so fast his head would spin.

Clearly, she was depraved.

She showered. It took three shampoo applications to get rid of the ice cream, and when she came out, her phone was ringing. Running for it, she stubbed her toe on her nightstand and went down like a brick. "Damn it, don't hang up, don't hang up!" she yelled as she crawled the last few feet to the phone. "Hello?" she gasped, a small part of her hoping it was Shayne.

God. She needed therapy. "I'm here, don't—"

Click.

"—hang up." *Damn it!* She sagged to the floor, her forehead to the carpet that definitely needed vacuuming. When the phone rang again, she nearly parted ways with her heart. "Hello!"

But in her ear came another click.

Huh. That wasn't Shayne. He would definitely not hang up. *No one* she knew would hang up on her, unless—

Oh, boy.

Unless this wasn't just a random annoying hangup. Maybe it'd been from her special psychotic stalker. A little creeped out, she rushed her morning routine and left for work as soon as she got dressed, needing to get out of her apartment before her fear gripped her.

The zoo's employee parking lot wasn't nearly as empty as it had been the night before, but she still didn't dawdle. Halfway across, her cell phone rang, making her jump. Shayne's name on the ID caused some other reactions entirely. *Be cool.* "Hi," she said as casually as she could with all her parts clamoring for his attention.

"Hi yourself. I just landed in sunny Las Vegas."

"Oh." He'd had a flight. Of course he'd had a flight. "So . . . you're calling because . . ."

"Because."

"Because what?"

"I'm calling just because, Dani."

That had a silly grin splitting her face. He hadn't dumped her. They were still on for their Just Sex. Her body let out a sort of shiver.

"Anything odd going on?" he asked.

Other than her heart had tightened at just the sound of him? And her nipples too? Oh, yes, her nipples were very happy to hear from him. "Nope."

"No more dead bodies?"

"Nope."

"No more break-ins?"

"Nope."

"How about hang-ups?"

She winced. "Well . . ."

"Tell me."

"A few hang-ups," she admitted. "I figured they were just a wrong number."

He didn't say anything, but she could practically hear him thinking. "I'm okay, Shayne."

"Actually, you're amazing, but that's another story

altogether. Look, just be careful, watch that sweet ass of yours. I'm fond of it."

God, look at her. *Grinning.* Just sex, she reminded herself. But she couldn't stop grinning. This was so bad. "I can do that. Have a good flight back."

"Will do."

"Good." She paused, then let it out. "Because I'm really quite fond of your backside too." Shocked at herself, she closed her cell—then laughed.

Her cell immediately vibrated with an incoming text message that had three words: "Tonight? Hot fudge."

Oh, God. This was ridiculous, this flow of euphoria that sex caused. Too bad it couldn't be bottled.

Dani's day was crazy. It didn't take her long to discover that scheduling and managing the other keepers, each with their own thoughts and agendas and temperaments, was a hell of a lot more challenging than she'd ever imagined. By that afternoon she'd listened to three grievances, broken up two fights— not between any animals but between two other keepers—and had redone the month's employee schedule four times.

Oh, and everyone hated her.

It wasn't until most of her staff had left for the day that she managed even a single moment to herself. It was six o'clock, time for food, her stomach proclaimed, but she couldn't leave, not yet. So she stood in front of the vending machine trying to decide between a relatively harmless bag of pretzels or the bag of cholesterol-crippling Twix bites. She slapped her pockets for change, but came up empty.

Damn, she needed her energy for the hot fudge.

Just thinking it had her insides going all tight and tingly, and anticipation rushed through her. What could he do with warm fudge that they hadn't done with the ice cream? She couldn't even imagine the possibilities, and that made the rush of lust even worse.

Definitely she should have the pretzels and save the calories for later. "Bob," she said when one of the night keepers rushed by her, "do you have change?"

Bob was fresh out of college on the East Coast. He was six feet five, weighed maybe one hundred and fifty pounds soaking wet, and dressed like he was still in middle school. This meant his jeans sagged to nearly his knees and his sweatshirt was at least a triple-extra-large on his extremely not triple-extra-large frame. A good wind could, and had, blown him over. Hell, just yesterday, one of the baby rhinos had knocked him on his ass when the thing had sneezed.

He didn't even glance at her.

"Bob?" She touched his arm, which jerked into the air as he fell backward to his butt. Looking up at her in surprise, he pulled out the earplugs to the iPod she hadn't seen.

"Sorry! I didn't mean to scare you!"

"Jesus."

"Do you have any change?"

He arched a brow. "You look desperate."

"I am."

Reena came down the hall and handed her two quarters. "How can you be desperate? You've got a hot guy giving you orgasms at night, and the dream job of a lifetime."

She said the first part of the sentence evenly

enough, but the last part didn't come out quite as much so, and guilt plagued Dani. "Reena—"

"Plus, there's the raise that goes with that dream job," Reena continued. "Which means that at least one of us won't be counting pennies at the end of every single month, or begging fellow keepers for change in front of the vending machine."

Recognizing trouble, Bob put his earplugs back in and hightailed it out of the hallway.

"The raise is minuscule," Dani told Reena quietly. "You know that."

Reena sighed. "I know. I do. I'm just a jealous bitch. Ignore me."

Dani slipped an arm around her, but instead of the hug that only two days ago would have been real and natural, Reena shifted so that there was some space between them. "It won't be long for you," Dani said quietly. "You'll get a promotion too."

Reena snorted. "Are you planning on leaving any time soon?"

"No."

"Then it will be a long time." Reena punched the vending machine and a bag of peanut M&Ms fell out. Snatching them, she walked away.

Dani bought the pretzels, then munched on them as she headed back to her office.

Candy, the floor's assistant, stopped her in the hallway. "I'm leaving, we're all leaving. Don't forget your meeting."

"What meeting?"

"I don't know. Someone from Global Supplies showed up with vitamin samples. They need your order."

"I didn't ask for any samples from Global. I don't use them anymore, I use ZooIts."

Candy lifted her shoulder. "Just relaying the message here. Oh, and you're the last one up here, so this is me, reminding you to lock up behind you."

"No problem." Dani moved back to her office, trying to formulate a gentle letdown for the Global rep. In front of her desk was a large case on wheels, signifying that the rep was here, somewhere, but Dani couldn't see anyone. "Hello?"

No answer. Maybe he'd stepped out to the restroom. Pulling off her sweater, she opened the closet door to hang it, and felt her entire world skid to a stop.

A body lay on the floor of her closet. An unmoving body.

"Ohmigod." She dropped to her knees. Was it a man? A woman? She couldn't tell because the closet wasn't lit and her own body blocked the light. "Can you hear me? Are you okay?"

The body didn't move.

"Oh, God, oh, God." She had to do something. She'd taken a medical class in college, she had the basics. Panicking was not on the list of things to do in an emergency, though she was doing a great job at that. Swallowing hard, she reached out to see if she could get a pulse, because that's what they did on TV.

The skin was cold.

Icy cold.

Jerking to her feet, she stumbled back, but then tripped over something she hadn't seen before, something that felt like . . . like a leg and foot. She had just enough time to feel her panic surge—she *wasn't* alone—but before she could process the thought, there was a burst of stars in her head and then blackness.

*   *   *

Dani opened her eyes. She was flat on her back in her office, legs draped over a stack of reference books she'd been meaning to pick up and reshelve. With a gasp, she sat up. There was no one in the office with her, or at least no one she could see.

But there was a sharp, grinding pain in her head, and she lifted her hands to hold it onto her shoulders as nausea rolled through her belly. Getting up? *Such* a bad plan. In fact, if she so much as breathed too quickly, she was going to lose all the pretzels she'd just inhaled.

Not good. Then she realized one of her hands was sticky.

With her own blood.

And that's when she remembered the rest—dead body.

She managed to crawl to her closet, and—

"Not again," she whispered, staring at the empty space.

No body.

Because even being on her hands and knees made her dizzy, she sank back to the floor and stared up at the ceiling.

She really was going crazy.

Chapter 17

Maddie set the phone down and glanced out the windows at the tarmac, where Shayne stood talking to their mechanic, and felt a familiar surge of affection and worry.

Familiar, because worrying about these guys, it was what she did. And in the past, she'd had good reason. Just last year, on a routine trip to Mexico, Noah had run into weather troubles and had crash-landed on a mountainside where one of their clients had died in his arms.

It'd changed him, that crash, and Maddie had worried herself sick about him. All of them had, for months and months, until he'd finally agreed to get back on the horse and start flying again.

Then, on his first flight out, he'd been hijacked by another of their clients, the desperate, terrified, cornered Bailey Sinclair.

Noah had reacted in a very different manner than they'd all expected—he'd fallen in love with Bailey. And somehow, he'd come back to them, the Noah they all loved. He'd found his way back to the living, and Shayne and Brody and Maddie herself had all breathed a collective sigh of relief.

Life had gone on.

But now Shayne seemed . . . different. In crisis somehow, and she didn't know what was going on, or how to help, how to make things better.

"What is it?"

In surprise, she looked up to find Brody watching her with those sharp eyes that missed nothing, including the fact that she'd changed her hair color again, dark brown now, or that she'd bought a new skirt.

An even shorter one.

It looked good on her legs. Okay, it looked great on her legs and she knew it, and for reasons not quite clear to her, or maybe for reasons perfectly clear, she'd wanted him to notice, and she wanted him to suffer.

He'd just come in from Cabo, where he must have spent some time outdoors either waiting on his client or working on the plane, because he had a tan going.

It worked for him.

Damn gorgeous grumpy man. Too gorgeous. Standing this close to him was making her . . . itchy. Making her want to shove him against the wall and press her body to his and kiss that grumpiness right out of him.

She could do it too.

But she wouldn't, of course she wouldn't. He didn't deserve her damn kiss. And she needed space. But in order to move out from behind the counter, she had to practically brush against him. She held her breath so she couldn't smell him—self-defense, because he always, *always,* smelled amazing—and then without a word headed toward the tarmac. She needed to tell Shayne about the phone call she'd just received. She needed to do her job, not be daydreaming about things that could never be—

"What's the matter?"

Damn it. "Stop following me."

"Then stop and talk to me. What's the matter?"

"Nothing."

"Nothing." He nodded, though he clearly didn't believe her. "I saw you the other night. On your date."

So he had seen her. Fine. She'd seen him too.

"Did it work out for you?"

"Meaning?"

"Meaning, did . . . did the rest of your night go well?"

"Are you asking if I slept with him, Brody?"

"That would be none of my business."

"That's right. It wouldn't." Once again she looked at Shayne, who was still on the tarmac.

Brody followed her line of vision.

"If you want him for yourself, all you have to do is say so."

Whipping her head toward his, she stared at him. "What?"

"You find him attractive."

"You mean because he has a penis?"

"I didn't say that."

"Then you'd better say something."

"You had an expression on your face—"

"Annoyance?"

"No. Frustration. Worry." His jaw tightened. "And something else."

"Spit it out."

"Arousal."

She stared at him in shock. *That was for you, you idiot.*

But Brody wasn't done pissing her off. "He's single right now, and—"

With a low growl in her throat, she reached up, grabbed his shirt, and shoved him back against the wall, then did as she'd been fantasizing about, pressed her body along the length of his and kissed him, hard.

There was a beat of utter stillness from him and then his hands came up to her face.

The almost reluctant touch fueled her frustration, her anger, her sheer lust. She hadn't planned on going anywhere with this but his mouth was warm and firm, and somehow also soft, and she licked his bottom lip until with a low, rough sound, he opened and thrust his tongue to hers.

And just like that, she went from seducer to seducee.

Holy shit, the man could kiss. His fingers slid into her hair, his thumbs sweeping her cheekbones in a soft caress that was in complete opposition to the feel of his long, hard body pressed so intimately to hers.

Then he changed the angle of the kiss, at once deepening it and gentling the connection so that she went from fury to straight-up desperate for him so fast her head spun.

And then they ran out of air. Somehow she found the strength to lift her head. To let go of his shirt. Stumbling back a step, she blinked the haze of desire from her vision and forced a glare. "Does that feel like I want Shayne, you arrogant, insufferable *ass?*"

He blinked once, slow as an owl. "Arrogant?"

"That's right. Your picture is in the dictionary next to the word."

He blinked again. "Insufferable?"

"Don't forget *ass*."

Still looking a bit stunned, he just stared at her. "You . . . you want me."

"There is no way you are *that* slow to have just figured that out." And then, knees knocking, she walked away. *Don't look back, don't look back . . .*

She looked back.

He was still leaning back against the wall as if he needed the support, looking both staggered and boggled.

And so damn cute she felt herself come to a stop. Damn it. "Brody."

He lifted his head, his eyes so hot she couldn't suck air into her lungs. "I'm going to tell Shayne about a phone call. He . . . he might need you."

Straightening, he went from passionate to concerned in a single heartbeat. "What is it?"

"The woman from the other night."

"The crazy one?"

"Shayne likes her."

"Shayne likes all women."

"This one's different."

He rubbed a hand over his jaw, the day-old growth there making a rasping sound that went straight to her good parts. "She's on her way to the ER. There was some sort of accident at her work."

"Shit." Apparently already completely over the kiss they'd just shared, he sighed and moved ahead of her to the tarmac door. There, he hesitated, glancing back. "We'll deal with what just happened later."

Or never. But Maddie nodded, and when he was on the tarmac, she let out a low breath and reminded herself that the kiss had been her idea, which meant she had no one to blame for messing up the best thing that had ever happened to her.

Shayne let Brody drive him to the hospital because it was easier than arguing. "Seriously. I could have driven myself."

"Are you kidding? Our insurance company is going to dump you if you get another speeding ticket."

"I don't have that many."

Brody sent him a baleful look.

"Okay, so I have a few speeding tickets." Shayne didn't care. He eyed the road, jaw tight, hardly able to breathe. Maddie had taken the call, so he hadn't heard Dani's voice, but Maddie had admitted she hadn't sounded so good. Dani had said only that she was at the ER, and that if it wasn't too much trouble, she needed Shayne to come and verify her sanity, preferably before she was questioned by the police.

The police?

Shayne had called Dani's cell, which had gone right to voice mail, then tried the hospital, but they wouldn't release any information except directly to a family member. Patrick had been next on his list, but he'd had to leave a message.

When Brody got caught in afternoon traffic, Shayne staved off a heart attack by calling the zoo. Their main switchboard was closed, and he couldn't get past it. "Take the 5," he directed Brody.

"It's bumper-to-bumper. I'm going over the pass.

What happened, anyway? I thought you two had your one-night already."

"It turned into two nights."

"How? I thought it was just sex."

It had been. Only then he'd gone back for seconds.

And wanted thirds. "I don't want to talk about it."

"Are you sure? Because you're looking like this is a lot more than sex, Shayne."

"Brody?"

"Yeah?"

"Shut up." He tried Dani's cell again, but it was still off. He slapped his phone shut. "Goddamnit."

"No answers?"

"Maybe if I call the hospital back and tell them I'm her husband—"

Brody choked and nearly drove them off the road.

"Jesus, Brody."

"I'm sorry. I've just been rendered stupid by the H-word that so easily flew from your lips."

"Just drive."

"Noah's right," he muttered, watching the road. "You are far gone."

"Oh yeah? And how does he know?"

"He said he recognized the signs."

"What signs?"

"The insanity, for one."

Shayne glanced at the speedometer. "You're driving like an old lady. Can you get it out of first fucking gear?"

"Old lady?"

"Seriously. Try second gear. Just for the hell of it, try third."

"What's going on, Shayne?"

"What's going on? Dani's in the hospital, and no one will tell me why. That's what's going on!"

When they finally pulled into the hospital parking lot, Shayne jumped out.

"Shayne, wait."

"What?"

"Just sex. Remember that."

Shayne rolled his eyes and ran through the double doors, going directly to the front desk.

A woman in scrubs stood there looking more than slightly harassed. She had a receiver to one ear, a radio to the other, and was eyeing a stack of charts in front of her, where the phone was lit up like a Christmas tree. She was barking orders at someone behind her; 211 was to get a sponge bath and 243 needed blood work. Someone in 316 needed a death certificate signed.

Which nearly gave Shayne a coronary.

"Dani Peterson?" he said. "I need—"

"Hang on." She tried to switch the top chart to the bottom of her stack and the entire pile tumbled out of her hands to her already cluster-fucked desk. "Oh, perfect."

"Dani Peterson?" he asked again.

"Hold on a second, I'm swamped."

"Dani Peterson."

When she glanced at him, he lowered his voice. "It's an emergency."

"You're in a hospital. Everything is an emergency." But whether it was the look on his face or her own humanity kicking in, she sighed in acceptance. "Okay. So you're Danny Peterson?"

"No." He willed himself to breathe, and also to access his patience, which he usually had in abundance, but it'd flown south for the winter. "Dani Peterson's here. I got a call about an accident, and I need to see her. Where is she?"

The nurse leaned over the keyboard and typed something. "Looks like the fourth cubicle on the left—hey," she called as he began running—"you can't go in there unless you're family!"

Shayne whipped open the curtain for the fourth cubicle on the left, but it was empty.

Except for the blood drops on the pillow.

His heart stopped. Just plain stopped.

"Ouch. *Ouch.*"

At the sound of Dani's voice, Shayne's knees nearly gave out, but he moved around the bed.

She was on her knees on the floor, holding her head.

"Jesus." He dropped to his knees too, and reached for her.

"No," she whispered, very carefully not moving a single inch. "Don't touch me. Don't even look at me."

"Dani—"

"Oh, God. And don't talk. Please . . ." With the care of the very inebriated, or from someone in bone-deep pain, she let out a careful breath. "Is my head still on? Because I think it's falling off."

"Where the hell is the doctor?"

"They're inundated right now. Some big traffic accident." She pulled a wad of towels away from her head, which came away red. "Oh, boy."

Jesus. As gently as he could, he pushed the compress back to her head and brushed her hair from her face. Pain made her eyes glassy, and he leaned in and touched his lips to her temple. "What happened?"

"Complicated."

Someone had hurt her, that was clear. The sheer amount of violence that was coursing through him shocked him. And told him something he already knew. *Not just sex.*

He'd deal with that later.

"I have to . . . get into this gown." She swallowed hard. "But if I move, I'm going to throw up."

"I'll help you."

"I'm sorry. I shouldn't have called you, but I was scared, and—"

"Shh." He reached for her, scooped her up.

She managed a sound that might have been a pain-tinged laugh, but let him set her on the bed. He grabbed the hospital gown and unfolded it.

"You've taken my clothes off twice now. Is three times going to be the charm, I wonder?"

"Charm?"

"The last time."

"Why?"

A sad smile twisted her lips.

"Dani? Why would it be the last?"

She'd closed her eyes and looked far too pale. "I figure you're either beginning to panic or at least feeling the need to hightail it away from me."

"Dani." He pulled off her shoes. She was shaking. Shock? God.

"Don't worry, I'll understand either way."

Would she? Because he wouldn't. "Dani, stop. We can talk about us later. What happened to you?"

"Honest. You can go, I'll be fine."

She'd be fine? She had a dent in her head, blood pouring out of it, but she'd be fine. Who the hell could walk away from her in this condition?

And why did she think he would?

Chapter 18

A uniformed cop stuck his head around the cur-tain of the cubicle. "Dani Peterson?"

Shayne looked at him. "Can I help you?"

"Who are you?"

"Dani's husband."

Dani twitched, then at the movement, held her head and groaned.

"We need to ask her a few questions," the cop said, then looked at Dani. "You told one of the night keepers that you saw a dead body."

A dead body? What the hell? Shayne looked at her, saw the wince cross her face.

"Yes," she whispered. "That's right."

"She's injured," Shayne said, feeling extremely tense. "This can wait."

"It'll only take a moment." The cop looked deter-mined. "Ms. Peterson? Where was this dead body?"

"It was in the closet of my office," Dani said qui-etly. "I don't know if it was the same one as before."

"As before?" The cop didn't look happy at this news. "What does that mean?"

"Dani, don't say anything else right now," Shayne instructed. He turned to the cop. "You'll need to wait until her doctor clears her before asking anything else."

The cop's jaw tightened but he nodded, then turned and left through the curtain, presumably to go get his clearance. Shayne let out a long breath and touched Dani's face.

She caught his hand. *"Husband?"*

Yeah. And he did not want to discuss the ease with which the word had rolled off his tongue. "Focus. Dead body?"

"You're probably wondering what the hell, right?"

"Yes. What the hell?"

"I saw the dead body again."

"So I heard."

"In my office closet." Lying back, she grimaced in pain. "Me and closets . . ."

"Okay."

"I know. Sounds crazy." She drew a shaky breath. "I thought so too, believe me."

"So what happened to you?"

"I have no idea. I'm thinking my mom and her crazy relationships warped me more than I thought."

"I meant your head, Dani. What happened to your head?"

"Oh." She made a sound that might have been a laugh. "After I saw the body, I staggered backward, and then I think I tripped over someone."

"Who?"

"Or thing. Maybe I tripped over something." She put both hands to her head as if she could hold it in place. "I don't know."

"Was someone in the office with you? Besides the dead body?"

Dropping her hands, she looked at him, with mismatched pupils. "You believe me about the body, right?"

Truthfully, he had no freaking clue what he believed, but he believed *she* believed. Before he could say anything, a nurse whipped the curtain aside. "How are we doing on that gown?"

Dani closed her eyes. "I'm doing better at not moving."

"We'll fix you up, don't worry. We're waiting on the x-rays."

"Maybe I can just hand my entire head over to you," Dani said. "Then you can fix it and sew it back on."

The nurse took the gown from Shayne's hands. "Here. Let me help."

"I've got it," Dani insisted.

"That's what you said a few minutes ago."

"This time I mean it." Dani reached up to unbutton her sweater. "Give me a minute."

"A minute, that's it. You're going to need stitches."

"Oh, goodie."

"It's okay," Shayne said. "I'll hold your hand." He'd hold her hand? *Who the hell was using his mouth?*

The nurse gave him the once-over. "And you are?"

That's what he would like to know. But whoever was in charge of his mouth just kept using it. "I'm with her."

"No one's allowed in here except—"

"Family," Shayne said, taking a good look at the back of Dani's head when the nurse turned her. His gut tightened. "And I'm not going anywhere."

"That's sweet, hon," the nurse told him. "But the rules are—"

"I'm her husband." Well look at him, throwing that word around like candy.

Dani stared at him. "You said it again."

Yeah. Yeah, he had.

The nurse raised a brow at him. "Husband?" She turned to Dani. "Why didn't you say you had a husband when I was charting you?"

"Uh, because I didn't—"

"Newlyweds," Shayne interrupted. "It's new. To both of us."

"New," Dani repeated softly.

"Ah, that's so sweet." The nurse smiled. "How long have you been together?"

"Two days," Dani murmured, eyes closing.

"Two days? Well, no wonder you forgot."

"It's one of those whirlwind things." Shayne's cell phone was vibrating. Pulling the phone out, he saw Michelle's name and clicked it over to voice mail. He'd talked to her earlier, gently explaining— again—that they weren't going to date. He realized that this being Michelle meant he was going to have to have that conversation several more times, but he'd deal with it later.

Soon as he dealt with his "wife."

"Whirlwind," Dani repeated, eyes still closed.

Okay, she was beginning to freak him out. "Is she okay?" he asked the nurse.

"How about you get your bride into her gown and I'll be right back with the doc. We'll see what we're dealing with then."

When she'd left, Dani let out a long breath. "Husband," she murmured.

"Don't even try to distract me." Because she

looked pale, and green to boot, he simply pulled her into his arms, where she proceeded to bleed all over his shirt.

"Sorry," she whispered.

"Don't. Don't even think about apologizing."

She let out a shuddery sigh and closed her eyes.

"Dani?"

"Shh."

"Dani, don't go to sleep."

"It's that or throw up. Just want to nap for a minute, 'kay?"

"Not okay." She was leaning against him in a trusting motion that had his heart in his throat. *"Dani."*

She didn't answer.

This time his heart completely stopped. He'd been through a lot of injuries in his lifetime. At ten, he'd fallen from an attic window to the ground thirty feet below when one of his brothers shoved him out before he'd had a good grip on the rope swing. Then there'd been the variety of nasty injuries from basketball, snowboarding, wakeboarding . . . But this, this standing here next to someone he cared about when she was hurt was far worse. *"Dani."*

"Shh. She's sleeping."

Sagging in relief, he took the gown from her hands and reached for her sweater. "Stay with me." There were a thousand tiny buttons down her front. He managed three before deciding he was never going to live through the others, so he tugged it up over her head.

"Hey."

That her protest came about five seconds after the fact, and was so weakly uttered, terrified him. She was wearing a pale yellow bra with a daisy between her breasts. His fingers brushed those breasts but he was so worried about her that he didn't even enjoy it.

Turned out her panties were also pale yellow, a pair of itsy-bitsy teeny-weeny string bikini bottoms with a daisy on each hip.

He tried like hell not to notice.

"Don't even think about taking off my underwear," Dani murmured. "I keep losing my underwear around you." Her eyes were still closed, her lashes black inky smudges against her cheekbones. "I'm not getting naked."

"Hate to tell you, babe, but you're already half there."

"Don't argue with your new bride."

He'd just pulled her arms through the gown when a guy in scrubs stepped through the curtain, holding a chart. "Dani Peterson? MRI time."

Because only one person could fit into the MRI machine, Shayne was sent back to the waiting room, where he was free to pace the length of the room.

Brody sat sprawled in a chair talking to Noah on his cell phone. "Yeah, he's here." His eyes cut to Shayne. "He's wearing a hole in the carpet."

A little girl sitting next to Brody tapped him on the arm.

He covered the mouthpiece and looked at her. "Yes?"

With a sweet smile, she pointed to the sign on the far wall that read: No Cell Phones in Waiting Room

Brody stared at her. "Yeah, hold on," he said to Noah. "I'm being told."

The girl put her hands on her hips.

Brody smiled sweetly at her and lifted a finger to signal he was almost done. "I'm telling you, Noah, he's as crazy as she is. Maybe we need an intervention—"

"She's not crazy," Shayne told him. "She's not."

"Noah, hold on. The guy lusting after the woman who sees dead people wants to talk."

Shayne tossed up his hands. "No one thought Noah was crazy for falling in love with the woman who hijacked him."

"We *both* thought Noah was crazy," Brody reminded him. "You flew all the way to Mexico to retrieve him, remember?"

"Ahem," the little girl said, looking very serious about this no-cell-phone thing.

With a sigh, Brody heaved himself out of the chair. Being six-foot-four, he towered over the tiny girl.

She didn't seem to care. She pointed to the door.

Brody glanced in disbelief at Shayne, who if he hadn't been worried to the point of nausea about Dani, might have laughed out loud at the way the big, badass Brody actually did the kid's bidding and moved to the door. On the way, he snagged Shayne's arm and pulled him along with him.

"Hey. I'm not leaving until—"

"Yeah, yeah." Brody didn't let go of him until they were just outside the ER doors, standing in the chilly night. Still holding the phone to his ear, he ran his sharp gaze over Shayne's face. "I'll ask him," he said. "Noah wants to know if you've fallen and can't get up."

"Jesus." He scrubbed a hand over his face. "I'm going back in."

"Wait. Noah says if you've fallen, it's okay—*What?*" Brody repeated into the phone. "No. I am *not* going to say that—"

Shayne grabbed the cell phone. "Noah? I'm going back in. Come get this asshole so I have a car here."

"Do you need anything else?" Noah asked.

"A lobotomy, maybe?"

Noah laughed softly in his ear. "Yeah, it does feel a little bit like brain surgery without the anesthesia, doesn't it?"

"What does?"

"Falling in love."

"No one said anything about . . ." Christ, he couldn't even say the L-word. *"That."*

Another soft laugh. "Right. Listen, you know Brody. He's going to tell you to take yourself and your dick home, that no chick is worth this much trouble. But I'm going to tell you to go with it. Because it just might be the best thing to ever happen to you."

"What's he saying?" Brody wanted to know, trying to hear.

"Just come get him," Shayne said, putting a hand over Brody's face and pushing him away. "Before I knock his big fat head against a wall."

"On my way."

"You," Brody said as Shayne shut the phone, "have completely lost it."

"Excuse me." A nurse poked her head out the ER doors. "Which of you is Dani's husband?"

Brody's eyes widened in horror.

Shayne ignored him. "Is she—"

"Back from the MRI. The doctor's heading in there right now. Did your wife suffer high blood pressure and stress levels before this accident?"

"Uh . . ."

"Because he's concerned about her stress levels."

Shayne forgot about kicking Brody's ass and rushed back inside.

"Husband," he heard Brody mutter as he moved. "Jesus. It's a fucking epidemic."

Two not-so-pleasant things about splitting one's head open? First, no matter what anyone said, getting stitches hurt like hell. And second, people tended to talk slow and loud around head-injury patients.

But the ice chips were nice.

And so was the fact that she'd somehow gained a husband. Dani glanced over at Shayne, who'd held her hand through the stitches, doing his best to distract her with sordid details of his wild youth. Not giving her time to freak out, he kept talking in that even, sexy voice of his, a running monologue of stories so funny she actually laughed while being stitched up. She looked into his face, into his amazing eyes, and felt her throat tighten.

She'd only known him for a matter of days, and already he was more there for her than anyone in her life. "Shayne."

"Yeah?"

"Thank you."

He smiled and brought their joined hands up to his mouth so he could kiss her palm, then went back to his storytelling. He told her how he'd met Noah and Brody, how they'd partied their way through high school and a good part of college before finally applying themselves in preparation for Sky High Air, and when he ran out of stories—all wicked, all utterly fascinating insights into the man—and there was still a needle being put in and out of her wound, he leaned in, put his mouth to her ear, and whispered other even more fascinating things.

Like, "Love your underwear."

This made her face go so red the doctor stopped to ask her if she was okay.

"Y-yes." She closed her eyes. "I'm fine."

When the doctor had gone back to his business, Shayne leaned in again. "That pale yellow bra? It highlights your nipples. Makes my mouth water."

"Stop it."

"Me?" the doctor asked.

"No. No, sorry," she muttered.

"I wanted to take them off," Shayne whispered.

This caused another rush of heat to her body, and she began to sweat.

The doctor noticed and frowned. "Nurse."

"Yes, doctor."

"Check her temp," he instructed. "Her color is way off."

Oh, God. "No. No, I'm fine," Dani hurried to say. "Really. Fine."

The nurse looked at the doctor and shrugged.

Dani carefully didn't look at Shayne again, though she heard his soft laugh, and recognized the way it made her belly quiver.

"I'll be happy to check your temp," Shayne whispered.

Did he enjoy torturing her? Of course he did. By the time the doctor was finished, her head ached fiercely, but so did the rest of her body.

Unbelievable. "Can I go home now?" she asked.

The doctor pursed his lips. "About your blood pressure and stress levels—"

"I'll work on that."

"Is it your job?"

She cut a look at Shayne. "Some."

"Maybe a short leave of absence to relax?" The doctor scribbled on a pad. "I can write something up for your employer—"

"No, don't. I really can't take a leave right now. I'll . . . try hard to relax."

"I'll make sure she does."

Both the doctor and Dani looked at Shayne. He smiled sweetly, even innocently, but Dani could guess how he intended to see her relax, and most likely it would involve him removing her pale yellow bra.

And matching panties.

That wasn't the question.

What was the question was whether or not she could weather another round of "just sex" without getting herself more hurt than she was at the moment.

Chapter 19

Dani stared out the passenger window, nicely dopey from the meds they'd given her at the hospital. "Hey," she said to Shayne.

"Hey yourself."

"We're here."

"That we are." He came around to help her out of the car, then slipped an arm around her when she weaved.

She wasn't hurting. The drugs had taken care of that. But she was floating nicely. Her brain couldn't seem to touch down on anything for long. Which was a shame, because she had a feeling there were things to touch down on.

"Come on. I'll tuck you in."

"And then leave?"

"No. We're having a sleepover."

"Oh, fun. With popcorn?"

Was that his jaw, all bunchy and tight? "Whatever you want," he promised.

"Really? 'Cuz I want hot fudge." She grinned.

He did not. He scooped her up in his arms, like she was a rag doll.

"I can walk."

"I know."

She set her head on his very broad, very nice shoulder, then pressed her face to his neck, loving the way he smelled, which was like heaven. "This really is way better than walking."

"We need a list," he said, carrying her up the stairs.

"Okay. The hot fudge. Then whipped cream, because I've heard—"

He made a sound that might have been a laugh or a groan. "I meant of people who don't like you, Dani."

"People don't like me?"

He got to her front door and propped her against it so he could slide his hands down her body, and she smiled dreamily. "Yes."

"Yes?"

"Yes to the touching."

"I'm looking for your keys."

"Oh."

He found them in her pocket and got them both inside, where he deposited her on her couch. "Stay right there."

Since she was dizzy and groggy, that worked for her. Plus, a secret part of her liked the bossiness. She could see him in her kitchen—with the place the size of a postage stamp, she couldn't help but see him in her kitchen—making her . . . aw. He was making her tea.

When he came back to the couch, he handed her the hot mug and waved a pad of paper she'd had by her phone, sinking to the coffee table in front of her. "Go," he said, pencil poised like a cute little secretary.

Only he wasn't little, and no one in their right mind would call him cute. Dangerous, yes. Edgy, yes. Sexy, double yes.

But cute? "Maybe like a cheetah. You know, cute from a distance . . ."

He blinked. "What?"

"You're cute."

He blinked again. "List all the people who would benefit from making you appear crazy."

"Cute *and* bossy." But she sighed and tried to put all the dangerous, edgy, sexy cuteness out of her head. Not an easy feat. "Well, my family has been calling me crazy for a few years now."

"Because you walked away from an inheritance."

"Edward wasn't my dad. It didn't feel right. Plus Tony and Eliza like all their billions of pennies."

"Tony and Eliza," he said, putting them on the list. "Who else?" He nudged her steaming mug up to her lips until she drank.

Earl Grey. Her favorite. She sipped, watching him over the cloud of steam that rose from her cup.

Or maybe that was the fog of nice drugs in her system. "You really are cute."

"We'll discuss my cuteness in detail after this."

She smiled dreamily. "What else can we do in detail after this? And does it involve the hot fudge?"

His eyes landed on hers, scorching. "No. It involves some of that relaxing the doctor insisted on. That I insist on."

"Oh." Huh. Yeah, he was pretty damn hot, all bossy and insistent.

"What about the woman from your work? The one you got the promotion over?" he asked.

"Reena?"

"Reena. She wouldn't . . ."

He didn't erase the name, just looked at her with surprising patience. Patience, plus that scorchness factor, and then the whole cute thing, really made him quite . . . "Irresistible." She smiled. "You're irresistible."

"You're high as a kite."

She grinned.

He sighed. "Who else?"

"No one."

"I'm sure there's someone."

"You're sure I've annoyed more people?"

"Yes."

She rolled her eyes, and then gasped and reached for her head. "Oh, bad. Very, very bad."

Tossing the pad aside, he dropped to his knees at her side. "You okay?"

"Not so much, no."

"I—" He broke off at the scraping sound. "What's that?"

It'd come from the other side of the front door. Striding over there, he whipped it open but no one was there. Just a package sitting innocuously all by itself.

"What is it?" she asked no one, because Shayne burst out of the front door and vanished from her line of sight.

"Hey!" he yelled, and then he was back in the doorway, holding someone by the scruff of the neck.

Alan, who shoved free and glared at him. "What the hell is your problem?"

Shayne bent to pick up the package and lifted a foil edge as if he expected a bomb. *"Brownies?"*

"Of course they're brownies, what did you think

they were?" Alan straightened his shirt. "And what are you, an ape?"

"I'm so sorry," Dani said to Alan. "Ignore him, he's—"

"Crazy?"

"Concerned about her safety," Shayne corrected. "Since someone's been stalking her. You a stalker, Alan?"

"*What?* Of course not." Circling Shayne, giving him a wide birth that would have been comical on any other day, Alan came in. When he caught sight of the blood still matted in Dani's hair, of the white bandage around her head, he stopped short. "My God."

"A little accident at work," Dani assured him. "Only five stitches."

"Stitches?" Going white as a sheet, Alan grabbed out for support, but nothing was there.

Then he flashed the whites of his eyes.

"He's going down," Dani told Shayne, who swore and lunged for him, unceremoniously hauling him back to the front door.

"Shayne, wait."

"Buh-bye," Shayne said to Alan.

To Alan's credit, he dug in his heels and tried to see past Shayne. "Dani—"

But Shayne shut the door on him.

"Ohmigod." Dani pointed to the door. "Open it up. Now."

Unapologetic, he moved toward her instead. "He's so going on the list."

"He doesn't belong on the list."

"Oh, he belongs on the list."

"Shayne, seriously. Did you see the way he nearly fainted at the sight of the blood on my head?"

Shayne's gaze lifted from the pad where he was furiously scribbling Alan's name. "So?"

"So you know if he's queasy at the sight of blood, then he's not hauling around a dead body to torture me with."

He narrowed his eyes. "I thought you were half delirious with pain."

"I am." She softened her voice, trying to distract him. "Delirious. Helpless. What are you going to do about it?"

"Don't even try to distract me with that tone."

"Which tone?"

"The sexy one that makes it so I can't think." Shayne stared down at the list while she stared at him.

He thought she had a sexy tone? One that made it so he couldn't think? Wow. She didn't think anyone had ever said such a thing to her before, and it cut right through the painkillers and activated her good spots.

Clueless, he was still studying his list. "I think we'll start with your siblings."

"Start with?"

"In the morning, we're going to pay them a little visit."

"They're in Tahoe."

"So?"

"So, it's like a nine-hour drive."

"But only a forty-five minute flight." He smiled grimly. "Luckily you know a pilot."

Her fear of flying reared its ugly head. "Is he the same guy who just threw my friend out on his ass, because I'm not sure I want to fly with that guy."

"How about the guy who has four broken fingers from you squeezing him while you got stitches? The guy who's good in an emergency, on the ground or in the air. You want to fly with that guy?"

"No. I don't want to fly at all."

"It's the best way."

"Says you."

He shook his head. "Dani. More people die in car accidents—hell, more people die getting struck by lightning—than in plane accidents."

"Has anyone at Sky High ever been in an accident?"

He hesitated, and she gasped. "You?"

"Noah. He crashed in Mexico last summer, but—"

"Ohmigod. What happened?"

He closed his eyes, then opened them on her. "He was hit by lightning, but—"

"*Ohmigod.* No. No, we are so not flying in any little tin buckets."

"Tin buckets? Are you kidding me?"

"No."

"It was a one-in-a-million thing, Dani."

She sighed, and carefully, very, very carefully, laid her head against the couch cushion. Just as carefully closed her eyes. The next thing she knew, her world was spinning as Shayne again lifted her in his arms.

"Whoa. Stop the ride, I want to get off."

But he just carried her down the hall to her bedroom.

"You don't have to do the he-man thing," she protested, but clutched at him, mostly because she loved having his arms around her.

"Maybe I like to do the he-man thing." He set her down on the mattress, gently, carefully, and then moved to the foot of the bed to pull off her shoes.

"What are you doing?"

"Putting you to bed." He came to her side and saw

the cursed buttons again. "Why do your clothes have so many buttons?"

"I like buttons." She yawned, hugely. "Shayne?"

"Yeah?"

"My eyes are closing."

"Let them."

So she did. "Mmmm," she sighed at the feel of his warm fingers brushing her skin as he spent the time to work the buttons now. Beneath she still wore that yellow bra, which he left on to work the zipper of her pants. When he tugged them down, he paused.

"You've already seen the panties," she murmured, eyes closed in exhaustion tinged with bliss.

"I know." He ran a finger over the strap on her hip. His breathing had changed, and now hers did as well.

And suddenly, she wasn't so tired. She opened her eyes to find him watching her in the dim light of the lamp by her bed. When he saw her eyes open, he stroked a strand of hair from her jaw. "Lift up," he said, and pulled the blanket from beneath her. But before he could cover her up, she scooted over in open invitation.

"You need your rest. You need to relax."

"Relaxing is out of the question."

"The doctor said—"

"I know. I just . . ." She lifted a shoulder. "Can't. There's too much racing around in my brain. I can't slow it down."

He made a soft sound of regret and kicked off his shoes. Then shrugged out of his shirt.

Okay, she liked where this was going.

But instead of stripping out of his pants, he only unbuttoned and unzipped, and then carefully lay down next to her.

"You didn't finish," she said in great disappointment.

He let out a low laugh. "You are not up for anything fun and naughty, so don't even go there." He pulled her in as if she was a China doll in danger of breaking, running his hands up and down her body in a gesture she was certain he meant to be soothing but instead began to warm her from the inside out.

"I am so up for fun and naughty." But she yawned, making him laugh again.

"Just let your eyes close." His fingers danced up her side.

Her nipples hardened in hope.

But he didn't touch them.

"Shayne."

"Shh." He played with the straps of her bra as if he couldn't help himself.

"Still not relaxed. In case you were wondering."

"It'd help if you stopped talking."

"You know I'm not good at that."

"Try. You've got to try to relax."

"Any ideas on how I could do that?" *Please, have some ideas.*

"No." But as if maybe he really did, his hand slid down her back, toying with the low waistband of her panties.

"Keep going."

With a laugh, he slipped his fingers just beneath the waistband.

"More."

He breathed another sound, a half laugh, half groan as he stroked her.

"Yeah," she managed. "Seriously. That's helping."

"Then why are you still talking?"

"Good question. Maybe I'm not . . ." She wriggled, and felt him. Hard. "Distracted enough. More distraction, please."

"Now who's bossy." But he slid that talented hand lower.

And . . . *oh, my God, yes* . . . even lower. "That's w-working. But you should keep going. Just to make sure."

"Should I?"

Sounding husky and aroused, he rolled her to her back, brushing his mouth to her ear. "Then stay," he whispered. "And don't move. Not an inch." Following this command, he slid beneath the covers, vanishing from her view. She couldn't follow his progress without moving her head, which would hurt. Plus he'd been pretty clear—don't move.

So she didn't.

She felt him unhook her bra, then skim it off, and then his mouth glided over first one breast and then the other, taking her to another place, where there were no headaches, no mysterious bad guys, nothing but this.

How long had they'd known each other? A few days? And yet he knew just how to touch her, how to taste her, as if he understood her body even better than she did, and she arched up helplessly until he put a hand low on her belly, holding her down.

Right. Don't move.

But staying still was so difficult, especially when that hand low on her belly slid down.

And . . .

Down . . .

Then slowly slid her panties to her thighs, then off completely, after which he made himself a home between her thighs.

He kissed her upper thigh.

She fisted her hands in the sheets at her side. "Uh—"

"A little bit more shhh would be good." He kissed his way to her other thigh, which he gently nudged, further opening her to him, making way for his broad shoulders. "There," he murmured in approval, using that low, husky voice with bunches of wicked promise in it.

She loved that voice.

Then he bent his head and made good on that implied promise, driving her with his voice, his tongue, his fingers, as he took her right to the edge.

Then pushed her over.

And when she came back to herself he was holding her against him, stroking her body with his hands. She wanted to speak, wanted to somehow return the favor, wanted . . . oh, she wanted so many things . . .

But with his warm heat surrounding her, all that delicious strength soothing her, taking her right into dreamland where slumber awaited, she could do nothing but sigh in bliss and drift . . . off . . .

Chapter 20

The next morning Shayne woke up to Dani hustling about her bedroom. "What are you doing?"

"Looking for a pair of socks. This'll probably come as a shock, but I'm not the most organized of people."

He blinked. She was already dressed, complete with white bandage around her head, protecting her stitches. She pulled her hair into a low ponytail. Immediately strands began to slip out and brush her shoulders. She sighed in exasperation but left them.

"Where are you going?"

"Work."

He stared at her in shock. Not a hell of a lot shocked him, ever. But this woman, with the drown-in-me eyes and the kiss that stirred him from the inside out, not to mention the sweet smile that always tipped his heart upside . . . she shocked him on a daily basis.

Make that by the minute. She shocked him by the minute. "Dani. You can't be serious."

"Why not?"

"Why not?"

"Because you have a concussion, and stitches."

"Had a concussion. Mild. I'm better, just a little headache."

"Your doctor told you to take it easy."

"I am. I will."

He'd always had low blood pressure, but he felt it rising now. "Okay, how about you don't go to work. Because the last time you went to work, your head was nearly bashed in. And the time before that, someone shot at you."

"And missed," she pointed out. "I've been wondering at that, Shayne. Why did they miss?"

His heart actually skipped a beat at the thought of the bullet *not* missing, tearing through any single inch of that flesh he loved.

"See, I think they missed on purpose." Leaning into her mirror, she applied lip gloss.

Peach, he was guessing by the color.

He loved peach lip gloss. "Maybe you were just lucky." His voice was a little hoarse. He'd gone a long time without overly engaging his damn heart, and she'd not only engaged it, she'd locked all missiles on it, in a matter of days.

"See, that's the thing. I'm not lucky." She rolled her lips together, spreading the gloss. "I've never been lucky." Her gaze locked on his in the mirror. "Do you know what I'm saying?"

"Someone's toying with you. I get that. But we've got a plan."

"The list is not a plan."

"Talking to everyone on it is."

"Talking? Is that what you were doing when you lifted Alan by the scruff of his shirt?"

He'd never been much of a fighter. Brody had always taken that roll. Noah too, when it'd been required. Shayne had always been like the middle brother, the peacemaker, the pacifist. But he didn't feel much like a pacifist at the moment. "I'll do whatever it takes."

She stared at him, then let out a disgusted breath of air. "You are being such a guy."

"What does that mean?"

"Nothing someone with a penis would understand." But she sighed. "You really think I should talk to my stepsiblings?"

"Hell yes, we should."

She just looked at him, not missing the shift from "I" to "we," but clearly deciding to pick her battles. "You have a flight today?"

"Just to Vegas and back. We could leave right after that."

She sighed. "I'll meet you at Sky High later, then."

"After you go into work?"

"Yes."

He felt a vein pulsing in his forehead. "Dani—"

"Look, I'm not letting this bastard, whoever he is, take my life away from me. I'm not going to lose my promotion because I'm afraid to go to work."

"This is asinine. You're putting yourself in danger."

"No. Trust me, I'm not going to be the stupid chick in the horror movies. But I am going to live my life."

"On your own."

"I think that's my only option at the moment."

"Are you kidding me? I'm here, right here, Dani, and I have been, but it's like you have built this wall between us."

"No. I let you in."

"Only after I knock it down every time. I'm tired of knocking, Dani."

She went still. "It's a habit," she finally admitted. "Being on my own. It's what always worked best for me."

"Really? Because from where I'm standing, it's not working for you, not at all."

"You want to go with me to Tahoe? You really want to do this."

"Yes. Hell, yes."

"Even though we're practically strangers."

Okay, that pissed him off, but he managed a smile, tight as it might be. "Actually, I think we know each other pretty damn well."

She blushed. "Our bodies, maybe."

"Yes. I know your body. I know all sorts of things about your body. I know, for instance, that you like it when I breathe in your ear, that you like it when I nibble my way to your breasts and—"

"Shayne—"

"I also know how to make you tremble and sigh my name in that little whispery pant that tells me you're close to coming. I know exactly . . ." Leaning in, he put his mouth to her ear, finding little satisfaction in the way her breath hitched. "*Exactly* how to make you fall apart for me, all over me."

"*Shayne—*"

"And my favorite part? It's that, Dani, it's you saying my name in that way you do. Makes me hard every single time."

She let out a shuddering breath.

"But I know more about you than that. I know you care about people with huge capacity. I know you are fiercely proud and live frugally to keep a job you love rather than ask your wealthy family for help. I know you have a secret lingerie habit that I am grateful for."

She blushed. "I don't have a secret lingerie habit."

Laughing softly, he hooked a finger in her top and pulled it out so he could peek in and see her purple and black lace demi-bra. "Oh yeah," he murmured. "*Extremely* grateful."

She shoved his hand aside, but her eyes were filled with things, things that made him ache.

"I know you, Dani. I know you love ice cream and sappy movies. I know that you hate airplanes, but that you just might like a certain pilot."

She turned away. "I've got to go."

"I didn't think you'd be the one running."

Whipping around, she pointed a finger at him. "I told you. I told you I don't want to do this. No dating."

"Just sex."

"That's right."

He shook his head, but had to laugh. "Do you have any idea how ironic it is that *you're* the one pulling away?" He rubbed his head. "God. Brody would so have a field day over this."

"Shayne—"

"No, it's okay, it's all good. I get it."

She let out a slow breath and nodded, grabbing her purse. Then she came up to him. With a hand on his chest, she leaned in and kissed him lightly on the lips. "Bye."

As she whirled away, he caught her hand and tugged her back, where he proceeded to capture her mouth and kiss her a whole lot deeper, hotter, wetter than her kiss had been, and only when she was thoroughly breathless and making those sexy lit-

tle panting murmurs in her throat, her fingers fisted
into his shirt, did he pull back.

"That." He nodded. "That's a good-bye, Dani."

Touching her lips, she stared at him, all glazed
and dreamy, which would have made his day if she
didn't drive him absolutely fucking insane.

Purse slung over her shoulder, sunglasses in one
hand, work ready, she glanced back at her bed.

She wanted to go back to bed.

With him.

She did not, however, want to do anything else
with him. And even accepting the ridiculousness of
the situation, even knowing that all his life he'd
been there, in that same place, it still hurt like hell.

On the way into Sky High, Shayne called Patrick,
who as usual was little to no help at all. The police
had the big, fat nothing. In fact, they had less than
nothing. Dani had claimed to see a body in front of
Sky Air, but there was no body. And no evidence to
suggest there'd been a body. She'd claimed to have a
break-in, but again, no evidence. Of course she had
been shot at, complete with bullets, but with no mo-
tive and no viable suspect, that was going down as a
random shooting.

Only Shayne didn't believe in random, or coinci-
dences.

As for the incident at Dani's work, since she'd
tripped over herself, or so it was assumed, with yet
again no body even though she'd claimed to have
one in her closet, there was nothing to go on.

Bottom line—at least as far as the police were concerned—the only danger to Dani was herself.

Frustrated, Shayne entered Sky High, checked in,

then went to conduct his preflight check, but found Brody on the tarmac with a gorgeous honey of a King Air, circa 1965. "Nice."

"I know. I think I'm in love." Brody stroked the sleek steel like a lover. His face was grease streaked, his hair standing straight up, no doubt assisted into that position by more grease. He wore his thread-bare jeans, signifying he was on maintenance duty. "What do you think?"

"She's for sale?"

"Yep. The owner's inside."

They both turned their heads and looked through the glass windows into the lobby. Maddie, gorgeous and outrageously dressed as always in black leggings, black knee-high kick-ass boots, and a silver metallic sweater that hugged her extremely huggable curves, was leaning against her desk smiling at a well-dressed man in his early forties. He was talking with his hands and a big smile, and Maddie, clipboard in hand, earpiece in, looking more like a superhero than a concierge, was smiling in return.

The man, clearly dazzled by her, leaned in and said something that had Maddie tipping her head back in laughter.

Brody frowned. "What the hell is he telling her?"

"Something funny."

"He's flirting with her."

"Jesus. Would you ask her out already? Or better yet, kiss her. Something. *Please.*"

Brody stared at him as if he was insane. "Why? Why would I kiss her?"

Shayne lifted a brow, but as he took in Brody's horrified, guilty expression, it came to him. "Holy shit. You've already kissed her."

Brody let out a sound as if his head had just gone

flat. Then the six-foot-four ex-linebacker and all-around badass shoved his hands in his pockets like a teenager and kicked the ground. He glanced into the terminal again and shook his head.

Shayne laughed. "You did."

"Shut up about it."

"What happened? She slug you?"

"Don't make me kick your ass."

"Hell, you could try. But then you'd have to tell Maddie why you sucker punched her favorite pilot."

"You are not her favorite."

"I am so."

"You're an idiot is what you are."

Shayne grinned. "That might be. But I'm not the idiot with a crush on our Maddie."

"Stop saying 'our Maddie.' If you were her favorite, why did she kiss me?"

Shayne's eyebrows rose. "So it really happened?"

Brody shoved his fingers into his hair and turned in a slow circle. "I think she did it because she was pissed off at me. Trying to prove a point."

"Yeah? Did she prove it?"

Brody dropped his forehead to the cool steel of the plane. "I have no fucking clue."

Shayne's grin spread as he burst into song. "Maddie and Brody sitting in a tree. K-i-s-s-i-n-g . . ."

"Shut up, you ass." He added a shove to the demand.

Shayne would have happily shoved back, but he didn't. Maddie might be flirting with the guy at the desk, but she also had an eagle eye on them, even though Brody was too miserably self-involved to notice. No way was Shayne going to piss her off, not when she had a temper like the natural redhead she was beneath all that dyed hair.

So he let Brody's shove take him back a few steps, making sure Maddie noted that he didn't fight back, and eyed the sweet plane. "You want to buy this baby?"

"It's way overpriced, but I think we can get him down."

Shayne stuck his head into the engine compartment and took a good look around, his heart sighing. "I'd marry her."

"No way. I saw her first."

Shayne looked at his lifelong friend, the brother of his heart. "What do you think it says about us that we run like hell from commitment to a woman, and yet this plane melts our circuits?"

"Shit. I have no idea."

Shayne nodded, and sighed. "We suck."

Brody lifted a shoulder. "At least we accept our flaws."

"Do you think the women in our lives could ever accept them?"

Brody stared at Maddie, then slowly shook his head. "Not if they know what's good for them."

Chapter 21

Late that afternoon, Dani entered Sky High's building. The place was nothing like the last time she'd been there. There were no festive decorations, no drunken revelers, no gorgeous man in the closet, and most importantly, no dead bodies.

No dead bodies.

She repeated it to herself so it would sink in. She was fine, she was good, she was—

Nervous as hell. How had she let this happen? *Flying*? She hated to fly, she really did. Why had she let him talk her into this? He was just a fling, a great fling, yes, but any second now he would fly right out of her life and—

"Hi. Dani Peterson, right?"

Dani looked at the gorgeous young woman who'd come out from behind the huge front desk and immediately felt like tucking in her own wild hair, not to mention tugging down the hem of her shirt to straighten out the wrinkles, but that might only emphasize the dollop of ketchup she had below one breast from the fries she'd not been able to resist at lunch. "Um, yes. I'm Dani Peterson."

"Nice to meet you," said the vision in black leggings and boots, with a silvery curve-hugging sweater that screamed cover model. "I'm Maddie. The concierge here. I saw you at the party the other night."

"Oh." Dani tried to remember seeing Maddie, but the evening was pretty much a blur, what with the mistletoe situation and then the dead body.

"With Shayne," Maddie clarified, perfectly evenly, without a single inflection, but somehow Dani knew that Maddie knew she'd spent most of her time in the closet.

But hell, Shayne probably spent lots of time with lots of different women in lots of different places. Maddie was probably completely used to it.

Proving it, the woman smiled easily, as if it was no big deal at all.

Because it wasn't, Dani reminded herself.

"He mentioned you'd be coming by. You're taking a flight this afternoon. To Tahoe. We're lucky the storm moved on. Weather's all clear."

"Oh." Goodie. "Great."

Maddie cocked her head to one side. "That was a loaded great."

"Yes. It was. Sorry."

Maddie had her dark brown hair artfully disheveled, the kind of disheveled that said she'd probably put a small fortune of hair product into it to make it look that way. The kind of disheveled that looked amazing—unlike Dani's own special brand of disheveledness, which came from genuine . . . well, disheveledness. Maddie's clothes were glitzy and wow, and because she had a body also straight from a magazine, she seemed glossy and perfect. Way too perfect for Dani to admit her fear of flying to.

"Are you okay?" Maddie asked.

Perceptive too. And most likely not afraid of anything, especially not of flying. "I'm . . ." *Terrified. Out of my element. Pick one.* "Fine. Terrific, really."

"Afraid of flying, aren't you?"

Dani sighed and gave up the pretense. "Unbelievably terrified."

Maddie smiled in sympathy just as the phone at her hip vibrated. She looked down, hit a button as she held up a finger to Dani. "Sky High Air, how can I help you?" She glanced out onto the tarmac, and Dani followed her gaze.

Shayne and another tall, good-looking man stood together. The wind was blowing, and they'd bent their heads close, clearly talking about the airplane they both stood next to.

Maddie shook her head. "I'm sorry, Michelle. Shayne's booked for a different flight right now, but Noah's free. We'll get you where you need to go. Yes, I'll tell Shayne you called." She clicked off. "Or not." Catching Dani's expression, she smiled grimly. "Don't worry. I only lie to people with crushes on one of my bosses. Where were we? Oh, yes. Your terror of flying. If you'd like, I have a cure for that."

"You do?"

"Oh, yes." She led Dani through the lobby, at the end of which was a small lounge and bar area, just as elegant and sophisticated as the rest of the place, complete with a large flat-screen TV showing a basketball game. Maddie moved behind the bar and pulled out a decanter and two shot glasses. "Would it help to hear that Shayne is an excellent pilot?"

"He's excellent at a lot of things," Dani muttered.

"Yes, he is. It was his influence with the investors that got Sky High up and running. And then there's his way with the clients. You've seen him. He could charm a tightwad out of his last penny."

Or the panties off a woman who'd told herself sex was overrated. "He's not quite as easygoing and laid-back as he seems, is he."

"Good for you." Maddie smiled. "He fools most people with that one. I'm glad you see past that ridiculous good-old-boy thing he puts out there to protect himself."

"Protect himself from what?"

"From getting hurt, of course."

Of course. Only . . . only she'd been the one protecting herself. Right? Because he didn't need to protect himself, not when he hadn't invested anything.

Or so she tried to convince herself.

"Sit," Maddie said to Dani, and pushed one of the glasses in front of her. "This whole place is really nice." Dani took a slow spin on the bar stool beneath her, taking in the atmosphere. "Ritzy but somehow cozy."

"Thanks."

"You?" Dani asked in surprise.

"I've always had a secret love of interior design. The guys let me have my way in here, or we'd be sitting on big beanbags. Single or double?" She lifted the decanter. "Might help when you get in the air."

Oh, God. She was going in the air.

With Shayne. "Double."

Maddie smiled and poured. "Can I ask you a question?"

Dani sipped, coughed, then sipped again, absorbing the warmth that slowly spread down her esophagus. "Okay."

"Is it flying putting that look on your face, or Shayne?"

"Flying," Dani said, finishing off her drink with a gasp. "No. Shayne—flying—*God*." She covered her eyes when Maddie laughed. "I have no clue. Men are like this big box of puzzle pieces, you know? Only I can't find all the edges."

Maddie refilled her glass and pushed it back to Dani. "I like you already. Cheers."

She slid her a sideways glance. "You expect me to believe that you have man troubles?"

"Honey, you have no idea."

Dani studied her a moment, saw the pain lurking behind her gaze. She lifted her glass and touched it to Maddie's, and then they both knocked them back.

Maddie set down her empty glass, blew out a long breath, and smacked her chest. "Yowza."

Dani choked and coughed and gasped so hard that Maddie had to come around the bar to smack her on the back. Finally she lifted her hand, signaling that she was going to live, swiping away the tears streaming down her face. "I'm okay," she wheezed. "It's hit my belly now, and it's no longer a fire but a nice toasty heat."

They drank to that and both looked out onto the tarmac, where the two obnoxiously handsome men still stood. After another long sigh, Maddie refilled their shots and lifted her glass in a toast. "To stupid, gorgeous men and the women who love them."

Again Dani choked. "Oh, no. No, no, no. You've misunderstood. I'm not in love."

Maddie poured herself another drink.

Dani shook her head. "It's not love."

Maddie just looked at her, and Dani looked back, and then sagged and tossed back her drink, down the hatch. "*Damn.* This sucks."

"Trust me. I know." Maddie filled Dani's glass. "I just turned down a most excellent date because I'm pining away after a most excellent idiot who did *not* ask me out on a date."

"Do you know what the problem with men is?" Dani asked, slurring more than a little bit. She was also warm, very, very warm. Toasty. Warm. Toasty, happy warm. "It's that they don't have enough blood to operate both heads at the same time."

Maddie laughed good and hard over that one, and so did Dani, until she fell off her bar stool. "Whoops," she said from the floor, which was surprisingly comfortable.

Maddie peered over the bar. "You okay?"

Dani grinned up at her, feeling a little flushed and a whole lot looped. "I'm good." She held up her glass. "One more, please. And maybe then I'll be able to face the flight and the gorgeous pilot."

"Gorgeous pilot?" Shayne stood in the doorway of the lounge, looking a little shocked.

Dani swiped a hand over the back of her mouth and stood, only she wobbled and then tripped over her own feet, and would have gone down if Shayne hadn't come forward and caught her.

She laughed and threw her arms around him. He was so tall, so warm.

So sexy. "Hi."

"Hi yourself." He sniffed her breath, then craned

his neck in Maddie's direction, giving her the evil eye. "She's drunk."

"Not quite," Dani told him cheerfully, then stared up at him, slightly cross-eyed. "You're so pretty." She slapped her hands on either side of his face. He hadn't shaved today, maybe not yesterday either. His hair had been finger tousled at best. She helped it along by moving her fingers through it. "So very, very pretty."

"And you're so very *toasted*. Dani, did you take any more of your pain meds today?"

"Of course. The doctor insisted, 'member?"

"Oh, I remember. And did you remember the part about not mixing those meds with alcohol?"

She blinked. "Uh-oh."

"Yeah. Uh-oh."

"Doesn't matter." She winked at Maddie. "Because I am ready to fly." She threw her hands out to simulate being an airplane, and nearly went down again.

Shayne swore and scooped her up against him.

"My hero," she sighed. "Always ready to slay my dragons." She set her head on his shoulder. "Someday I want to slay your dragons too, Shayne. All of 'em."

He looked down in her face in shocked awe. "What?"

"Fly me, Shayne. Or should I fly you?"

He seemed to lose his words for a minute. "How about I fly you this time, okay?"

"Okay." Snuggling in, she closed her eyes and yawned. "Wake me up when we get there."

*   *   *

Maddie watched Shayne carry Dani out the door. He looked a little bowled over and a whole lot gobsmacked, and she couldn't blame the guy. If what she suspected was true, he was falling every bit as much as Dani clearly had, and falling hard. He wouldn't go down easy, that was for sure, but she did envy him the fall.

Thinking it, she set her spinning head to the bar, letting the cool wood hold her upright. God, she envied the fall. But it was just as well.

She didn't have anyone to catch her. No hero, no one to slay her dragons. Nope, she was entirely on her own.

Nothing new, she reminded herself, and with a deep breath, lifted her head.

Look at that. She wasn't alone after all. Nope, Brody stood in the doorway where Shayne had been only a moment before.

Watching her.

She lifted her chin and pretended she could see straight. "What can I do for you?"

They hadn't spoken since The Incident.

AKA the kiss.

Actually, kisses, as in plural, because there had definitely been plural kisses. And correction. *He* hadn't spoken to *her*. In fact, he'd downright avoided her.

But now his piercing eyes missed nothing as they touched down on the decanter, with only an inch of brandy left in it, to the shot glass in front of her, empty. His jaw tightened.

And her stomach slipped, all the way down to her tippy-toasted toes. Because she knew what he was going to say.

"I thought you don't drink," he said.

Yep. That was what she thought he'd say. And she didn't drink. Anymore.

Mostly.

Except the rare occasion when her courage and bravado and toughness failed her. It'd all been slipping for some time now, and she'd needed a boost.

A liquid boost. "I'm off duty."

"I can see that."

She carefully put away the brandy and washed the two glasses, extremely aware of him watching her. With equal deliberateness, she walked toward the doorway, intending to get her purse and call for a cab, but she came to a dilemma.

He still stood there, and despite her walking directly toward him, he didn't move aside, leaving her with the choice of asking him to move, or touching him.

She wanted to touch him.

All over.

Naked.

With her fingers *and* her tongue, and then her fingers some more.

But since that was undoubtedly the brandy talking, she bit her lip rather than say so. She was sloshed, yes, but she knew him. He wouldn't have sought her out unless he needed something done in regard to work, so chances were that he was thoroughly disgusted, annoyed, or just plain pissed off. Knowing it, she averted her gaze and didn't look directly into his face.

His gorgeous face.

But then their toes touched, and she was forced to tip her head back and glance up at him.

He merely arched a brow, silent.

The bastard, forcing her to make a move either

way. Except in his eyes she did not find disgust, annoyance, or temper.

Just . . . oh, God . . . heat. Such bone-melting heat that her knees wobbled. "If you'll excuse me." She accompanied this request by moving into him, certain that he would fall over backward in order to get out of her way before they touched.

He didn't. In fact, he didn't move, which had her shoulder brushing his chest. "Brody, seriously. If you'll just . . ."

This time he shifted, not away, but into her, just enough that she couldn't have gotten by him if she wanted to.

More than her shoulder touched him now; it was a full body contact, her front to his, and she froze to the spot, barraged by the memory of the last time they'd had full frontal contact.

When she'd kissed him.

When he'd kissed her back.

It had been unlike any kiss in recent memory, and that wasn't just the alcohol clouding her thoughts, but the utter truth.

He kissed like no other.

And she wanted another. Too bad her pride gripped her by the lapels and straightened her wobbly legs. "You're in my way."

"Don't you think we should talk about it?"

"About Shayne and Dani?"

"No." Leaning in, he forced her back against the doorway and planted a hand on either side of her face.

Suddenly it was *her* turn to shrink back from the contact. Not because she didn't want to touch him, because oh, God she did, but because she was just tipsy enough to know that she wouldn't be able to stop at one touch.

"The kiss," he said, his mouth only a whisper from hers. "Should we talk about the kiss?"

She licked her lips and shook her head, her gaze locked on his mouth. "I don't think talking about that is a very good idea right now."

"You sure?" His mouth was tight. Grim. *Worried,* she realized with surprise.

"Because we're employer and employee," he murmured. "And it was wrong for me to let it happen."

Okay, it was about guilt. She got it now, though she wished she didn't. He didn't want her to sue him for sexual harassment. Funny, because she'd been the one doing the harassing. "Don't worry, it was nothing."

He just looked at her, and finally she dropped eye contact because holding eye contact and all this body contact at the same time was pretty much nearly as good as sex. It was certainly causing the same reactions within her body. If he only knew . . .

With a low oath, he abruptly pulled away and turned his back.

Yeah, he did know.

"Get your stuff," he said over his shoulder. "I'll drive you home."

"I don't need—"

"Just get your things."

Fine. If he needed to assuage his guilt, she'd let him save her the cab fare. Crossing the lounge for her purse, she caught sight of herself in the mirror. Eyes glossy, cheeks flushed.

Nipples hard.

He'd seen, of course. He always saw, and no

doubt, her body's reaction to him had freaked him out. Good to know some things never changed. With a sigh, she grabbed her purse and walked out ahead of him, head high, hoping he was watching her pretty damn fantastic ass and kicking himself for being so stupid as to let her get away.

Chapter 22

Shayne carried Dani through the lobby. He had a strand of her hair in his mouth and her belt was cutting his ribs. But she felt warm and soft, and was looking at him as if she wanted to jump his bones.

"Shayne?"

"Yeah?"

She looped her arms around his neck and grinned at him. "Have I mentioned I like it when you carry me?"

She had brandy breath, and he still wanted to kiss her.

"Shayne?"

"Yeah?"

"I also like it when you look at me like I'm someone special to you. Because you're someone special to me."

"You're going to be sorry you admitted that when you're sober."

"Why?"

"Because when you're sober you don't like me as much, unless we're in bed."

Her smile faded as she stared up at him. "Then I must be a very stupid woman when I'm sober."

He used his foot to open the door to the tarmac. A gust of wind rolled over them and he hunched over her to protect her from it, which effectively brought his face closer to hers.

She sighed. "Very stupid."

He took her down to the first hangar, where he'd had his Cessna fueled up for their trip.

Inside the plane she looked around. "It's tiny," she said in an extremely small voice. "Very tiny."

"It's a six-seater." He plopped her down across the two seats behind the pilot seat, then grabbed a blanket and spread it over her. "Plenty big enough."

"What are you doing?"

"I'm assuming you got yourself in this condition so you can sleep through the flight."

"Well, there's that . . ."

He turned back and looked down at her, so sweetly sprawled in the seats. "And what else?"

She covered her eyes.

Huh. He crouched beside her. "Dani?"

Uncovering her eyes, she hit him with the full potency of her gaze, which if he'd been standing would have staggered him.

"Can you handle the truth?" she whispered.

No. "Yes."

"You're freaking me out as much as this flight is."

"Me? Why?"

"Because . . ." She shook her head. "I don't think I'm drunk enough for this."

"Talk to me, Dani."

"Why didn't you tell me that Sky High Air exists all because of you? That without you it wouldn't exist?"

"Because that's not true."

"It's your money."

"And without it, we'd have come up with something else."

"You handle all the client relations. You bring in all the clients."

"I'm president of operations. You know that."

"You *are* Sky High Air."

He shook his head. "Why are we having this conversation?"

"Because you're not who I thought you were, okay? Because you're not just the laid-back, easygoing, fun-loving playboy who sleeps with anyone with a pretty smile. You're . . ." She sighed. "More. A lot more. And I don't know what to do with that."

"You're not making sense. At first you didn't want to be with me because I was that guy. Now you're pissed because I'm not?" He shook his head. "Maybe I should be the one drinking."

She rolled away from him. "You know what? Don't listen to me."

"Now that's a deal." Rising, he turned away too, happy to not have this conversation, because he was this close to humiliating himself and begging her to want him for more than just sex. "I have to do the preflight check. Wait here."

Grateful for the fresh air, he stepped off the plane, and as he did, a shadow stepped in front of him.

Michelle.

He bit back his sigh. She had a private jet that they housed here in this hangar. She was a frequent flier, a real jet-setter who lived and loved the lifestyle, so it wasn't unusual for her to be here.

What *was* unusual was for her to be here and him

not know it. Maddie usually kept him apprised of which client was on the premises.

But then again, Maddie had apparently clocked out early today to have shots with Dani.

In any case, Michelle smiled at him. A tall, gorgeous, stacked brunette who'd graced many a lingerie catalog in her modeling days, which she'd just recently left for higher, loftier aspirations—acting—she was so beautiful it actually hurt to look at her, and Shayne had definitely enjoyed their two dates.

And their activities on that second date.

But even as she lifted her gaze to his, he remembered what had driven him away—her naked, overwhelming ambition to have a diamond on the ring finger of her left hand.

And then there was the other thing. She'd never made him ache. She'd never made him think of her 24/7, even when he was in the air.

Even when he was sleeping.

And she sure as hell never drove him to complete and utter frustration the way the woman on the plane behind him did.

"I have a change in plans," Michelle said. "I need a flight to San Diego."

"I can't."

She arched a brow in surprise. Not many people told Michelle no. "You can't?"

"I can't. Did you talk to Maddie?"

"She said you were booked and that Noah could take me."

"Great." He pulled out his cell phone. "I'll check your takeoff status."

"But I want you—" Michelle broke off and cocked her head at something behind him. "Hello. Who are you? A Sky High employee?"

Dani had poked her head out of the plane. "No. I don't like planes."

Shayne sighed and when Dani stepped down to the tarmac, he introduced the two of them, and when Michelle shook Dani's hand, she asked, "So you're a client?"

"Then . . ." Michelle glanced back at Shayne. "You're his date."

"I don't think so," Dani said. "Because I told him I didn't want to date and he believed me, so . . . no. No, we're not dating. We're just . . . Well. I'm not exactly sure."

Shayne felt Michelle's gaze sizzling his skin. "Calling Noah," he said, punching in Noah's number.

"No, don't. I can find him myself." Michelle didn't move, instead looking Dani over. "Good luck with him. You're going to need it." And with that, she turned around and walked away.

Dani arched a brow, or tried, but in her inebriated state, she couldn't quite pull it off. "You really do have a special way with women."

"Yeah. I'm a keeper, all right."

She didn't say anything to that, just sort of weaved, and then turned to take the few steps back up into the plane. On the last one, she tripped, abruptly vanishing into the plane with a thud.

"Dani?" Leaping up the steps, he peered into the interior of the plane.

She'd hit the floor. Rolling to her back, she waved a hand. "I meant to do that."

With a sigh, he scooped her back up and got her into a seat.

"I'm okay," she said, eyes closed.

His gaze touched over her face, and he felt his heart constrict. "Yeah. You are."

Her eyes opened, and though they were more than a little glossy, she gazed up at him. "I like him, you know," she whispered.

"Who?"

"The guy you really are." Lifting a hand, she tried to cup his face, ended up smacking him instead. "You ought to show him more often."

He just stared down at her.

She laughed a little, then closed her eyes again, and with a shuddery sigh, fell asleep.

Shayne landed in Tahoe, arranged for tie-down services, ran through his postflight check, and still Dani didn't stir. He went into the lobby, grabbed a tray of food from the café there, and went back to the Cessna.

As he entered, Dani lifted her head, then winced and held it. "Is it morning? It feels like morning."

"It's seven. At night. How's the head?"

"Concussion plus hangover. Not pleasant."

Setting the tray down beside her, he watched with some amusement as her nose wriggled and her eyes lit. "Burger and fries?"

"It's all yours."

She dug in with gusto and a smile, and when she'd plowed through most of it, she sat back and sighed. "Thanks. You do good morning-afters. Or evening-afters."

He never had. Normally he was running for the hills from any kind of "after."

When she saw his expression, her smile faded. She stood, straightening her clothes and her hair. "Sorry. I forgot there for a moment. You don't do af-ters."

"Dani—"

"Nope, it's okay. I knew that about you going in. It's why I didn't want to date you. What do we do now, rent a car?"

"Maddie arranged for one already. Dani—"

"No, let's just go." Nodding, she moved around him to the door, careful not to touch or look at him, so he pulled her back around.

The look on her face dared him to say what was on his mind. "Dani, I don't know what the hell I'm doing here. I don't know what comes next."

"Well, let me help you. Nothing comes next."

"Maybe that's not what I want."

"Really? What do you want?"

He wanted to say *whatever makes you happy*, or anything that would make her stop looking at him like she was looking at him now, as if he was about to disappoint her and she was okay with that.

"Tell you what. You let me know when you know." Pulling free, she stepped off the plane.

Resisting the urge to thunk his head against the wall, he followed her out.

"Don't say anything about my job." Dani whispered this to Shayne on the porch of her mother's Tahoe house. Somewhere inside were her siblings, on a weekend getaway. "The job makes them crazy."

"Okay."

Nodding, she went to knock, then turned back to him. "And don't say anything about my car either. When they're reminded of my financial situation, they're always afraid I'm going to change my mind and need their money."

He nodded.

But again she hesitated before knocking. "And nothing about—"

"Dani."

"Right." She nodded. "I'm stalling. I realize that."

"Then knock."

"Okay." But she just stood there, heart thumping in her chest.

"Dani? You okay?"

"Terrific." But she wasn't. She wasn't even close. She was being stalked by someone who wanted her to look crazy. She was falling in love with a man she'd told she didn't want to do anything with but have sex. Overwhelmed, she closed her eyes, then drew in a deep breath. "Just terrific." And she would be, even knowing that when they got to the bottom of her rather unique problem, it would be over between them.

And she was okay with that.

Or she would be, soon as she repeated it enough. *You're not keeping him, you're not keeping him . . .*

Damn it, she wanted to keep him.

But she'd known what would happen, known it from that first night when she'd been stupid enough to think one kiss would be enough.

One kiss would never be enough, not for her, not with this man. But that was her own damn fault, and she'd get over it.

On her own.

Shayne sighed, reached past her, and gave a decisive knock-knock-knock. She glared at him but he just shook his head.

Such a damn guy.

A damn guy who didn't know how to take the just-sex thing to the next level, and she was okay with that. She had to be, because she'd told him she was.

Her stepbrother opened the door with a glass of champagne in one hand and a ski bunny in the other. He had an unlit cigar hanging out a corner of his mouth and a ridiculous party hat tipped to one side of his head. "Surprise—" He broke off, then sighed. "Oh. It's you."

"We need to talk."

Tony sighed. "Hang on." He shut the door in her face.

"Ah. Family love." Shayne nodded. "It's overwhelming, isn't it?"

And just like that, the tension drained from her and she laughed. *Laughed.* So did he. He got it. He got her. And something else. Even though she didn't want to, she got him too. "Thanks," she whispered, and turning to him, pressed her mouth to his jaw, meaning to just give him a quick little peck for being there, just to let him know that even though she knew that he knew that he was a big chicken shit when it came to them, she still was grateful for him being here with her.

But at the last moment he turned his head and she accidentally caught his mouth with hers, and the quick little kiss didn't feel so quick or so little when his hands tightened, pulling her in against him.

The front door opened again, and Dani broke free, a little blown away by how quickly he could draw her in and make her forget absolutely everything.

Her stepsister stood there this time, wearing a frown and a little black dress that surely cost more than a month's salary. She glanced at Shayne in surprise, obviously not able to figure out how Dani had possibly snagged him. "Dani? What are you doing here? Someone tell you about the party?"

"What party?"

"We're having a surprise party for Mom."

No. No one had told her, mostly because clearly she hadn't been invited, but that didn't surprise her. "I just need to talk to you a moment."

Eliza glanced at her watch. "I've got half a minute."

Dani let out a breath. "Okay, well, someone's trying to make me look crazy. There's a dead body—"

"A *what?*"

"A dead body," Dani repeated. "And it keeps disappearing and then reappearing. And then there's the fact that someone was in my apartment, and then shooting at me in the parking lot at work, and then the dead body again, this time in my office, and then the concussion. And frankly, the police are starting to doubt my sanity."

Eliza laughed. "Starting?"

"*My* half a minute," Dani said. "Someone isn't trying to kill me so much as trying to make me look crazy. Maybe so that a certain someone and her brother could ensure their full inheritance."

Eliza gave one slow blink. "You mean me."

"Is it? Is it you trying to get me committed to the loony bin?"

Eliza lifted her champagne glass and drained it. "Tony," she called weakly over her shoulder. "Do you by any chance have a plan to have Dani committed to the . . ." She looked at Dani.

"Loony bin," Dani provided helpfully.

"Loony bin?"

Tony reappeared, minus the ski bunny. "What the fuck?"

"Well . . ." Eliza grabbed her brother's drink and drained that too. "Danielle's just stopped by to ask us a question, a simple one, really. She'd like to know if we're the ones who have a dead body, one that keeps disappearing and reappearing, and are we also the ones who have entered her apartment without permission, shot at her in her work parking lot, and . . ." She turned to Dani. "I'm sorry. I forgot what came next."

"The dead body again," Dani said helpfully. "In my office."

"Right. And then the . . ."

"Concussion. Which led to the someone trying to make me look crazy to the police."

Eliza turned to Tony. "This is where we come in, apparently."

Tony looked at Eliza, and then together they both burst into laughter.

Shayne frowned. "What the hell is so funny?"

Eliza had to lean on her brother, but finally she wiped away her tears of mirth and sniffed. "Oh, God. It's beautiful, really."

"What? What is beautiful?" Dani demanded.

"Your ridiculous need to prove yourself all on your own, without family or friends or help of any kind, has finally come back to bite you on the ass."

"I don't have a ridiculous need . . ." Dani trailed off when Tony lifted a brow. "Okay, maybe I do. A little. It's just that you guys never wanted to include me."

"Oh, no," Eliza said. "You're not putting this on us. I'm drunk, but not that drunk. From day one you looked down your perfect, surgery-free nose at us. Face it, Dani. It wasn't that we were too good for you, but that you were too good for us."

Dani just stared at them, letting the words sink in. Was that—could that be true? Really?

Eliza sighed, and as a waiter passed behind her with a tray full of drinks, she nabbed two and handed one to Dani.

Dani stared at it. "I can't."

"See? Too good for us."

"No, it's just that I overindulged earlier." Had she disliked Tony and Eliza just because they'd had money? Had she distanced herself as if she was too good for them? She'd certainly had the fiercely independent thing down by the time they'd come into her life . . . Oh, God. Was this all her fault? "So this has nothing to do with your dad's money?"

"Did you by any chance see how many zeroes are on the end of our trust-fund accounts?" Eliza smiled, and it was surprisingly free of cynicism and sarcasm. "I don't think you've ever really looked, but let me tell you what. We have enough, Dani, more than enough, without what was set aside for you."

She could only stare at them. "So you don't care if I go after it."

"Nope. And here's the kicker," Tony said. "We don't even care if you're really crazy."

"But hey, as long as you're here," Eliza added, "you could come in and pretend we're all one big loving family, and yell 'surprise' when your mom gets here. That would be nice."

"She already had a party," Dani pointed out.

"Yes, but this is your mother. She likes multiple parties."

Chapter 23

Back in Los Angeles, Shayne walked Dani to her door. He had a sinking feeling in his gut that this was it, that when he said good-bye here, she was going to walk out of his life.

"Thanks for the flight," she said, turning to face him. "It was almost painless."

The "almost" hung in the air, while the pain she'd just professed not to feel sat in her eyes and grabbed him by the throat. "Dani, you sure you don't want me to come in?"

"Not necessary."

Just down the hall, Alan's door opened, but instead of Alan, a pretty brunette came out, straightening her slightly crooked clothes with a silly little smile on her face.

"Oh," she said in surprise and pulled up short. "Dani."

Dani blinked. "Reena?"

"Reena . . . from your work Reena?" Shayne asked.

Dani nodded, her eyes on the woman. "You . . . and Alan? But . . ." She looked blown away. "But . . . when?"

"We met when he brought you pizza that night, remember? And then you turned him down for another date, so that left him free." She lifted a shoulder. "And I needed a pick-me-up." But she softened. "You're not mad, right?"

"I'm not mad. Of course I'm not mad." Dani glanced at Shayne, then back at Reena. "I'm just . . ."

"Surprised? Yeah, well, other people have stuff going on too, Dani. Other people get lonely, have needs, too."

"I know that."

"Do you? Because it seems like sometimes you don't."

"Reena—"

"No, never mind." Reena rubbed her eyes. "I'm sorry. I just don't want this to be a problem."

"It's not."

"Okay, good. Then I'll see you at work."

"Wait." Shayne glanced at Dani, who was looking a little shell-shocked. "Wait up."

Reena looked him over. "I know you. You're the rich pilot. Not sure which karma god Dani kissed lately, but she's on a roll."

Shayne asked, "You think nearly getting killed, several times now, is on a roll?"

Reena's smile faded as she turned to Dani. "Can you believe I nearly forgot? Did they catch the shooter?"

"No," Shayne said. "Nor the person who was in her office. The one who caused her concussion and five stitches."

"What?" Reena grabbed for Dani's hand. *"What?"*

"You don't know what happened to her at work?" Shayne asked.

"Oh, God. Something else? I haven't been in, I had today off. What happened. Reena's self-protective smile had vanished, replaced by a freaked-out expression that could have been faked but seemed genuine. "Dani? What happened?"

"There was a dead body in my closet."

"A dead . . ." Reena staggered back against the wall. "My God."

"I freaked, tripped over someone, and fell. Knocked me unconscious."

"Oh, Dani."

"When I woke up, no body."

Reena just stared at her, slack-jawed, and slowly shook her head. "Have you considered the fact that you must have royally pissed someone off?"

"Yes, actually," Shayne said.

Reena looked at him as understanding dawned. "You think that I—My God. She's never pissed me off."

"What about the promotion?"

"Well, yeah, I was jealous," she admitted to Shayne. "And then there's you . . . I mean, hello, have you looked in the mirror?" She looked at Dani, eyes luminous. "I know I can be a jealous, petty bitch, but I'm not a vindictive one. Tell me you know that."

Dani stared at her, and then nodded. "I know it."

"Okay, good." Reena hugged her hard, then pulled back and looked into her eyes. "Stick with him until this is over. He's pretty, but he also looks fairly capable, as far as guard dogs go."

Shayne watched her go, then found Dani watching him.

"She comes off the list too," she said very quietly, then turned to her door.

"The list is getting a little short for my comfort." For the first time he really had no idea at all what she was thinking, and he decided he liked it better when she wore her emotions out on her sleeve.

She unlocked her front door, opened it, peered inside, then turned to face him, one of her fake, polite smiles crossing her lips. She'd been giving him the fake, polite smile ever since the flight back.

"Thank you," she said.

He looked at that fake, polite smile and tried to figure out where it was coming from. "I think we should talk, make a new list."

"I'll do that. Tomorrow."

"By yourself."

"Yes." She stepped over the threshold, still careful to block his way.

He got it. He wasn't coming in. Under any circumstances. "Dani."

"Yes?"

Since she was looking over her shoulder into the dark apartment, he tugged her around.

Another brief flash of that fake, polite smile. "We've already said good-bye."

So he hadn't gotten tired of her as planned. That was scary enough, but nothing to the fact that somehow the tables had gotten turned and she'd tired of him. Letting go of her, he just stood there, a little stunned, and ridiculous as it seemed, a whole lot hurt. "Fine."

Cocking her head, she gave him a look. "What's fine?"

"Every damn thing."

"Now you're just pouting."

He gaped at her. "I am not pouting. I never pout. But if you think the fact that you're tired of me means I'm going to let you walk in there alone after all the things that have happened to you, you *are* crazy."

A funny look flashed over her face. "You . . . think I'm tired of you?"

"Sure. It happens. No hard feelings." Now he flashed her his own personal brand of the fake, polite smile and turned away.

And this time, it was her turn to grab him and force him around. "You think I'm tired of you," she repeated.

Given her incredulous tone, he had to reassess. "Uh—"

"Are you kidding me?" With jerky movements, she yanked open her purse and pulled out a string of five condoms. "I bought these to keep on me because you and I? We tend to need them in a hurry. I've never bought condoms in my life, Shayne, so you tell me. Is the fact that I did, that I went to the store, trolled the condom aisle, and picked out a box just for you the actions of a woman who's *tired of you?*"

Before he could respond, she'd tugged him inside her apartment, kicked the door closed and shoved him up against the wood with shocking strength, then clamped her lips on his.

That's when all the blood in his head drained for parts south as her mouth ravaged his.

Finally, when he was breathless and stone hard, she lifted her head. "Does that feel like I'm *tired of you*, Shayne? Or this . . . ?" She tore one of the condoms off and slapped it against his chest.

"Jesus." His vision actually blurred. His hands

went to her face, guiding her mouth back to his. He had to have her mouth on his, now, right now.

Her hands were already pulling open his pants and tearing at the condom packet when he spun them around, pressing *her* to the door now, needing the leverage. Her top went sailing over his shoulder, as did her bra. "Kick off your shoes," he commanded as he dragged down her pants, taking her panties with them, leaving her completely and perfectly naked as he slid his hand between her legs, groaning roughly at how ready for him she was.

"Told you." She yanked his shirt off and sank her teeth into his shoulder. "Not done with you yet, damn it."

He stroked her with his thumb and her head thunked back against the door, exposing her throat for his mouth, where he did some biting of his own. Lifting her, he wrapped her legs around him, which opened her more fully to him, and helpless to the pull, he sank in deep with one powerful stroke.

Just her low gasp of sheer pleasure turned him on so much that he had to go still a moment. "Don't move," he demanded gruffly. If she did, if she whispered his name in that sexy-as-hell whisper, if she so much as breathed, he was going to come.

"Have to." She rocked her hips, and his vision blurred.

"God. Dani, not yet." Gripping her tight, he held her still, but she sighed his name and he felt lost. Just as whenever he was with her, he was also found. Terrifying, and utterly, overwhelmingly simple.

"Oh, Shayne," she said, sounding as if maybe, just maybe she felt the same way. She was wet and hot, sucking him into a chasm of pleasure so deep he couldn't see his way out. Didn't want to see his way out. This wasn't just sex, he knew that now. This was a heart and soul connection, and he opened his mouth to tell her, but she fisted her hands in his hair and bit his lower lip, tugging on it, bringing a sweet stab of pain until she released it and then licked the spot while he pounded into her, the sound of her hips hitting the door, of him sinking in and out of her driving him to the very edge of his mind.

Past the edge, where there was no cognitive thought, only the sensations. Hot and wet and deep and overwhelmingly amazing. It was all he could do to hold on to her. "Dani, I'm going to—"

But she burst first, his name on her lips as she came all over him in gorgeous, violent shudders that sent him skittering into it with her. Then his knees collapsed, and they sank to the floor in a tangled, naked, damp, and sweaty heap.

"Jesus," he breathed. "Did you get the license of that truck?"

She rolled to her back and stared up at the ceiling, and even stripped of all energy from the wild sex, he recognized trouble. Coming up on one elbow, he looked into her face. "Why do I get the feeling we just had make-up sex without making up, after a fight I didn't understand?"

"That wasn't make-up sex. That was just sex."

Okay, definitely, he'd missed the fight. Damn, he hated that. "Come here."

She didn't. "Do you always cuddle and talk after sex?"

"I wouldn't call lying on the wood floor, butt-ass naked, cuddling."

Turning only her head, she gave him a long look. And he had to concede. "No. I don't usually cuddle and talk afterward."

"So why me, Shayne?"

He wished he knew. When she made a soft noise and turned away, he pulled her back. "If I had the answer to that, this would be simple, but . . ."

"I know. Not simple."

"I'm working on it. I swear I'm working on it."

She stared at him for a long moment, then nodded and set her head on his chest. A gift. She was this rare, precious gift. Pulling her in close, he held her tight and did some ceiling watching of his own, wondering what the hell was wrong with him that he couldn't just tell her.

After a few minutes, Dani pulled free and stood up.

"We have got to start making it to a bed," Shayne murmured, and rolled to his back in all his naked glory, and there was lots of glory. "Where are you going?"

Throat tight, she managed a smile. "Just getting some water." She couldn't have said another word without giving herself away, that being the fact that she couldn't hide from it anymore. This bone-deep, desperate, insatiable yearning clawing at her? *Love.* She moved into the kitchen for the water she didn't really need and tried not to panic.

And failed.

Gripping the counter for strength, she pressed her head to the cool tile and gulped for air.

She loved him.

"Dani."

Jerking upright, she turned around just as Shayne flipped on the light, and she realized two things at once.

One, she was still naked, and standing beneath

the harsh fluorescent kitchen lights in that state was probably a worse nightmare than getting caught in a green mask with an entire carton of ice cream and one spoon.

And two, there was a piece of paper stuck to her forehead. Shayne's gaze narrowed in on that, and also naked, he strode toward her, but even with the unflattering light cast over him, he still stole her breath.

Pulling the paper from her forehead, he looked down at it, face tight with tension.

Peering over his arm, she went still at the words she read: *You're next.*

Chapter 24

They turned the note over to the police, who scratched their collective head and sort of went, "Oh, guess someone *is* after you."

Duh.

Dani offered to let Shayne sleep over after that. Of course he said yes, after running home to get Bella, who was ecstatic at the field trip. Dani looked at the determination on his face, the determination to keep her safe, and felt something warm deep inside. He had a sense of responsibility an annoying mile long.

But it hadn't been responsibility that had made her come so many times in the night that she'd lost track.

The next morning, she got up to go to work.

"Oh, no," Shayne said. "Not this again."

"What do you suggest I do?"

"Something that doesn't require you leaving my sight." While the words were thrilling, the intent behind them was not. He was scared for her, worried beyond belief, but neither of those things was something one based a relationship on.

And God help her, she'd figured out that *that* was what she wanted—a damn relationship. She was tired of being on her own, tired of fighting off her emotions for him, of not letting him in because she was tough and independent. She could be herself and still have a guy in her life. *Him* in her life.

"Come with me," he said.

"Where to?"

"Trust me?"

She looked into his eyes, not all that surprised to realize she trusted him more than she'd ever trusted anyone.

She let him drive, but instead of taking her to his house as she'd expected, he took her and Bella to Sky High.

"I'm not ready for another flight," she told him, hugging the dog. "I haven't had any alcohol."

"I just have a quick flight to Santa Barbara."

"And you, what, think I'm going to sit and wait for you?"

He came around the car for her and pulled her out, holding her hips, pressing her back against the car as he looked into her eyes. "You won't be alone here."

"I'm capable of taking care of myself."

"More than," he affirmed, sliding his fingers into her hair, holding her face up to his for a long, sweet, slow kiss that pretty much melted all her resolve. "But this isn't about you, Dani. It's about me."

"That's ridiculously Neanderthal."

He closed his eyes, then opened them again. "I'm worried about you. I'm so goddamned worried about you that I can't see straight, not even to fly."

She stared up at him, her throat tight.

He glided his thumb over her lower lip, his gaze on her mouth, which he covered with his for another extremely nice kiss. "You turn me upside down." He pressed his forehead to hers. "So completely, fucking upside down."

What did that mean? Before she could ask, Bella barked with enthusiasm to get inside. Shayne took her hand and led them inside. He waved at Maddie, who was at the desk talking into a radio while working not one but two keyboards and looking like a supermodel while she was at it. She waved at Dani, handed Shayne a stack of files, tossed Bella a doggie cookie, and went back to multitasking.

Shayne took Bella to his office, then brought Dani onto the tarmac, where they walked past two hangars. They entered a third, a huge steel building housing four planes, all shiny and gleaming and looking very expensive. "Are these all yours?" she asked, awed in spite of herself.

"Those two." He pointed to the two planes in the back. "The Moody's on the left, the Learjet on the right." He gestured to the front planes. "That's a Piper, it's Brody's new baby. Cost a pretty penny, and once we fix her up, she's going to be the new girl on the block. The other's a Beechcraft. It's a client's, in for some regular maintenance."

They walked up the middle of the hangar, between the planes, and Dani swallowed hard. She felt so small in here. But then Shayne opened the Lear and nudged her inside, and she gasped.

It was like looking into a beautiful, elegant, sophisticated house. A mansion. The interior was all plush, soft-looking leather, the carpet as thick as a forest. "But . . . it looks like someone's living room."

"I know." Nudging her in, he shut the door behind them.

"We're not—"

"Not going up, no. At least you're not." He led her down the body of the plane and opened a door at the end, which opened to a mouth-dropping master bedroom suite that might have been ripped right out of *Architectural Digest.* "There's a TV," he said, lifting a remote, "a small library, and hell, there's even an exercise bike. Make yourself at home until I get back."

"And then?"

"The kitchen's fully stocked."

"Shayne. You can't baby-sit me forever. You have a life. Flying. Running Sky High Air. Perpetuating that lazy, sexy image."

He came back to her, a frown on that sexy mouth. "Yeah, my life's full. So's yours. And I've lived my life just the way I wanted to, I won't deny that. Neither would you. But maybe I'm . . ."

She stared up at him. "What?"

"Maybe I'm ready for some changes."

Well, if that didn't send her heart skittering. But he looked unaccustomedly uncertain, and she wasn't used to seeing him look that way. Not this man, who'd never doubted himself, not once. "Changes or not," she managed. "I'll handle whatever comes."

"On your own, right? Just like always?"

Was there an option? "Of course."

"Of course," he echoed quietly. "Dani." His hands came up, cupped her face, his fingers sinking into her hair. "Maybe I'm not the only one who should be thinking about making changes."

What the hell was that supposed to mean? She was fine, just fine—

Okay, she wasn't exactly fine.

In fact, she knew exactly what he meant. She'd been a loner, too independent. She closed people out.

But she was going to work on that. She just didn't plan to reveal her heart to the man who was most likely to break it. "Shayne, seriously. I can't just live here."

"Just today. Give me that much."

When she only stood there, he made a low, rough sound in his throat and pressed his mouth to her temple, then her ear. "Come on, has it been that bad hanging with me? Have I been that bad to you?"

Memories of the past four days pelted her—Shayne playing the relaxed, smooth host of her mother's party, him coming to her aid whenever she'd wanted, and even when she hadn't, anticipating her, which took an excellent judge of character, not to mention the depth of caring.

And that, that caring, was what kept tripping her up. No, he wasn't who she'd thought he was.

He was better.

And she wanted him. "No," she whispered, her voice hoarse and just a little bit raw. Damn him for making her admit this. "You've been wonderful. *Amazing.*"

With that endearingly crooked smile, he lifted one of her hands to his mouth. "Okay, then. So the problem is?"

That you're going to break my heart. That you are breaking my heart.

"Dani?"

Knowing now what she had to do, hating what she had to do, she turned her face into his throat and just breathed him in, wishing she could bottle him up and keep him forever. But if she let this go on much longer, it *would* kill her. "The problem is me, Shayne. All me."

He went still for a beat and pulled back a fraction. "I've used that sentence. That's an I'm-dumping-you sentence."

She just looked at him.

"You are. You're dumping me," he said.

Cutting my losses . . .

"*Why?*"

"Shayne—"

"No. Don't give me more of that it's just you crap, okay? Don't give me any excuses, just the damn truth."

"Okay." She stepped back. She needed space for this one. "I'm protecting myself."

"I thought we were past this. I'm not going to hurt you."

But you already are . . . She couldn't help it, her love for him was spilling all over, and as she looked at him, with all that love most likely completely obvious, something in his eyes changed. Filled with the knowledge of what was already wrong.

She loved him.

She nodded. "It's for the best, really," she managed. "I'm going to be busy with my work, and you're also extremely busy."

"Yes." But he shook his head in the negative. She'd have sworn his eyes were suspiciously shiny as he pulled her in.

A hug.

A good-bye hug.

His body was warm against her, and she wanted to cry so she tried to pull free but he held on. "For me," he whispered, and she found her arms winding up, around his neck, pressing closer.

He let her in, fisting his hand in the back of her shirt as if maybe he couldn't quite bring himself to let go.

Their eyes met. His mouth curved slowly in a smile that reached his eyes but was sad, so damn sad she actually felt her heart crack. Then he leaned in and kissed her. A good-bye kiss. An *I'm sorry I can't be more for you* kiss. A *you're breaking my heart* kiss . . .

She clung. Only for a moment, she told herself. A moment was all she needed, but that moment turned into two . . . and then they were straining toward each other, hands colliding for purchase, suddenly breathless and not so suddenly all heated up.

It was crazy. It was wrong. And she didn't care.

"What time's your flight?" she gasped as he slipped a hand beneath her shirt and cupped a breast.

"I can't remember." His thumb stroked her nipple. "I can barely remember my own name. Dani, what the hell are we doing?"

"Saying good-bye in the same way we started this whole thing." She pushed up his shirt, then leaned in and kissed a hard pec.

Breathing unsteadily, he yanked out his cell phone. "Maddie? What time's my flight? An hour? Great, thanks." Tossing the phone over his shoulder, he urged Dani toward the couch, then gave a little push so that she fell into it.

Following her down, he put his mouth to her ear. "This is crazy."

"I know. But I can't stop. Please, don't stop."

"No. No stopping." Her shirt flew over his shoulder, along with her bra, and he sucked in a breath at the sight of her. "God, you're gorgeous."

"Okay, don't talk. I can't say good-bye this way if you talk—"

Her words stuttered to a halt when he sucked her nipple into his mouth, playing the other one between his fingers and thumb.

"So gorgeous," he murmured, his mouth still full. "Sorry, can't seem to stop talking." Her shoes, pants, and panties went the way of her other things, until she was completely naked beneath him. "Or touching you . . ." He slid a finger into her, groaning when he found her already wet. He put his face to her belly. "God, Dani. You do me in. Every single time . . ." He kissed his way to her hip, licking and nibbling, leaving her an anticipatory, trembling, needy mass of quivering nerve endings . . . Good-bye. This was good-bye . . .

"Can you really walk away from this?" His shoulders wedged her thighs open so he could look his fill. "Can you?"

"I . . . don't know. Shayne, I'm feeling really naked."

"I like you naked." Gently he stroked her with his thumb, once, twice, tugging a soft cry from her lips that she couldn't hold back.

She was completely undressed, open to him, and he was still fully dressed. But then he replaced his fingers with his mouth . . .

And then a most impressive erection . . .

All of which brought her right out of herself, and then again when he came too. It took a while but she slowly came back, in his arms, face-to-face, their hearts racing.

As one.

How ironic was it that their hearts could beat as one, when their minds and souls couldn't?

Wouldn't.

Chapter 25

The one thing Maddie had gotten from her parents—good genes. She tended to use those genes to her best advantage. Especially on a day like today, when she was still stinging from the other night. The night Brody had driven her home without a word. Not a single mention of their kiss, nothing.

So she'd decided not to mention it either. She wore a baby-soft angora sweater and a little black skirt with fuck-me black heels. Today, she fit the secretary fantasy down to the last little bobby pin.

She was going to show Brody.

Exactly what she was going to show him, she really had no idea, other than she was suffering, so he needed to suffer right alongside of her. To that end, when she saw his car pull in the lot, she came around the front of the desk and perched a hip on one corner, crossing her legs so that her skirt rose, accenting her runner legs that she knew could make a grown man drool.

But Brody had the nerve to walk in the door with

his cell phone to his ear, his coffee at his lips, and head straight for his office.

Not so much as a glance.

Bullshit if she was going to let him get away with that! She cleared her throat, which had him taking a quick glance over his shoulder.

Executing an almost comical double take at the sight of her, he simultaneously dropped his cell phone and spilled his coffee down the front of him.

Oh, yeah. Payback was a bitch. It took all she had not to grin, but damn, suddenly the day was looking up. Way up.

"Shit." He brushed at his coffee-stained white shirt. *"Shit!"*

"You already said that."

Over his now half-empty coffee mug, he glared at her. "You did that on purpose."

"Did what?" She accompanied this with her best innocent smile as she put a box of tissues on top of the counter.

He yanked a handful and pressed them to his shirt. "You know damn well what." He gestured to her body. "You look . . ."

"Yes? I look what?"

Crouching, he grabbed his phone. "You made me hang up on Noah, damn it." He flipped it open and hit a number. "Noah? Sorry." He stared at Maddie. "Got distracted. I'll call you back later."

Oh yeah, the day was definitely going to be a good one.

Brody slapped the phone shut against his thigh, pulled his coffee-soaked shirt away from his skin, and winced. "Ouch."

"Maybe you ought to be more careful."

"I need to change."

"There's two clean shirts in your closet."

"Thanks."

"Okay, don't thank me, it's my job."

He looked a little baffled at her snooty tone. Stupid, stupid man.

After another long look, he turned away, all long and hard muscled and badass, soaked in coffee.

"Brody?"

He glanced back. "Yeah?"

"I looked what?"

"Nothing." He turned away again, but she'd have sworn he mouthed, "Hot, you look hot"—in an extremely unhappy tone.

Glad he was suffering, she moved behind her desk, burying herself in work, of which she had plenty. She had leases to prepare and three important flights to organize, two of which were for W-VIPs.

Whiny Very Important Persons.

No problem. She happened to specialize in W-VIPs, and prided herself on being able to please any client they'd ever had. She could fulfill any special request, acquiring and getting delivered the most difficult and rare of items, and make it look easy.

First W-VIP, Mr. Komomoto. Noah would be flying him to Aspen, and en route Mr. Komomoto would expect a full course dinner of the highest caliber. Today's demand—er, request was Alaskan crab, which she was having delivered from a five-star restaurant.

Second W-VIP for today? Michelle, one of their richest—and most annoying—clients.

It wasn't often Maddie felt sorry for Shayne. Who could feel sorry for a guy who looked like he did, had the money he did, and was as talented as he was? But he'd gone out with Michelle, what, maybe twice, before making it clear that he wasn't interested in

more, which she'd not taken well. For the past two
weeks, she'd called every day, multiple times, making Maddie her own personal sounding board. Ha!
Maybe the person Maddie should feel sorry for was
herself.

In any case, Michelle wanted to fly to Mexico and
had a special in-flight request. She wanted an ice
bath. Odd, yes, but then again Maddie found most
of the rich and famous were very odd, but it didn't
matter what she thought. A request was a request,
and it was her job to fill it.

It was her job to fulfill every wish.

She just wished Brody had a wish for her to fulfill . . .

"Is Shayne ready for me?"

Maddie looked up from her computer, managing
to keep her features in a polite smile. *Speak of the
devil.* Michelle stood there looking Barbie-doll perfect as always in a Prada suit, every hair in place, lip-
stick perfect, towing a large designer suitcase behind
her.

Maddie pulled Michelle's flight file. "You're early.
That's no problem, I'll call your pilot."

"Shayne. Shayne's my pilot. He's my everything."

Cuckoo.

"He is." Michelle let go of the handle of her suitcase, and it fell over with a solid thud. "Whoops."
She looked around. "Is Shayne here yet?"

Yep. And probably doing the wild thing with Dani
in the Learjet, if she had to hazard a guess. "You
know he's seeing someone."

"He's seeing me. I've made sure of it."

"You've . . . what?"

Michelle smiled.

Maddie sighed. She didn't owe Michelle anything, but as a fellow member of the female species, she had to try to get through to her. "Look, this is none of my business, but—"

"You're right. None of your business. Not at all." Michelle leaned over the counter. "Don't try to understand, because you can't."

"Okay." Another job requirement, ignoring rudeness. Her eyes were on her computer screen as she entered Michelle's information for the flight.

"You've made some changes. Your hair. Your nail color."

Maddie's gaze was still on her screen. "Wow, that's pretty observant. Are you stalking me?" she joked.

"Not you."

Maddie went still, and when she looked up, Michelle raised her eyebrows like yes, you idiot, you've finally got it.

That wasn't all she raised. She had a gun.

Pointed it right at Maddie.

Whose heart stopped short.

"Ask me what's in my suitcase."

She swallowed. "What's in your suitcase?"

"Actually, it's a who. Kathleen."

Maddie crept her hand toward the phone. "Kathleen," she repeated softly. My God . . .

"She's dead, of course." Calmly, Maddie yanked the phone cord out of the wall before Maddie could get an open line. "I was trying to pin it on Dani, but that bitch isn't easy to pin. How about you, Maddie? You look pretty capable and tough, but I'm thinking everyone has their breaking point."

Okay, surely someone, anyone, would come in and see what was going on. "I'm sure I have no idea what you're talking about."

"Brody. Brody's your breaking point."

Oh, God.

"Try to call for help again, and I'll kill him next. In fact, do anything to annoy me and I'll kill him. Clear?"

Maddie forced herself to breathe. "Crystal."

"Yep, just as I said, everyone has their breaking point. And I'm thinking now I should have just started with you. You, my dear, are my ticket out of here."

The hell she was. So she'd been a little slow on the uptake, they all had. For one thing, Dani didn't have a crazy stalker.

Shayne did. "So really," Maddie said, "your problem is that you've gotten yourself hooked on an inappropriate man. Rookie mistake."

"You know, you really should talk nicer to the woman who's going to marry one of your bosses."

Maddie managed a laugh. "You haven't done your homework. Shayne isn't the marrying type."

"Seriously. I'm holding a gun on you, you're supposed to be groveling and sniffling and desperate to get me whatever I need. And what I need is Shayne."

"Sorry to be contrary, but I'm not going to help you."

From behind the gun Michelle was pointing directly at Maddie's head, she smiled coldly. "Yes, you are. Where is he?"

Maddie arched a brow.

"I know that you know exactly where he is and what he's doing." In emphasis, she cocked the gun.

Which sounded much scarier than it did in the movies. "Okay, let's not doing anything stupid here."

"Stupid? Of course not. I'm never stupid. Stand up, Maddie."

Uh-oh. "Actually, I can't. I'm really tired, and—"

"Stand up *now*."

Maddie stood up. "So why did you go after Dani?"

"I've gone after all of them. Marie, Kathleen, Suzie . . ."

"But . . ." Maddie shook her head. "Those were women Shayne only dated once."

"I know. One little scare each and they all ran like hell. Can you imagine?"

Maddie blinked. "*You're* the reason he couldn't get a second date?"

Michelle gave a little bow.

"He thought he was losing his touch."

She smiled.

"But Dani wouldn't scare, I'm guessing."

Michelle's smile faded. "You need to be quiet now."

"You really screwed up there."

"Be quiet."

"Because by going after Dani, you just pushed them together. You realize that, right?"

"Shut up!"

"In fact, they're together right now, they're probably f—"

The gun went off. Maddie slammed back into the wall, white-hot agony shooting through her body.

Michelle frowned at the smoking gun. "Now look what you made me do."

Shayne awoke with a start. He and Dani were still on the Lear, in the master bedroom.

On the bed.

Entwined.

They'd fallen asleep. Must have been all the late nights and extremely gratifying sex.

Or maybe it was the fact that suddenly he had more on his mind.

Like Dani.

All the time . . .

And then he realized what had woken him. They weren't alone. Someone was standing over them in the dimmed room. "Hello?"

The shadow twisted, then vanished.

As he heard the sound of the plane door closing, he leapt up and flipped on a light.

But he and Dani weren't alone now either. There was a body with them, crumpled on the floor, and he'd recognize those kick-ass heels anywhere.

Maddie. With blood pooling beneath her. *"Christ."*

In the bed, Dani sat straight up, confused and baffled. "What?"

Heart in his throat, Shayne tossed her his cell phone and dropped to the floor. "Call 9-1-1," he commanded hoarsely and put his fingers to Maddie's throat, where he found a pulse, slow and beady, but there. Thank God. "It's Maddie." And it was bad, very, very bad, but even that wasn't the worst of it.

Because whoever had shot Maddie was just outside the plane, waiting for them.

Chapter 26

Dani's fingers shook as she tossed Shayne his pants. Pulling on her clothes, she dropped to the floor next to Shayne. "Police are on their way. Ambulance too. Ohmigod, is she—"

"Alive. She's alive."

Dani gulped for air. Alive was good, very, very good.

Maddie's eyes fluttered open. "Shayne?"

He leaned over her, grabbing her hands. "Right here, I'm right here."

Maddie gasped. "She's completely lost it." Her face was a tight mask of pain. "Goddammit, getting shot hurts."

Shayne was peeling her shirt away so he could see the wound. "Maddie, you're bleeding like a sieve."

Dani leaned over Shayne and saw that Maddie had a bullet hole in the region of her collarbone. One that was pumping out a shocking amount of blood.

Maddie coughed. "Shayne—"

"Don't talk," Shayne begged her, pulling his shirt from the foot of the bed and pressing it against Maddie's wound.

"Listen," Maddie said, grabbing his hand. "She's not Dani's stalker. She's yours."

Shayne gently pushed her hair from her face and cupped her jaw. "I love you, Maddie, you know I do. But when you talk, you're pumping blood out like a hose. So shut the hell up, okay? Just shut up and hold on."

"No. Please." She licked her dry lips. "Get Dani out of here, okay? Or Michelle'll shoot her too."

Michelle? Dani looked at Shayne, who appeared just as shocked as she.

"She's been scaring off all your dates since she became a client and fell all in psycho love with you," Maddie managed. "But Dani didn't scare off— Oh, God." She closed her eyes, her face pasty white and damp with perspiration.

"Maddie," Shayne said hoarsely. "We've got help coming, so you just hang on. You hear me? Hang on." He pulled back to look down into her face. "Christ." Setting her back on the floor, he checked her pulse.

"Is she—"

"Alive." His mouth was grim. "The bullet went all the way through. Maddie?"

No response.

"Shock is going to set in." Dani covered her with a blanket from the bed. "We have to keep her warm."

A funny ping sounded, and Dani would have sworn something whizzed right by her ear as the window cracked above her.

And then the wall splintered.

"Down." Shayne accompanied this demand by fisting his hand in Dani's shirt and tugging hard. He hunched over both her and Maddie, craning his neck, eyeing something behind her. "We're sitting ducks in here. We have to get out, and that's our only chance."

"What is?"

"Back door. Come on." Hoisting Maddie up into a fireman's hold over one shoulder, he grabbed Dani's hand and yanked her to the exit on the opposite side of the plane. "Stay low." He cracked the door.

They were facing the steel wall of the hangar. Five feet to the right was a door to a long hallway that led to the maintenance and mechanic's offices. "There." But just as he reached for the door, another ping ricocheted off the steel doorway above his head.

Before Dani could draw a breath to scream, Shayne shoved her ahead of him, around the back of the plane. In front of them was one of the golf carts they used to transport clients and their luggage back and forth from their planes to the lobby. Shayne carefully set Maddie in the back. Dani hopped into the passenger seat while Shayne took the driver's side and turned the key.

The engine was loud, and as Shayne hit the gas and held the wheel with his left hand, he shoved Dani's head down with his right, keeping his hand there as if he could protect her from getting shot. He took a hard right, and Dani let out a breath, thinking they were going to make it, but then came the staccato beat of bullets against the steel wall of the hangar, close enough to make her ears ring.

"She's shooting up the Lear! Hold on!" he shouted.

He wasn't kidding, because suddenly it felt like they were in a spin and Dani was flung hard against the door. But just as she braced herself, they spun in the other direction and she slammed into Shayne. "God, what about Maddie?"

"She's wedged in," he told her grimly.

Bleeding to death . . .

Oh, God, this was bad, so very, very bad. More bullets, and Dani bit her lip to keep her scream in.

"Christ, and now the Piper," Shayne muttered and took his hand off Dani's head to put both hands on the wheel, which he promptly tugged hard to the right.

From Dani's vantage point, she caught sight of a plane wing, and then just the ceiling of the hangar, which was a series of rafters and wires and lights. And then she saw it.

A flash of leg.

Female leg.

"She's above us," Dani gasped. "In the rafters."

Pop, pop, pop.

"And the Moody. Goddammit, that's not even ours!" He made a hard right, and the engine coughed. Stalled.

Died.

"Fuck." He pulled Dani out of the seat and then grabbed Maddie as if she weighed nothing. "I'm going to kill Brody for being too damn cheap to upgrade that cart!"

"Do we have a plan?"

"Yes. Run like hell. Behind the Beechcraft—"

"The what?"

"Behind that plane ahead of you is the maintenance closet. It's built like a tanker."

They rounded the back of the plane, with Dani's
skin literally leaping at every heartbeat, expecting to
be pierced by a bullet at any second.

Instead, Shayne yanked open the door of the
closet, set Maddie down and then shoved Dani in
after her.

"What—" she started but he put his fingers over
her mouth.

"Stay in here, you'll be safe."

Oh, God. She snagged his arm just as he turned
away. "Where are you going?"

"To make sure you stay safe."

He was going to play the hero. "No, Shayne—"

"I have to stop her. We have other clients on the
premises."

"She's got a damn gun!"

"She won't shoot me. I'm going to draw her away
until the cops come." He waited until she thought
about exactly how true that was—Michelle didn't
want Shayne dead, she wanted him very much alive.

"She's crazy," she whispered.

"Nutso. So swear to me you'll stay here."

While he went out there, unprotected.

"Dani. Swear to me." He closed his eyes, then
leaned in and put his mouth to her ear. "I can't do
this with you right next to me, a target." His voice
was low, hoarse. "I can't think when you're out
there, a target."

A huge admission, one that reached into her soul
and warmed it. "She's in the rafters," she whispered.

"I know."

She fisted her hand in the front of his shirt, dragging his face to hers. "Don't get hurt. Not one hair on your head. Swear it."

"I won't get hurt." He covered her hand with his until she loosened her grip on him, then kissed her once, his eyes on hers as he slammed the door in her face.

Chapter 27

Dani kneeled on the floor of the maintenance closet and checked Maddie's wound.

"Shayne," Maddie whispered.

"He'll be right back."

"Oh, God, he went after her? Stupid man. Why are all men so stupid?" She struggled to get up. "So stupid."

"Maddie, stay down. Please, stay down. You're bleeding."

"Shayne—"

"He said she wouldn't hurt him."

Maddie, eyes closed, shook her head. "She's got a past date of Shayne's dead in her suitcase." Her eyes, feverish and glossed over, met Dani's. "She's taken a right turn out of Saneville, Dani."

Dani stared at her. "So she's going to hurt him."

"Oh yeah. She's going to hurt him. And Brody too." Wincing in pain, she clamped a hand over her shoulder and gritted her teeth. *"God."*

The sound of another gunshot split the air. Steel on steel.

"She's going to hit her own damn precious plane," Maddie gasped. "The idiot."

"One of those planes is hers?"

"The Beechcraft is in the northeast corner. She treats that thing like her baby."

Dani leapt to her feet. "I have a plan."

"Do you have a gun?"

"No."

"A knife?"

"No."

"Honey, then you don't have a plan."

"Something needs to happen to her plane to distract her."

Maddie nodded. "I knew I liked you."

"Good, huh?"

"Brilliant. *Shit.*" Maddie tried to reach up into her own skirt but gasped in pain and fell back, face pasty white. "I have a knife. Take the knife."

"Are you kidding me?"

"Do I look like I'm kidding?"

Dani reached up Maddie's skirt, found her garter and a—"You really have a knife up your skirt."

"If Michelle gets a hold of Shayne, she might— she could make him fly her to Mexico. Where she could get away."

Dani looked down at the knife in her hands. "So I need to stop her."

"And do not, and I repeat, *do not* get yourself hurt. Shayne will kill me if you do, and—" She broke off to grimace in pain.

"Maddie—"

"And . . ." She let out a breath. "I really like my job."

"I'll keep that in mind." Dani slipped the knife into her pocket, then peeked under Shayne's shirt at Maddie's wound.

"I'm not dead yet."

"Go."

Right. Go. Dani cracked the door and peeked out.

Utter silence.

But then, from the far side of the hangar, came a scraping noise, and another. Good. Wherever they were, whatever they were doing, they were doing it far away. Heart in her throat, she slipped out of the closet and backed up against the wall, next to a stack of boxes, where she hoped like hell she was completely out of sight.

She could see the tail of Michelle's plane now, and when she moved around the boxes and hid behind a set of portable stairs, she could also see the landing gear. The tires of the landing gear.

Slipping her hand into her pocket, she fingered the knife. If she popped the tires, the plane wouldn't be able to take off. Felt like a good plan. She ran across the floor toward the phone—

"Ah, there you are."

Uh-oh. Dani slowly tipped her head up. High in the rafters above her knelt Michelle, still looking as if she should be on the cover of a Victoria's Secret catalog, not holding a gun.

But she was.

Aimed at Dani. But then the gun shifted, and re-aimed—at a spot in the rafters across the way, at the figure of a man steadily making his way toward her.

At Shayne, who wore only his jeans, no shirt, no shoes.

No weapon.

"No," Dani gasped. "Don't shoot him. Please don't shoot him."

"Oh, I'm not going to shoot him. He's going to fly me out of here." Michelle sent a smile toward Shayne. "Soon as I set up the tragic scene here, of course. Shayne? Be a good boy now, and go get my baby ready to fly." Holding the gun on a very still Shayne, she turned her attention back to Dani. "Look at that. He doesn't want to leave you."

"Michelle," Shayne said very quietly.

"Do you love him?" Michelle asked Dani. "Do you love my pilot?"

Shayne pulled himself a little closer to Michelle, who suddenly whipped her head in his direction. *"Don't."*

He went still, but not Dani, who took the last step to Michelle's "baby" and slipped her hand into her pocket for the knife.

"Goddamnit, answer me!" Michelle screamed, suddenly not looking so much Victoria's Secret as ready for a straitjacket.

Dani stared up at Shayne. She couldn't see his expression clearly, but she could sense his disbelief that she'd left the safety of the closet, his frustration at being held at gunpoint, helpless, his anger that there was nothing he could do to protect her.

"Do you love him?" Michelle yelled to Dani.

Anguish too. There was just enough anguish in his eyes that Dani nearly staggered back. "I do," she whispered. She cleared her throat, her gaze never leaving Shayne's. "I love him." Her eyes burned, her throat tightened at the look of shock and awe on his face. "I love him very much."

"Well." Michelle stared down at Dani, who'd have

sworn the crazy model's eyes actually filled with tears. "Then you're definitely going to have to be taken care of." Her voice was thick and hoarse. "Aren't you?"

"No—" Shayne started forward, but Michelle's head whipped toward him, gun at his chest.

"Do not defend her. Ever. We're going down. We're going down and I'm going to do what I have to, and so are you. You're going to fly me out of here."

In the split second that Michelle's attention was on Shayne, Dani scooted behind the landing gear tires, which she sincerely hoped would absorb any flying bullets. God, she really hoped that as she stabbed the first tire.

"You cannot make me fly you anywhere," Shayne was saying.

Dani could hear his voice clearly far above her as she crawled on her hands and knees toward the next tire.

"Yes, Shayne, I can," Michelle assured him. "And you know why? Because I have the gun." But then her scream of fury bounced off the walls as she discovered Dani gone.

The gun went off then, and Dani, crawling the last few feet between the tires, actually closed her eyes. Such a girl thing to do, but blindly she stabbed out with the knife and blessedly connected with the next tire at the same time that she heard another furious scream.

"Not my baby, don't you touch my baby!"

Then something slammed into Dani's arm, spinning her around. Dropping the knife, she hit the cold floor. On her back now, she had this great view of the ceiling, through a funny haze that was slowly taking over her vision. She couldn't hear, couldn't really feel.

But she could see. And what she saw stopped her heart—Shayne, diving at Michelle. Both of them flying through the air toward the ground, hitting the wing of the plane, bouncing off it, and vanishing from her line of vision.

Oh, God.

She closed her eyes for a moment, and flashes hit her eyelids, like flipping through a yearbook of her memories. Walking into her mother's party and running, quite literally, into Shayne. Kissing him in the closet. A flashing dimple when he grinned at her. Every time he'd ever been there for her . . . *"Shayne."* She sat up, gasping at the pain in her arm, and found herself next to the landing gear.

All flat now.

Everything sort of spun a bit and she put her hands on the ground to try to anchor herself just as an eye-popping white light blinded her, along with the loudest clanging she'd ever heard.

Oh, God. The light. She was going into the light—

"She's here!"

And then she was hauled up against a chest. A bare, bruised chest.

Shayne's. Dani blinked at him. "Are you dead too?"

"No." He rocked her in his arms. "And neither are you."

She blinked, and things came into focus. The huge hangar door, open now, letting in the sun.

The light.

Police were everywhere, and Maddie was on a

stretcher with two paramedics and Brody leaning over her. "She's—"

"Alive too. God, Dani. When she shot you—"

"I wasn't shot. I think I'd know if I was shot." But it was in his eyes, so she looked down at her arm. Oops. Her sleeve was wet, dripping down her fingers onto the floor.

Blood.

There was a paramedic at her side too, and he tore her sleeve off, revealing a deep, nasty-looking bloody gash—

A bullet wound. "Uh-oh."

"Dani?"

Yeah. That was her name. But it was the most annoying thing. Her ears were ringing, her vision going gray . . .

When her eyeballs rolled up in her head, Shayne knew she was checking out.

"Got her," the paramedic said, and caught her. They wheeled her past the police, who were dealing with a screaming Michelle, who was yelling about her "precious baby." Shayne, more viciously pissed and worried than he'd ever been in his life, wished someone would shut her the hell up. One of the officers was handling her suitcase, which Shayne now knew held Kathleen's body.

The dead body that had haunted Dani . . .

Brody was watching Maddie get loaded into an ambulance, and he glanced over at Shayne, pale and terse.

"Is she—"

"Still breathing. Dani?"

"The bullet grazed her arm."

Brody nodded, tough and stoic as ever, but there was a look in his eyes that said he was an inch from losing it.

If something had happened to Maddie—

Shayne would have to deal with that, with all of it; the guilt, the torment, the anguish.

Later.

For now, there was the living to take care of.

"I want to see her," Dani insisted to the nurse. She sat on the cot in her ER cubicle, all stitched and bandaged, and nicely loaded on pain meds for the second time in as many days. "I need to see Maddie."

"She's resting."

Okay, resting was good. Alive was good. "And she's going to make it."

"She's out of surgery. She's going to make it."

Thank God. The only thing that could have been better than that news was having it delivered by Shayne. He'd been with her while she'd been treated, once again holding her hand, stroking the hair off her face, smiling into her eyes, but she knew his smiles now, and the one he'd given her had devastation all over it.

He blamed himself for everything.

And sure enough, afterward he'd been taken from her to be x-rayed, then treated for his own various scrapes and bruises including a broken ankle, and he hadn't returned.

Noah had popped in to check on her, saying he'd drive her home when she was ready, just to come get him out of Maddie's room.

But she didn't want Noah, she wanted Shayne, damn it. "I'm okay to get up," she insisted to her nurse, who sighed, shook her head, and stepped aside.

Dani tested her wobbly legs and locked her knees. No more passing out. She had to be strong to shake some sense into Shayne. Or shake the guilt out of him. Either way.

She found Maddie's room two doors down from hers. Noah was sitting in a chair while Brody paced.

"She's asleep," he told her.

"Surgery went okay?"

The men looked at each other and her stomach sank. "What?"

"The bullet shattered her collarbone and destroyed some muscle. They don't know how much mobility she'll recover."

"Oh, God," Dani whispered.

"Come on," Noah said gently, taking her arm. "You need to go rest."

She let him lead her into the hallway. "I want to talk to Shayne."

Noah sighed. "Dani—"

"You can either take me to him, or I'll find him on my own."

"He's not good, Dani. He's blaming himself."

"I can help him."

"How do you know?"

"Because I love him."

Noah just looked at her for a long moment, then nodded. "That's probably the one thing you could have said to convince me. Come on." He turned her toward the outside doors, but just before they went out, he stopped her. "He's not going to want to listen."

"I know."

"He's going to try to push you away."

"Don't worry, I'm tougher than I look."

Some of the worry left his gaze. "I believe you are." He took her outside, where a dark shadow stood propping up the outside wall, arms and legs casually crossed, though there was nothing casual about the tension and violence simmering just beneath his surface. "Jesus, Noah."

Shayne.

"She wanted to see you."

"She should be in bed." Shayne grabbed the single crutch leaning next to him and limped forward, coming into clear view when he passed beneath the light. His face was pale, taut with tension, his eyes shadowed as he took her arm.

Noah leaned in and gave Dani a quick kiss on the cheek before leaving them alone.

"You don't belong out here." Shayne pulled her back inside the ER. But just before her cubicle, she put her foot down. "Wait."

"Dani—"

Brody caught sight of them and frowned. "Christ, Shayne. Make her sit down."

"I'm trying!"

Dani put her good hand on Shayne's arm, which leapt beneath her fingers. The man was wound up tight. "I don't need to sit down."

"Dani."

"I need you. You, Shayne."

He closed his eyes, lifted his hands. "I can't. I can't do this." He pivoted away. "I'll get Noah."

She stared at his back, aching for him. "Shayne."

He stilled, but didn't turn back to her.

"You didn't say you loved me back."

He jammed his hands into his pockets.

"I'd say I was sorry for blurting it out to you, but I'm not. The thing is, I've never said it to anyone. I've always kept my heart sort of locked up tight, you know?"

A low sound escaped him, and he bowed his head. "I know."

"But then I told myself it was time to change, and then I met you, and I'd promised myself to do things different. Hence that whole closet kiss thing. I let my heart have its own way, and at first it freaked me out because of what could happen to it, but then, somehow, I put myself on the line anyway, I really let myself live, and although I pretended that it was just sex, it was more. So much more, Shayne. It was amazing, and you should know, I have no regrets."

"Dani—"

"*None.* And Shayne? You shouldn't either."

At that, he turned to face her. "Kathleen is dead because of me. Maddie almost died—"

"But she didn't."

"And you—"

"Standing right here looking at you." She smiled. But he shook his head. "It's not that simple."

"No, it's not. You need time to think, to grieve, to get past all of it, and you should take that time. But when you're done, I'm still going to be here, looking at you."

He closed his eyes, then opened them again. "I nearly got you killed."

"Nearly doesn't really count." She touched a cut on his cheekbone. Then leaned in and kissed it. "I might have said it because she asked, but I meant it. I love you."

A rough sound escaped him and he slipped his

arms around her, carefully pulling her in for a hug before looking into her eyes. "I love you back. Damn it. I love you so much it's killing me."

She felt her eyes fill. "I know."

"You know?"

"It was in your eyes when you looked at me from the rafters."

"No, that was sheer terror."

"And also when Michelle pointed the gun at me."

"Again, sheer terror."

"Love."

He sighed. "Yeah." He touched his forehead to hers. "That too."

"And when you sat at my side in the ER, holding my hand when I got stitches again."

"That was pain. You squeezed my fingers really hard."

"Love," she insisted.

With a sigh, he pressed his mouth to her jaw, then her lips. "Love."

She nodded, then wobbled. Relieved when he slipped his arms around her even though he was none too steady either, she smiled up at him shakily as they propped each other up. "Aren't we a pair."

"Yeah. We are. You're the best thing that's ever happened to me, Dani."

Her heart caught at that. "I am?"

"Oh, yeah. You are." He flashed a hint of his dimple. "Maybe you can retract that whole just-sex thing now. Maybe you'll even undump me."

Dani caught a glimpse of movement to her right. Noah and Brody were in Maddie's doorway, unabashedly listening. From behind them, in her bed, Maddie waved weakly.

Dani looked at Shayne. "Maybe we could take this someplace more . . ."

"Private?" Shayne nodded, and opened the first door they came to.

A closet.

He looked inside at the supply shelves and laughed. "You have got to be kidding."

Dani pulled him in. "It's perfect. Don't you see? We've ended up where it all began."

Looking as if he'd just won the lotto, Shayne nodded and pulled her into his arms, right where she belonged.

The Sky High series begins with
SMART AND SEXY,
available now!

Noah Fisher needed a double-diamond ski slope, a hot ski-bunny babe, and a beer, and not necessarily in that order.

Mammoth Mountain, here he came.

He studied the gauges in front of him, then stroked the dash of his favorite Piper. "Don't worry, baby. The weather's going to hold for us."

Hopefully.

He put on his headset, then took a moment to lean back and draw in a deep breath. His first flight in six months. Man, he was ready to get into the sky, heading for that desperately needed R&R.

R&R, and hopefully that ski bunny . . .

With that in mind, he okayed his takeoff and began to taxi down the runway, the scent of the burrito Maddie had left for him on the copilot's seat making his mouth water. Within five minutes, he was ten thousand feet and counting as he headed toward his utter freedom.

God, he loved, *loved*, being up here. Here there

were no distractions, no memories, nothing but a spattering of cotton-ball clouds and azure sky as far as he could see.

Just what the doctor had ordered.

He checked the instruments and then the horizon. Ah, yeah, conditions were good. The Piper was doing her thing, as always. She was a classic, though not necessarily a beauty, which meant that most of their customers wouldn't have given her a second look.

Their loss.

She flew like a dream. He could fix her up real pretty, he knew, and then everyone would be clamoring for her, but he didn't feel the need to share her.

As he leveled out, he grabbed a stowed-away chocolate bar to munch on before the burrito. He'd always eaten his dessert first, because hell, once upon a time, he hadn't known when and where his next meal would come from. Chewing, he began to picture the weekend ahead: the slopes, the wind in his face, powdery snow up to his knees as he plowed straight down the mountain, his hair blown back by his own speed. . . .

Then he pictured the sexy ski bunnies waiting in the warm lodge afterward, and one of those rare but genuine smiles tugged at his mouth.

Yeah, a sexy ski bunny—or two—was key to this whole event. She'd be an expert in erotic massage, of course, and ready, willing, and able to do . . . well, pretty much whatever came to mind.

And plenty did.

At the thought, he actually smiled again.

Yes sirree, his muscles were getting quite the workout today, after six long months of neglect. Thanks to his crash, it'd been a long time since he'd fantasized about women, or even craved sex at all—

A rustle sounded from behind Noah, startling the shit out of him, but before he could react, something jammed into his shoulder, something that unbelievably felt an awful lot like a—

Gun?

"Keep flying," said a ragged voice. "Just keep flying."

Holy shit. Noah craned his neck. The soft, fuzzy blanket he kept on the backseat was on the floor now. She'd been hiding beneath it, and yeah, the person behind him was most definitely a she. Once upon a time, he'd been considered an expert on the species, and despite her gruff, uneven tones, her voice shimmered with nerves.

Female nerves.

Unbelievably, he'd just been hijacked by a nervous woman with a gun. He tried to get a good look at her, but the gun shifted to his jaw, shoving his head forward before he could take in more than a big, bulky sweater with a hood down low over her face—

"Don't turn around," she demanded. "Just keep us in the air."

He could. He'd been a pilot ever since the day he'd been old enough, flying on a daily basis, either for a job or on a whim, into a storm or with one on his ass, without much thought.

He was giving it plenty of thought now. "Hell, no." His fingers tightened on the yoke. *Goddamnit.* "What the fuck is this?"

"You're flying me to Mammoth Mountain."

"Hell, no, I'm not."

"Yes, you are. You have no choice." Then she let

out a disparaging, desperate sound and softened her voice. "Look, just get us there, okay? Get us there and everything will be all right."

Yeah, except that she didn't sound as if she believed that line of crap, and he sure as hell didn't believe it either. Worse, he suddenly had a nasty flashback to another of his flights that had gone bad, six months ago. Only in that one, there'd been no gun, just a hell of a storm in Baja Mexico, where he'd hit a surprise thunderstorm, one with a vicious kick. That time he'd ended up on a side of a mountain in a fiery crash, holding his passenger as she died in his arms. . . .

So really, in comparison, this flight, with a measly gun at his back, should be a piece of cake. Just a day in the life.

Knowing it, he swiped a forearm over his forehead and concentrated on breathing. Maybe she was all talk, no show. Maybe she didn't really know how to use the weapon. Maybe he could talk her out of the insanity that had become his life today. "How did you get in here?"

The gun remained against his shoulder, but not as hard, as if maybe she didn't want to hurt him. "No questions, or I'll—"

"What? *Shoot?*"

She didn't answer.

Yeah, all talk, no show, he decided, and reached over to switch his radio on, then went very still at the feel of the muzzle just beneath his jaw now.

"Don't," she said, sounding more desperate, if that was even possible. "Don't tell anyone I'm here."

Hell if he'd suffer this quietly, and he braced himself for action, but then she added a low, softly uttered, *"Please."*

Jesus, he felt like such a fool. Who the hell was she? She'd been careful to stay just behind him, just out of range of his peripheral. He could smell her, though, some complicated mixture of exotic flowers and woman, which under very different circumstances he'd find sexy as hell.

But not today, the day that was quickly turning into a living nightmare. He couldn't believe this was happening. Not when he was getting back on the horse. Wasn't that what Shayne and Brody had told him to do, *get back on the horse.*

And he had.

Was.

Hence the ski/fuck-his-brains-out weekend.

What the hell was in Mammoth that was worth hijacking someone? And why was she so desperate to get there? Instinct had him checking the gauges, looking for a place to land.

"No." The gun was an emphasis, back to pressing hard between his shoulder blades. "We're going to Mammoth. Just like you planned."

"I didn't plan for this."

"You have a passenger now, that's all. Everything else is the same."

Yeah, he had a passenger. A shaking, unnerved, freaked-out desperate one.

Give him a thunderstorm in Cabo any day over this. . . .

"There's no need to panic, or do anything rash," she said, and he wondered if she was talking to him—or herself.

"Yeah, well, if you're insisting on coming along, then sit." He jerked his chin toward the copilot seat next to him, because he wanted to see her, wanted to know exactly what he was up against.

"I'm fine right where I am."

Hell if he'd have her at his back with a gun jammed against him for the next hour. "Sit. Down."

As if for emphasis, they hit a pocket of air, and the plane dipped. With a gasp, the woman fell backward into the seat behind him.

Noah smiled grimly. He wasn't stupid, and he hadn't been born yesterday. Actually, he hadn't even been born in this country at all, but in England. He'd ended up here, orphaned as a teen, where he'd proceeded to beg, borrow, and steal his way to his dream.

A life of flying.

And she was not going to take that life away from him.

"You did that on purpose." Her voice was tight and angry. "Don't do anything like that again."

He hadn't done it in the first place, but he could have, and *would* if he got the chance and could manage it without getting his head accidentally shot off, because he really hated it when that happened. "Who the hell are you?"

"Doesn't matter."

"What's in Mammoth?"

"Doesn't matter."

Great. A stubborn female. Who happened to have a gun.

Never a good combination.

He glanced back and wasn't happy to see her standing again, directly behind him so that he still couldn't get a good look at her.

"Don't." Once again she shoved the gun into his back, a situation of which he was quickly tiring. Right before his crash, adrenaline had pumped through him, but it was nothing compared to what flowed through his veins now.

Then he'd been scared, to the bone.

Now he was pissed. To the bone. His radio crackled, and then Shayne's voice filled the cabin. As a team called Sky High Air, they had a fleet of three jets, three Cessnas, two Beechcraft, a Moody, a Piper, and a Cirrus, and access to others via a leasing network, and had just constructed a building to house them all instead of working out of a very expensive leased wing at LAX. It gave them their own hub, a fixed operating base for their picky, finicky clientele, complete with maintenance and concierge services.

Not bad for three punks who'd once been nothing more than sorry-ass teenage delinquents.

"Noah?" Shayne asked via radio. "You there?"

"I have to answer that," he told his hijacker. "Or he'll know something's wrong." Without waiting for her response, he pushed the button on the radio. "Here."

"Just checking in on your inaugural flight."

He was doing fine. Great.

If he forgot about the gun digging into him.

"You okay?" Shayne asked.

Noah hated that his friend even had to ask, but could admit, at least to himself, that the past six months had been just rough enough that Shayne felt he had to. "I'm . . ." He pushed back at the gun. "Hanging in."

His kidnapper remained silent, tense.

"Brody's flying Mrs. Sinclair to Aspen," Shayne said. "At least so she says, but she's had us ready-up four times this past week, only to correct at the last minute. I don't see today being any different."

The idiosyncrasies of the rich and famous didn't bother him any, as long as they paid for it, but just the words "Mrs. Sinclair" made the butterflies in his stomach tap-dance.

Mr. Sinclair had been a forty-year-old trust-fund baby who'd built huge resort complexes in every party town along the West Coast while showing off his much younger trophy wife, Bailey Sinclair, an ex-model, a woman who screamed sophistication and elegance.

Not to mention her *muy caliente* factor.

But her husband had bitten the big one three months ago in a mysterious hunting accident, and they hadn't seen much of the missus since then. She was probably off spending her husband's billions of dollars, and . . . and hell.

Bailey Sinclair was intelligent, and sexy, stubborn as hell—three of Noah's favorite qualities in a woman. She had strawberry blond, wild flyaway hair that framed her face in a way that seemed as if maybe she'd just gotten out of bed and wasn't averse to going back. Her baby blues were deep enough to drown a man, and her mouth . . .

Christ, he'd had entire day-long fantasies about her mouth. Truth was, she was his living secret crush.

It was pathetic, really. Getting weak-kneed over another man's wife.

Even if that man was dead.

But he was a little busy today, so it was probably time to get over Bailey Sinclair.

Cold turkey, pal.

"She's already on board and locked up in her stateroom," Shayne said. "And if the rumors are true—"

"Rumors?"

"That she's selling everything off . . . then she's probably going for one last hurrah. Said she was taking a sleeping pill and just to wake her after arrival."

Noah could picture the sleek honey of a plane on the tarmac. It didn't take much for his imagination to go farther and see the gorgeous, lush stateroom on board, the huge king-sized bed covered in the best of the best silk, and Bailey sprawled on it, her hair streaming across a pillow, her long, willowy body barely wrapped in satin and lace—

Scratch that.

No satin, no lace.

Nothing but Bailey. Yeah, that might help him get over himself real quick.

If he lived through this, that was.

"Be careful," Shayne said.

"I will be, Mom. Thanks."

"*Mom?*"

"Better than old lady," Noah said, checking the horizon, ignoring his "passenger" while Shayne huffed out a low laugh.

"Smart-ass," he muttered, and clicked off.

Yeah, that was him: Noah Fisher, smart-ass. Among other things. And actually, he'd heard them all: selfish bastard, good-for-nothing lout, cocky SOB. . . .

That most of them were completely one-hundred-percent true didn't keep him up at night. Nope, he saved that for the nightmares, of which he now had a new one.

He glanced at his altimeter and airspeed indicator. Everything looked okay. Everything *was* okay, because he'd checked and double-checked over the static-system vents and Pitot tube for foreign bodies, like the bird that had fucked him just before his crash. All was clear right now. Good to know. He would not be crashing tonight.

"Thanks," said the woman at his back, "for not giving me away."

He did some more ignoring, and the silence filled the cockpit. Reaching out beside him, he lifted the brown bag from which came the most heavenly scent on earth—his burrito. *Bless you, Maddie,* he said silently to Sky High's concierge. She always stocked him with his favorite fast food. "Hungry?" he asked his hijacker. He hadn't had a real mother, but he still knew how to mock politeness.

"Just fly."

"Suit yourself." He opened the bag and stuffed a bite into his mouth. His taste buds exploded with pleasure, and to be as annoying as possible, he moaned with it. "You have no idea what you're missing."

"Looks like I'm missing a boatload of calories." She sounded tense enough to shatter. "Can't you fly faster?"

Yes. "No."

"How much longer?"

"As long as it takes." Taking another bite—if he was going to die, it wouldn't be hungry—he checked the instruments, the horizon.

Still no weather between here and there, and he supposed he should be thankful for small favors. "So . . . what's your story?"

She didn't respond. Shocker.

"You rob a bank?" he tried.

Nothing but the disquieting sensation of the gun against his skin.

"Kill someone?"

The silence seemed to thicken, and his gut clenched.

Great, she'd killed someone. "Oh, I know," he said conversationally. "Your rich husband has a ski bunny at your Mammoth cabin, and you're going after them."

She choked out a laugh utterly without mirth. "Can you fly without talking?"

He opened his mouth to give a smart-ass reply to that, but the gun at his back pressed into him and shut him up. Yeah, okay, maybe he could fly without talking.

For now.

The adventure continues in SUPERB AND SEXY!
Here's a sneak peek at the third book in
the Sky High series,
available now!

The man pulled up in a rumbling, bad boy Camaro like he owned his world, and Maddie had good reason to know he did.

Brody West owned his world all right, and completely rocked hers.

What the hell was he doing here?

It'd been a long time since she'd seen him. Six weeks, two and a half days, and waaaaay too many minutes. Not that she was counting.

But to be honest, that she hadn't seen him was all her own doing. She'd left town to recover.

To think.

To make a Plan with a capital P.

Hence staying in the mountains where no one could bother her—including Brody.

Especially Brody.

With him, no contact was good contact since they clashed at every turn, bickered when they weren't clashing, and in general, brought out the worst in each other. She hadn't even thought about him while she'd been gone, sitting here on the porch of

the log-style cabin that she'd rented for its rustic, isolated beauty, emphasis on isolated.

Okay, so she'd thought about him. She just hadn't
wanted to think about him. Probably, she was just
overreacting. Honestly, maybe it wasn't even him in
the car.

And yet, she knew better. Her body knew better.
The simple act of hearing the engine rev had made
the hair on the nape of her neck rise in sudden, unexpected awareness.

Yeah, it was him because she felt . . .

God, she felt so much, but thunderstruck led the
pack, though an undeniable excitement came in
close second.

He was here, forty-five miles off the beaten path
from his home in the Burbank Hills to the Angeles
Crest Forest.

But *why*? Why wasn't he holed up in his office,
or on one of his planes he loved more than anything, working himself into an early grave as he liked
to do?

She knew that he, along with his partners Shayne
and Noah, wanted her back at work, seemed desperate for her to be back. Shayne had told her yesterday
on the phone that Sky High had gone through four
temp concierges in the time she'd been gone on
leave, all of whom Brody had chased off with his
sunny nature.

Translation: he'd been brooding and edgy and
terrifying.

Yeah. Sounded like him.

But the brooding and edgy thing had never bothered her much. Maybe because she'd always been
drawn to the bad boys. The reason for that was sim-

ple. Bad boys wanted the same things she did—no strings attached.

She didn't do strings.

Outside, Brody turned off the Camaro, and silence filled the air.

A heavy, weighted, questioning silence.

And suddenly, Maddie's chest felt too tight. Damn it. She let out a long, calming breath, which of course, didn't work. It never worked. Neither did just sitting at the window staring down at him, but God, she was tired, and still recovering. Yeah, that's what this asinine weakness in her knees was—recovery. Because it sure as hell wasn't for him.

No way.

They didn't even like each other . . .

And yet she leaned over so she could see out the window again, past the tall twin pines trying to block her view of the nearly six feet, four inches of rough and tumble, sexy as hell male as he unfolded his long legs from the muscle car.

Her pulse took another unfortunate leap. The last time she'd seen him, he'd been in his pilot's uniform, and even though it was ridiculous and juvenile and wrong, it had turned her on. The thought of seeing him *out* of it? Even more so.

Yeah, she had a problem. She'd been shamelessly, secretly crushing on him all damn year. But that was her own humiliating secret, and one she'd take to the grave. And here was another—that fateful last day at work six weeks ago now, when she'd been just a little ticked off that she couldn't get him to notice her as a woman, she'd dressed solely to gain his attention—miniskirt, snug cami, teetering heels, the whole shebang. She'd been gratified when it'd worked, when he'd executed a comical double take at her and then spilled coffee down the front of his shirt.

Mission accomplished. He'd most definitely noticed her as a woman.

The excitement level had been so high she couldn't stand it. And then she'd smart-mouthed a psychopath and gotten herself shot, and her life had been put on pause.

Fast-forward to now.

Shutting the driver's door of the Camaro, he stared at the cabin. He wore a T-shirt, cargoes, and scuffed boots, all in black, emphasizing that world-class bod she'd spent many, many days drooling over while pretending to work.

Unlike her, the man was genetically incapable of pretending anything. Nope, he rarely bothered to hide his thoughts, especially as they pertained to her, thoughts that had at one time or another run the gamut from baffled to that one time she'd done the unthinkable and pressed him back against a wall and kissed him.

And for that one blissful moment, he hadn't been vexed or grumpy. He'd been stunned and aroused and all sleepy-eyed and sexy with it.

Not now, though.

Now he stood there, tall and sure, a frown on his face, his dark hair falling carelessly across his brow, and at just past his collar, longer than one would expect a pilot's hair to be. She knew that it wasn't that way because he cared about being in style, but because he simply forgot to get it cut. Sometimes she thought he'd forget his own head if it wasn't attached.

The only things he never forgot were his damn planes or his business. Sky High Air was an exclusive, luxurious, sophisticated airline service. Pretty damned hilarious considering that the three guys who ran it had been troubled youths, to say it kindly. They'd started Sky High last year by the seat of their pants and their collective wits. They'd put their heads and bank accounts together, managing, barely, to eke enough money to get it going, then keep it going.

But a miracle had occurred. The LA rich and spoiled had discovered them, *loved* them and the services they provided, and all the buckets and buckets of antacids they'd consumed over the cost of the start-up were finally paying off.

Below, Brody stopped on the walk and looked up.

She held her breath. Hard to believe they made geeks in such outrageously magnificent male packages, but there it stood, looking for her.

His eyes were hidden behind mirrored aviator sunglasses, but she knew them to be a mesmerizing pewter gray that could turn to ice or flame given his mood, and they were filled with secrets she'd never managed to plumb.

They drove her crazy, those secrets. She'd always wanted to know their depths, wanted to know what made him tick, his likes, his dislikes . . . and the yearning had driven her even more crazy.

Had.

Because she no longer had the luxury of dreaming about him. She had other things to dream about—things like life and death.

But he didn't know that as he headed for the door. Around his neck were the earphones for his iPod, which probably had Linkin Park blasting out at decibel levels uncharted. How the man hadn't gone deaf was beyond her, but that wasn't what she wondered as her gaze ran all over him like he was cotton candy. No, she wondered how she was going to keep her hands to herself if she had to talk to him one-on-one . . .

Get a grip.

After all, his partners had stolen her heart from day one, too, and she didn't want to jump them. Shayne and Noah were bad boys as well, and when she'd gotten the job working for them, the rebel inside her had rejoiced to find a place where she belonged. She loved them both, loved them like the older brothers she never had.

But nothing about her feelings for the edgy, brooding Brody was brotherly.

Nowhere even close.

Very annoying, and hard to hide as well, though she'd managed. She always managed, no matter the task. Cool as a cucumber, that was Maddie, always.

She needed to find that cool now. Oh boy, how she needed to find that cool.

Not easy when that dark, silky hair of his called to her fingers, and then there was that lean, angular face she wanted to touch, or that tough, muscular body she wanted to lick from top to bottom.

Damn it, she'd told herself she was over her little schoolgirl crush, over whatever it was about him that melted her brain cells, not to mention her bones, leaving her a ridiculously vulnerable puddle of longing every time he so much as looked at her.

She was tougher than this.

But not with him.

That thought came out of nowhere, and she beat it back, along with the knowledge that he, unlike any other man she'd ever met, had somehow sneaked past her defenses, past her carefully erected brick walls, and saw the woman beneath.

He stopped walking. Stopped and tilted his dark head up to the second story window, and then seemed to look right into her eyes.

Oh, God.

Unprepared for the reaction that barreled through her, she actually sat there, still, rooted to the spot for one long heartbeat.

"Who is that?"

Maddie jumped as her sister came into the room. Tiptoed, as if someone was still on her trail, in the jerky, self-conscious movement of someone used to being pushed around.

Goddamnit. "No one, Leena. It's okay."

Leena leaned over Maddie's shoulder, gnawing her lower lip between her teeth as she took in the man on the walk below. "My God," she murmured and shivered.

Yes, Maddie thought. My God. Brody induced that reaction from her, too.

"That's not no one."

True enough. She took another quick peek and felt a shiver herself, not of fear of that impressive size and height, but because she knew what that impressive size and height felt like full frontal and plastered up against her. "It's okay. He's my boss."

Leena let out a low breath as she stared at Brody. "You work for *him*?"

"And two others. Three pilots."

"You work for three men like *that*?"

No use telling her that not all men were manipulative jerks who ruled with their superior size or fist. That was something she'd have to learn on her own.

After all, Maddie had.

"You can't let him in," Leena said, a growing panic in her voice, a panic Maddie felt as her own.

Because Leena was right. She couldn't let him in. Couldn't because there was far too much at stake here.

No matter that she and Brody had unresolved issues, mostly hers. There were other more pressing issues, issues that had nothing to do with him.

Serious issues.

Like those life and death issues . . .

If she let him in, he'd take one look at her and know something was wrong because brooding and edgy as he might be, he had the intuition and instincts of a panther—sharp and unwavering.

In Brody's world, things were black and white. Right and wrong. When something was broken, he fixed it. If someone needed him, he moved heaven and earth to do whatever needed to be done, and he would do so for a perfect stranger.

Maddie was no stranger, perfect or otherwise.

Yeah, he'd want to help.

Only he couldn't.

No one could.

Staring down at Brody, her pulse raced with a horrible mixture of yearning and wariness. Him showing up was the worst thing that could have happened, for the both of them.

Not that he could know that or the fact that she was in over her head in a way she hadn't been since he'd hired her and unknowingly given her a much needed security that she valued above all else.

But apparently unable to read her mind, he headed straight for the front door, his long-limbed stride filled with a casual ease that said even if he'd known about any potential danger, it wouldn't have stopped him.

God, she loved that about him.

Beside her, Leena made a sound of distress and wrung her hands together.

Maddie's reaction wasn't much different. Her heart took another hard knock against her ribs. She had no idea what it was about Brody's attitude that went straight to her gut—and several other good spots as well—but with that scowl on his face, he looked every inch the wild, bad boy rebel pilot that she knew him to be.

And from deep within her came a new emotion, one she hadn't thought still existed inside her.

Hope.

It made absolutely no sense, no sense at all, and she quickly squashed it flat because that particular emotion, or anything close to it, had no place here, and she'd do well to remember it.

That was the hard part. Remembering it.

"Maddie," Leena whispered.

"I know."

For all of their sakes, she had to get rid of him. *Fast.*

GREAT BOOKS, GREAT SAVINGS!